Redeeming Eve

NICOLE BOKAT

PIATKUS

First published in Great Britain in 2001 by
Judy Piatkus (Publishers) Ltd
5 Windmill Street, London W1T 2JA
email: info@piatkus.co.uk

First published in the United States in 2000
by The Permanent Press, New York

The moral rights of the author have been asserted

*A catalogue record for this book is available from
the British Library*

ISBN 0 7499 3248 1

Printed and bound in Great Britain by
Mackays of Chatham plc, Chatham, Kent

The New School for Social Research and lives in Montclair, New Jersey with her husband and two sons.

Also by Nicole Bokat

The Novels of Margaret Drabble:
"this Freudian family nexus".

3ᐸ

Acknowledgements

Many people read this novel in one incarnation or another who deserve my thanks. They include: Ed Levy; Naomi Rand; Laurie Lico Albanese; Tanya Priber; Marie Theberge; Suzanne Roth; Pamela Satran; Deborah Maher. With special thanks to Susan Shapiro, Robert Miller, Mary Pat Champeau, and to my pal and copy editor, Lynne Lisa. Thank you to Judith and Martin Shepard of Permanent Press and to my wonderful agent, Jeremy Solomon, for his unwavering support.

All my love and gratitude to my husband, Jay, for believing in me, reading through countless drafts, and for all his encouragement over the years. And, to our two beautiful boys, Noah and Spencer: they are talented enough to do whatever they please with their lives.

To my father, Peter Bokat (1932-1999):
For your unfailing love, support and kindness.
You are sorely missed.
To my mother Mona Bokat, for everything.

Prelude
1996

"The intellect of man is forced to choose/ Perfection of the life,
or of the work . . . ."   —Yeats, "The Choice."

IN ONE SHADOWY crevice of her mind—that private place in
which so many accurate perceptions had been ambushed—
she recognized the truth: she was leaving her husband and
her baby daughter. Yet Eve remained in her seat, belt
buckled, book in lap, eyes closed for take-off and told
herself: I need to do this; *this* is my true fate. She could
rationalize that she'd be home soon enough (whatever
enough meant to a six-month-old and a floundering
husband). Still, in one hand, she clutched the black and
white photograph of newborn Gemma and prayed: Don't
hate me, little one. As the plane taxied down the runway,
Eve listened to the whirling sound of compressed air in the
cabin and the melodic voice of the airline attendant reciting
safety instructions. A thrill of fear rushed through her: in
less time than it took to complete a day's work, she would
be in London. In the morning, she'd head out to the
University, track down Professor Wellington and rekindle
her old life.

Eve had made this momentous decision three days ago.
She simply couldn't wait out the seasons of Wellington's
sabbatical: the ice-gray winter, in which her husband was
finally beating depression and she had, shockingly, broken
off from her mother for the first time; the tease of spring;
and, then, the second summer of head-pounding humidity
and a cranky child (her beautiful girl—but she pushed this
thought out of her mind) too young to even lug to the town
pool. It was more than a little uncharacteristic of her: the
short time that had elapsed between forming the idea and
her actual escape. After charging the one-way ticket on her
credit card, she'd placed an ad for a nanny in the town
paper, then confronted her husband with what she'd done.

She'd expected him to explode in anger; instead he'd lost his balance on the shabby living room rug that had curled up in one corner. Eve had reached out a hand to help him but, instinctively, he recoiled from her and steadied himself by grabbing onto the arm of the couch. A smirk distorted his face but Eve knew it was from terror as well as rage. "What kind of mother would just leave her baby?"

"A bad one," Eve whispered.

He began to pace, his hands in fists. "Okay, okay. Let's look at this great escape plan of yours. Who do you expect to take care of Gemma while I'm looking for a job *and* working?"

"I've put an ad in the *Reporter* for a child care person." Eve put her hands above her head as if to stop an avalanche from burying her under rubble. "I know you don't have the money. I've sent a letter to my mother and asked her to arrange for payment. She can afford it. She owes me after humiliating me on television."

That's when he slumped over just as surely as if he'd been punched in the gut. When he looked up into her eyes, he was crying. "I thought you were finally happy again. How could you do this?"

His question reverberated in Eve's mind even as she whizzed away in a cab to Newark Airport before the first light of morning.

"'I have none of the usual inducements of women to marry. Were I to fall in love, indeed, it would be a different thing! but I never have been in love; it is not my way, or my nature; and I do not think I ever shall. And, without love, I am sure I should be a fool to change such a situation as mine.'"
—*Emma*

OF COURSE, EVE knew that Jane Austen never looked at life after her heroine's marriage: the swelling of Elizabeth Bennet's belly, the agony of childbirth, the potential that Mr. Darcy could lose his fortune. What intimate knowledge did Eve's idol have about these things, herself an "Affectionate Aunt, The Author," a woman who found children noisy and intrusive? As a literature student of the late twentieth century, Eve was well versed in the *truth*, the long history of women writers who embraced the life of the mind, cool and airy, crisp as celery, in place of motherhood, a chaotic, fragmented business, composed of all kinds of unsanitary fluids. Women wanted to believe that things had truly changed, that contemporary scholars and authors could now balance the changing table next to the writing desk as evenly as Madam Justice balanced her scales. What was there to say? Eve was smug in the assurance that they were wrong.

The night before her thirtieth birthday, Eve dreamed of Jane Austen poised at her writing table, quill pen in hand. Although the narrator of this dream, she could not see the words. Yet, she knew that the author was composing the exclamation in *Pride and Prejudice:* "'Jane will be quite an old maid soon. . . . She is almost three and twenty!'" The author's/Eve's mother, dressed in a hangman's black cape, stood over her shoulders, hissing this sentence in her ear: "Both my daughters are spinsters!"

So, it was fitting that Eve awoke at near dawn to talk of marriage.

"I know it's early, but I just *had* to call," her best friend, Annie, whispered into the telephone. "Now, promise you won't be mad?"

"Not if you were molested by your lab rats." Eve elbowed her way up in bed and turned her clock radio around; at night, she hated to see the glowing green numbers taunting her with years of insomnia.

"Eve, listen to me! I have some news that couldn't wait." There were a few seconds of silence and then Annie said, "I feel bad because of you and Graham. But, here goes: Arthur proposed last night."

In her mind's eye, Eve heard Annie's little girl voice—the voice from their childhoods sung out so high it was nearly shrill, "Happy Birthday to you, Happy Birthday to you." She could picture her friend at seven years old, the tallest girl at Eve's party, frizzy hair tamed by a red head-band to match that awful red velvet party dress which made Annie look gangly, like a boy wearing his sister's clothes. "Happy Birthday, Dear Evie, Happy Birthday to you!"

"Are you upset?"

"Not at all," she said, lying. Now things would change permanently between Eve and her best friend. "I want to hear all about it, but I have to call you back later. Like morning, eastern standard time?"

"Oh, I'm so excited, I almost forgot to wish you a happy thirtieth! Happy Birthday! I love you, Evie."

After hanging up the phone, Eve rolled around in bed for a few minutes, then kicked off her blankets. Finally, she switched on a reading lamp and picked up her copy of *The Complete Jane Austen, Volume One,* skimming it for a quick fix of wisdom.

It was her father who first gave Eve a copy of Jane Austen's *Letters* for her sixteenth birthday, soon after she'd discovered *Pride and Prejudice,* a world as perfect and disciplined as the ballet. She loved the notion—unheard of in her childhood home—that passion and restraint could be embodied in one person. Up until that point, when feelings sprouted like wild plant life inside of her, Eve perused her psychiatrist father's library for answers; the books had titles like: *Characterological Transformation, Psychoanalytic Theory of Neurosis, The Anatomy of Human Destructiveness* and *The Etiology of Schizophrenia.*

Night after night, she'd lie in bed, listening to her father, his voice croaked with worry about his sad lineup of patients: holocaust victims, manic depressives, women contemplating the cool feel of razor blades against their skin. In the viral gray of her room, a teenage Eve heard her parents refer to "clinical depression," "borderline personality combined with narcissism," and "bipolar disorders." The sound of the diagnoses made her feel as if she were choking in a pool clogged with mud and algae. She'd reach for her journal and make her adolescent entries: "I want to grow up to be like a Jane Austen heroine, and say things like 'she's out of sorts' instead of 'exhibiting suicidal tendencies.' Is that at all possible in this family?"

Her parents had insisted she see a psychoanalyst throughout her adolescence: Dr. Ackerman. She'd been getting pulsing headaches in school and the scores on her standardized tests were slipping; her teacher claimed it wasn't because she couldn't handle the work. Dr. Ackerman actually had a bust of Freud on a shelf. He would sit with his hands folded on his desk and clear his throat when he wanted her to talk. That sound always made Eve feel as if she'd demonstrated some depraved flaw in her character, as if she'd purposely shown up with her shirt unbuttoned or vodka on her breath. Even then, Eve knew—from studying her father's voluminous *Standard Edition of Freud*—that everything she said was going to be linked to some sexual feeling she'd inadvertently distorted.

She could remember, perfectly, her eleven-year-old self lying in bed, on the edge of sleep, the night her parents decided to send her into therapy. She'd been staring at the sky which was such a deep luminous black, it had reminded her of those velvet wall hangings of puppies and Jesus she'd seen at flea markets. Her parents jarred her into full consciousness:

"For Christ's sake, Maxine, I don't understand this at all. Her scores on this last battery of exams don't match her intellect at all. What's Eve got to be so anxious about?"

"You know better than anyone how irrelevant that question is. She has nothing to be anxious *about;* she just *is.* She's *your* daughter, that's all. I *sailed* blithely through school, in the indomitable Goodman way. My mother skipped two grades and was not shy to point it out. It has nothing to do with intelligence or capability, Daniel. It's just the way you Sterlings are wired." Dramatic sigh. "Oh, never mind all that. Let's just get her to see someone twice a week."

Eve had rammed one fist into the side of each thigh. *She'd show them.*

And, she had, no thanks to any intrusive muddling in her psyche. She'd done gloriously well, achieving all her goals with the precision of a Chinese painter.

Now, Mr. Knightley, her white long-haired cat, looked at Eve with uncaring green eyes and then jumped off her bed. "Just like a man," she said, but decided to follow his lead; she would not get any more rest that morning.

For breakfast Eve tried to create a watercress omelet. Unfortunately, her longing for domestic elegance rarely manifested itself in practical ways. Impatient by nature, she could not bear to cook; either she turned off the heat before the food was ready or became distracted by another chore and burned the meal. Today, she lowered the flame and went on a quick search for the novel she was reading; by the time she came back, the eggs were browned all over. After pouring herself hazelnut coffee with cream into a French porcelain cup, she got back into bed with just the drink and some toast, the *Times* crossword puzzle, and a pile of her research notes. "Don't bother wishing me a happy birthday," she shouted at the telephone, thinking of her ex-boyfriend Graham, of his pinkish-white chest, sprinkled with blond hair, his slightly-rounded shoulders, his darting blue eyes. She pictured him at home: he'd be hunched over at his desk, his dandelion soft hair swept over his face, his small fair hands covered by his ragwool sweater. He read with such total devotion that his book was like an oxygen mask; he simply couldn't be separated from it. Beneath a thin, blond mustache which she used to love to lick, he'd be smiling, the right side of his mouth curving up a bit.

Eve was mulling her way through her *Pride and Prejudice* notes when the phone finally rang. It was barely ten, too early for her friend Dee, who alternated nights waiting tables at a café with singing torch songs in a downtown speakeasy in her sad, throaty voice. She whispered to the cat, "Please be Graham."

"Hi," Eve's mother sighed in her "I'll try to get through one more day," voice.

"Hi, Mom."

"Happy Birthday. Are you okay? Please be okay as a *favor* to me." Maxine Sterling sighed. "I *know* this business with *that boy* has you upset."

"I'm not upset, Ma, and Graham's not a boy. He's thirty-two."

"He seemed like such a good match for you, so smart, so hard-working. Too bad you couldn't wangle a quick marriage and a very profitable divorce out of him. *Just kidding!*" Sigh. "I can't say *I* won't miss his money or his dedication to his studies, very admirable. Oh, at least you have career goals. I *mean* it, Eve, I *do*. I just got off the phone with your sister. Ohhhh, God, she's just so confused."

"Annie's getting married."

"COULDN'T she have waited until tomorrow to tell you? Oh, who wants to marry an accountant anyway?"

"He's a tax lawyer. And, *I* don't want to get married."

"Of course you do," her mother declared. "You're just upset right now. Wait until he realizes what he's missing. Who's he going to find more beautiful, intelligent, and accomplished than you?"

"It doesn't matter to me who he finds." Eve put her notes on her folding table and walked to the kitchen, trying not to become entangled in the phone wire.

"God! Thirty. Another lifetime. Do you know, when I was twenty-nine, your sister was in kindergarten already." She blew out an exaggerated sigh. "I hadn't even started my doctorate; I was too busy making your peanut butter and Fluff sandwiches for lunch. I still had two long braids down my back and wore knee socks." Eve began tapping her foot nervously. "I just wanted to make sure you were all right. Are you all right? Are you sure you don't want me to take off from the hospital today? Will you be lonely? Ohhhh, you'll be okay. You're *always* okay. See your friends and we'll do it tomorrow for brunch."

"I'm fine, Ma. How'd your group go?" Eve's mother—a social worker whose specialty was rescuing the infertile from despair—conducted her couples' support groups every Friday morning in her home office. She had a waiting list a legal pad long, filled with the names of those who crooned, "Maxine is the best therapist on Long Island."

The virtuoso of desperate souls emitted a loud sigh. "Oh, the usual: Sally Perroni accused her husband of caring more about the Jets than her uterus. Granted she's been through in-vitro six times already and is discussing using her brother-in-law's sperm as an alternative . . . her husband's sperm count is low to top it off. Poor things, dear God. . . . Why not go to football games, I say? Let's face it, men can't deal with pain. Although the Italian men are usually better. The WASPS are the worst but it's not their fault, it's in their blood."

"Graham's a WASP," Eve offered, scrubbing the burnt egg off her Teflon frying pan.

"Of course. But he talked about Philip Roth to me. He was very smart and polite and rich. But not funny. *Graham* was not a funny man. Ohhh, well, humor isn't everything. I mean look at Annie's little friend. And she seems to like him. There's really isn't any *accounting* for taste, no pun intended. So, what're you doing today? I'll take off from work and come to your place, if you want." Sigh. "No, really, I *should*, Eve. It's your birthday. I *really* can."

"I have plans. Dee's taking me out to lunch," she said, watching a roach scramble for safety down her drain.

"How's her writing paying off?"

"Not the big bucks. She's singing, though, for a little money."

"You girls pick lucrative careers, I must say. *Big* money-makers."

Eve squashed the bug in time, a small birthday victory. "I thought you wanted me to become a literature professor. Besides, not all my friends are poor. What about Annie? She's marrying Arthur and she'll make her own money."

"Good for her. Let her play with her rats. I hate psychologists *as a group*. All that research with rodents makes them crazy. Although not Annie, of course. And, I *do* want you to finish your degree. If I could do it over (big sigh here), I'd use my degree differently. I'd become a college professor."

"You want to teach my remedial courses for me? I'd love to be able to concentrate on my dissertation proposal." Eve said, spraying with a new, more powerful brand of insect killer.

"No, I want to go to the bathroom, I'm sorry to say. I haven't had a chance all morning. What could I say, 'I'm sorry Sally Perroni, that your uterus is empty and your husband is insensitive, but I really must go relieve myself?'" Maxine always seemed to call at her most inconvenient moments: either her bladder was about to burst or she was falling asleep from exhaustion or she was starving at the end of a work day. Eve referred to this habit as: "I'm such a martyr, I don't even have time for my own bodily functions complex." Her mother promised, "I'll call you later. I must go back to work. Have fun with Dee. And *please* try to have a happy birthday. Stop studying for one day, for God's sake. Isn't that proposal done already, anyway?"

This was the same routine Eve had gotten all her life: her mother as push me, pull you. Up until her second year of high school, Eve danced four days a week and practiced cheerleading on Thursdays. Her muscles were taut from neck to fingers to high arched feet. But she felt as though

15

she was going to be snapped in two from trying to make her body into an "instrument of art," as well as a support system for the home team. Her mother would fly from her father's office—where she had just begun seeing couples part-time—to her pastel blue VW bug, canvas pocketbook slipping off her shoulders, scarf untying from around her neck. She would race Eve around town, from school to her lessons, her papers, with phone numbers of clients scribbled on them, littered the floor of the car along with mints and a ten-year-old orange lipstick. Maxie's relentless devotion to Eve translated into her daughter's firm belief that she was destined to lead an extraordinary life, a burden that felt as heavy as rocks stitched into her clothes.

When Eve confessed that she wanted to quit cheerleading, her mother said, "I had two wishes when I was your age: to be a cheerleader and to sing with a band. I never got my first wish but, as you know, I met your father the one summer I got to sing in that club downtown. Sometimes, doing what you really want leads to other things. I was there when you tried out for cheerleading, Eve. My God, you were practically hysterical; you wanted it so much. But, listen, you're not *me*. If you feel it's too much, don't do it. It's just you're so *good;* you make it look so easy. Can't you just have *fun?*"

When Eve applied to her doctoral program in British Literature, her mother had sighed, "I stopped taking English classes at City because it wasn't the place to meet boys. So, I majored in educational counseling because that was one of the things young girls were told to do at that time. It was a different world. I'm so proud of you for following your dream." But, one telephone conversation later, she moaned the fact that: "My children are going to be poor forever."

This morning, after hanging up the phone, Eve listened for awhile to the wail of a car alarm; such a beseeching noise, it seemed to be warning the world of genuine peril. Then, she dressed in jeans, a forest green sweater, and black boots. She turned on the radio to Annie Haslam singing, "Wildest Dreams," and applied black mascara to her light brown lashes, rosy blush, shell pink lipstick.

Dee rang the bell two hours later; despite Eve's good intentions, she was furiously grading her worst classes' sad-looking, scribbled papers. "Sterling," Dee yelled into the intercom, "Open up, it's me, Glassman."

"Hi," Eve said as she opened the door to her friend. Small, olive-skinned Deirdre was decked out in her all black, with bangle bracelets and a leather jacket. "Happy adulthood, kid," Dee smiled and kissed her friend's cheek.

"Maybe we should do this quick. I have a ton of grading to do."

"Jesus! Why do you always act like you have more work than God? When are you going to stop hiding out in school and start living your life?" Dee hooked Eve's arm. "It's your birthday. Tell all those illiterate students of yours that you took the day off to get laid."

"I wish. I'm as chaste as a nun. I dreamed about Graham again. It was my birthday and he said he couldn't take me out because he had too much work. He was copying all of *Clarissa*, the unabridged 2000-plus page version, onto file cards."

"You should write down your dreams and make them into one of those bullshit postmodern novels about alien-ation and chaos. Make some bucks out of all this self-punishment."

"We're not having this conversation again," Eve said, as she put one arm through her camel-colored wool coat.

"You love school the way I love fucked-up men," her friend said, pulling her out the door. "We're the perfect complement to each other. Let's go. I'm taking you to Telly's Place for brunch. You can lick your wounds later."

"I don't have wounds. *I* was the one who broke up."

This was not altogether true; although, she meant it to be. Graham had dressed quickly after they'd last made love at her place. He was always in motion, reminding Eve of Mercury, wings at his heels. "I can't do this anymore," he'd said when she tried to hug him afterwards. "Neither one of us is going to change. I'll always say a couple of nights is enough for me; you'll keep complaining that you're lonely."

17

She'd flung herself off the bed, crying in a hiccuppy way, her tears of revenge acting as adhesive, gluing strands of hair to her cheeks, her robe falling off her shoulders. She opened her file cabinet, pulled out pictures of them together in Rome and ripped them up. When she got to one of herself sitting alone on the steps of a *pensione,* looking depressed but pretty—elegantly thin with her elbow-long curly hair, intense eyes and sharp-boned face—she'd paused. She asked, "Why tear myself up?" When she got no response, she shouted, "Good luck in your next sadistic venture." He shrugged and calmly saw himself out. She had not heard from him since.

"You would have stayed with him if Graham wanted to get married," Dee said.

"Do you ever listen to me?"

"Every word. I just chalk up what you say about yourself to pure fantasy."

"Very funny."

The November air was biting, the sky an almost dizzying blue and streaked with clouds which resembled friendly apparitions. As they weaved through the streets of the West Village, delicious smells escaped from cafés: the rich roast of espresso, buttery brioches and croissants stuffed with sweet Empire apples and smoked ham. Dee related the most recent escapade with her latest lover; while talking, she chomped on a large wad of gum which she added to by periodically picking new pieces out of her skirt's huge front pocket.

"Get this: Sunday night, we have this fantastic time. He actually tells me he loves me. Monday night he comes over, unexpectedly, and asks if I can get away this weekend. He knows I have no money, so he offers to pay for us to fly to Florida for a long weekend. I manage to get off from work. I'm psyched, I'm packing. And, so last night, he calls and says he has to work both Saturday and Sunday cause his partner has to go out of town. It's an emergency, and besides—he sort of adds this real quick, like he's trying to be casual about it—he needs to think things over, maybe we're rushing things."

"You *know* what I think," Eve said, by rote. Dee shuffled through lovers so quickly one marveled at her slight-of-hand. "I think you should dump him."

"Oh, it's over. Definitely. He's a shmuck," she insisted, waving her arm exaggeratedly in the air, as if signaling for the planes to land.

"You deserve better. That will be a hundred dollars."

"Right. If I wanted a new shrink I'd have called Annie Sunshine." Realizing that Eve had stopped short, Dee backed up and asked, "Did I hit a nerve?"

"Annie's getting married," Eve announced and slapped her friend on the shoulder. "She called me at sunrise this morning, she was so excited."

"No," Dee crossed herself in a swift, choppy gesture. She was Catholic on her mother's side. "Of the three of us, not Annie!"

"She's the most settled, it makes sense."

"Corpses are settled, Sterling," Dee said, "but not known to be fun in the sack. Never mind. Who wants to get married anyway. . . ? I mean when you really think of it, it's not much of an achievement. Any idiot can do it. All you need is another idiot."

"Let's just eat," Eve said as she swung open the door to Telly's Place, a cramped, noisy hangout, done in dark wood with lilies-of-the-valley in black vases at each table. (Trashing Annie was Dee's way of testing her allegiance, Eve knew. But, it would remain with Annie, whom she'd loved since they met, at five years old, in ballet class. She'd spotted Dee in a graduate seminar on Modern American Poetry at Columbia University and found her oddly compelling.)

Dee made a beeline for a spot near the window. Once seated, she took her time lighting a thin beige cigarette. "Want to pig out and split the banana pecan whole wheat pancakes?"

"Sure, why not? Who's going to see me naked?"

"Hart?" Smoke streamed out of Dee's nose, dragon style and she glared at her friend. "You've failed to mention how your date went." And she looked at her watch set in a thick silver band. "It's been over three days. I think you owe me since I set you guys up."

"He's very nice," Eve said tactfully. "He's just not my type."

"Don't be such a *snob!*"

"And you're not?"

"Not when it comes to getting laid."

Convinced that too much solitude was interfering with her usually flawless productivity, Eve had agreed to a go out with a man named Hart once her birthday began to approach. He was a casual acquaintance of Dee's, someone who'd shown up with a date to several of her infamous parties.

"I do mostly commercial still lifes," he'd said. They were seated at a dimly-lit steak and seafood restaurant of his choosing. Eve couldn't help but wonder if this was his typical "first date" scenario, since the waiters had flown right to them and were buzzing around. "I've been doing cosmetics recently, which are actually very boring. I also do video focus groups—market research stuff—freelance for a friend of mine who has his own video business."

Eve nodded, slightly dazed. Even before Graham, she'd only dated academics, with a couple of poets thrown in for spice. She imagined herself landing in a different part of the country, startled that just a few hours away the landscape and weather could be so different from one's homeland. Sneaking a look at Hart when he excused himself to use the men's room, she admitted he was attractive. He had a very long face which reminded her of someone in a Modigliani painting and large brown eyes, the kind that should have reflected melancholy, but in which the expression was pleasantly nonplussed.

They'd ordered coffee and Hart smiled a crooked, tentative smile with the left side of his mouth. "Jane Austen, right?"

"Right."

"All that school. I've got to hand it to you, I couldn't do it." There was a long silence. "I guess you don't have much time for other things."

"Well, I also teach," she said. "And I'm not a total recluse; I have friends, as you know."

"Oh. I meant hobbies."

"Hobbies, what's that?" she smiled. "Haven't you read about the decline in leisure time in America? I do crossword puzzles every Sunday morning. Does that count?"

"I didn't mean to put you on the defensive," Hart laughed. "I seem to have more hobbies than most people, probably because I spend a lot of time alone. It's the nature of freelance. But then, writing a dissertation has got to be lonely."

"I play the flute. But pretty badly."

Hart perked up like Mr. Knightley when he smelled his food; leaning into her, he said, "My ex-girlfriend was a professional flutist." Those words were like the bells at the races: now the horses would come galloping out. "You're a little like her," he added in an excited voice. "Well, I mean, you're not, but the way you approach your work reminds me of Diana." He shifted in his seat. "She's very passionate about her work also." He leaned closer to Eve and confessed, "It took me a year to recover from a nine month relationship. Finally, I decided to just thrust myself back into the world."

"I'm sorry," Eve said. With her foot, she tapped out the moments—like morse code—until she could excuse herself and escape from a eulogy of past love affairs into the ladies room.

"I'm over her now. She moved to St. Louis to play with the orchestra there. I like to keep up with her career, but that's it."

"It's nice if you can stay friends."

"I don't know if we were really ever friends," he cupped his chin in one hand. "I tended to romanticize more about our relationship than I actually lived it. You know how slow men are to grow up."

"Adult male: an oxymoron," Eve said.

Hart gave another half smile, but then jumped right in again with a lengthy explanation of his experience with this woman, this Diana, how he put her off without knowing it, how, on the night he confessed to her that he loved her, she broke up with him. "She had already said goodbye without my knowing what was happening. By the time she told me what was going on, she was over me," he said. "We weren't too good at verbal communication. You know, a flutist and a photographer."

"You seem pretty verbal to me," Eve said, the dull misery beginning with an ache above the eye. The idea of returning to her empty apartment made her feel worn out, slightly less than visible, sheathed in smoke. When still with Graham, she had cherished her solitary days because she knew they'd be capped with a dinner in Soho, a meal that promised stimulating conversation accompanied by expensive French wine. After the breakup, she'd accused herself of being totally crazy to have stayed so long with someone who she could never love. Annie, in her professional capacity, deduced, "You two were well suited. His money made the life of a student more palatable. You were his exotic Russian Jewess. You know, neither of you want to compromise an inch."

Hart said, "You must have no trouble communicating, being a writer."

"Reader," Eve corrected him.

"Reader," he acknowledged, his eyebrows furrowed, mystified. "But you're writing your thesis, that has to count, right?" His deep, round eyes had gazed directly into hers.

"I'm not any kind of artist, if that's what you mean."

"Well, what are you writing about? What's your *theme?*"

"I don't usually talk about it."

"Oh, c'mon. I'm really interested."

She shifted in her seat and smiled faintly. Outside of her small circle of friends, she was uncomfortable discussing her intellectual ideas. She knew—that to the average person—scholarly work usually sounded quaintly irrelevant, self-indulgent, or incomprehensible. The perfect fodder for ridicule. She cleared her throat and said, "The tentative title is *Emma's Entitlement: Jane Austen's*

Feminist Models. It's basically explaining how Austen's heroines are more powerful feminist models than many of the female characters in twentieth-century literature who reveal a disturbing propensity for masochism."

"I was just thinking about that yesterday," he said.

"Very funny."

Hart had paid for the meal after she made a fainthearted protest. He drove her downtown, and once parked outside her building, asked, "Do you ice-skate?"

"I used to when I was a kid."

"You never forget. It's like riding a bicycle. I haven't been to Rockefeller Center in years. You want to go Sunday?"

"I don't know; I'm not in great ice-skating shape."

"You look okay to me," he said, with no sexual overtones whatsoever.

"I should do work. . . ."

He had touched her hand lightly. "It sounds like you work enough."

"Okay. But talk to me later in the week; I may still bow out. . . ."

"You won't. You're not the bowing out type." At the entrance of Eve's building, he'd pecked her cheek. Then he'd scurried off, quicker than the white rabbit.

Dee lit another cigarette and said, "So, to recap the week's events: Hart's nice but not your type and Annie Sunshine's getting married."

"For my birthday. Let's all be friendly."

"You know I like Annie, as much as I can like someone who orders those shoes from L. L. Bean. What're they called?"

"Topsiders. Who cares what she wears on her feet?"

"Right, right. It's the headbands I love most. So, Annie's going to marry Arthur Schwartz. Unless she began having safe sex with someone new?"

"No," Eve said, raising the cream-colored coffee mug in a toast to her friend's impending nuptials. "It's Arthur."

"Well, bless her. Bless them both, actually. I mean it. As Granny Rose always says: every pot has its lid." She shook her head and her earrings chimed as the silver tongues slapped together. "Can you imagine living with an accountant?"

"He's a tax lawyer, actually."

"Same cliché."

Smoke circled around Dee's small face; her lips were pursed and red, like a rose that couldn't quite bloom. Her almond-shaped green eyes were lined with a black pencil on the lids. She looked, as always, pretty and worn out.

Eve had a headache from the smoke and the two cups of coffee she'd consumed waiting for the food to arrive. She leaned her head in the palm of her hand. "It's not that I'm not happy for them," she said. "It's just so strange how differently we feel on this issue. I mean, I need to be firmly established in my career before I even *consider* marriage. It's weird. We used to think we had parallel lives."

"Why do you still compare yourself to her?" Dee snapped. "What's the difference if Annie is getting married, anyway? If you love school so much and don't want to get married so much, then everything is wonderful."

Eve nodded. "It is. Don't look at me that way, Dee, and stop being so bitchy. I'm just feeling a little isolated these days. I need a change of scene. I'm thinking of going to London for a few months to work on my thesis in another setting."

"All that cold fog will make you feel less isolated. Why don't you give yourself a break and let down your morals? Have sex with someone just for fun."

"Because that's your style, not mine."

The banana pancakes arrived quickly, cheering them up. "I got you two cool presents," Dee said, after quickly downing several bites, soaked in syrup. It was marvelous to watch Dee eat; she was like a religious fanatic who had been fasting for days and had finally broken down.

"I thought this breakfast was my present."

"I'm not *that* cheap, Eve. You can pay for your own breakfast." Dee reached into the enormous black sack she always carried and handed her friend a book wrapped in white wrapping paper with photographs of semi-nude men on it. Inside was a hardcover book entitled, *Debunking Freud*, and it was written by a famous French feminist that Eve had yet to read.

"Didn't you once see a shrink who conducted sessions in French?" Dee asked.

"Yes, to help prepare me for those awful language exams in college when I was blocked. As far as I'm concerned, passing those exams was the only useful thing that ever came out of therapy for me. The rest of it was bullshit. You should agree with me, after that last primal scream idiot you saw. Thanks for the book, Dee. It's great."

"That's part one, part two is better."

It was a black silk teddy with a garter belt. "Well, I hope I get the opportunity to wear it some day," she said, by way of thank-you. She held it up and thought: it's just the right size for Mr. Knightley.

That evening, Eve played the one message on her answering machine. "Happy Birthday, my number one beautiful, accomplished, talented grandchild!" Grandma Henrietta's craggy voice exclaimed. "My word, it's hard to believe that you are thirty years old, since that makes me a hundred and fifty two! Please call me back and give me a clue as to what I should get you as a gift for this momentous occasion. Grandpa wants to get on the wire. Hold on." The phone clanked against the kitchen counter top, and Isaac grumbled, "I'm coming. Hold your horses." Then, her grandmother added, "I hope you're out having a grand old time. Taking a little break before delving back into that important work of yours. I love you, Evie."

After listening to her grandfather's good wishes, Eve crawled into bed with her book, *Self-Deception in Emma*. A half an hour later, the phone jarred her out of studies.

"Hi," Hart said into to the machine. "I just called to tell you I had a . . . nice, no, better adjective, umm . . . interesting, no, stimulating (no, bad connotations), lovely, that's good . . . I had a lovely time the other night." Eve smiled and lifted the receiver. "Sorry," she lied, "I just walked in."

"So did I. I was walking my dog."

"I didn't know you had a dog. I had an Irish setter and an English sheepdog growing up. Now I have a cat. Mr. Knightley."

"Amanda's a mutt. What did you say your cat's name was again?"

"Mr. Knightley. It's from Jane Austen's *Emma*. Remember from Sophomore Survey?"

"No. We didn't have Sophomore Survey at Queens College. Or, if we did, it didn't make an impression on me. Amanda's named after Katharine Hepburn in *Adam's Rib*. Have you seen it?"

"Of course. It's one of my favorite movies."

"Really? I've only seen it once. A couple of months after breaking up with Diana, this flutist I told you about, I rented it. It made me so lonely that the next day I went to the Animal League and got Amanda. It's nice that someone knows if I come home."

"Cats barely notice," Eve said. There was a lull in the conversation.

"What other movies do you like?" Hart finally asked.

"Oh, comedies, especially classics, standard stuff."

"What about *Born Yesterday?* It's one of my favorites."

"I love it," Eve said, and when Hart voiced surprise, she added, "I do have a sense of humor." She turned to glance at her face in the mirror. Despite her pale complexion and the lines beginning to form around her mouth, she looked lovely with her greenish gray eyes and pre-Raphaelite auburn hair.

"Listen, what are you doing tomorrow night?"

"Working," she laughed. "So I can take the time out to see you at the ice rink on Sunday."

"I guess I'm being too pushy."

"Don't worry about it." She watched the smile form in her mirror.

Eve thought that she went to bed feeling happy. But in her dream that night, the women in her family surrounded her: her grandmother, her mother, and her sister. They were holding rocks in their outstretched hands, closing in on Eve, who was frozen still from fright. It was an enactment of Shirley Jackson's *The Lottery,* the story she'd just taught in her Introduction to Literature class the previous week. A wispy dream voice narrated that, in spite of their love for Eve, her family would have to sacrifice her. Unlike the plot of the story, they had chosen her purposely. Eve had not lived up to expectations in a timely enough fashion. Granted, it was a pagan ritual, but it was necessary for the survival of the Goodman/Sterling tribe.

Letters

"Those who tell their own Story . . . must be listened to with Caution." —Jane Austen, *Sandition*

London, England
December 2, 1996

Dear Professor Wellington:

This letter is to inform you that I've arrived safely in England and am looking forward to meeting with you. I was wondering if you'd had the chance to read over the paper on Jane Austen that I'm presenting at the Nineteenth-Century Literature Conference in Bristol? I sent it DHL, as you suggested during our telephone conversation on November 22nd. I would very much appreciate your feedback in as timely a fashion as possible (since your input is invaluable and the date of the conference is fast approaching). Please feel free to call me here at the hotel and to reverse the charges.

I look forward to meeting with you after the first of the year.

Sincerely,

Eve Sterling

December 3, 1996

Brookfield, Connecticut
USA

Dear Eve Jael,

(Does anyone even call you that anymore?) Honey, are you okay?

Do you remember the summer you were thirteen and spent a week with Grandpa and me in Connecticut? You tried to be nice about the fact that you were wasting part of your break from school with the old fogies, but I knew the whole time that you wanted to escape. You always reminded me of me—you know how the story goes. When your mother finally came to after having been knocked out giving birth, she took one look at you and screamed, "Oh, my God, she looks just like Nettie," and promptly fainted away. Well, of course, it's one of my favorite family anecdotes because, even on your first day on earth, you were linked to me.

Anywho, after going off on a tangent like that, I'll try to get down to business. (I'm getting old and I haven't been good for anything since Grandpa got sick, so please excuse the digression.)

I couldn't get the straight story about you from your mother or father. To her credit, your mother has been discreet. But, I did learn your whereabouts from your sister who mumbled something about your needing to go to England to do research for your dissertation.

Sweetheart, is this true? Is everything all right? I'm worried about you taking off like that, with the new baby and all. Do you have that newfangled illness, post-partum depression? Or is it too long after Gemma's birth for that? Tell you what, I'll read up on it.

Please write to me and let me know what's going on. I love you so, my darling first granddaughter!

All my best thoughts are with you,
Grandma

"'Mama, the more I know of the world, the more I am convinced
that I shall never see a man whom I can really love. I require so
much!'"   —Marianne in *Sense and Sensibility*

"IN JANE AUSTEN'S novels, the author manipulates events so
that the heroine is granted the good fortune of finding her
best marriage partner," Eve typed into her old word
processor, the next morning, after breakfast. She thought: in
life, one has to beguile fate to meet one's own advantages
much the same way. Eve decided, then and there, to
construct a concise schedule to ensure the completion of her
doctorate within a year's time.

"So, how'd your birthday go?" Maxie sighed into the
phone, a half-hour later.

"It's okay, Mom. You don't have to check on me."

"I'm not *checking*. I'm concerned. Can't I be
concerned? And speaking of checks, I just sent you one for
two hundred dollars to help you with your rent on that hole-
in-the-wall of yours this month. I know you didn't ask, but
I did it anyway. For your birthday. So, I earned the right to
be concerned *and* to pry." She laughed.

Eve sat up and adjusted the beige throw pillow under
her neck, while her mother asked, "Well, are there any men
on the horizon? I mean, for company, to pass the time with
until you're where you want to be in life."

"I made a date to go ice-skating with a man named
Hart." She wondered why she was telling her mother this
when Maxine would just hoard her vulnerabilities, like a
squirrel storing nuts to chew up later.

"Ice-skating? Hart? What kind of name is that? Is that
his real name?"

"No, Ma. He's a biker. He's in a street gang. Hart. Like
the writer: Hart Crane."

"Oh, forget it. Never mind. Ice-skating is *cute.* Do you

like him? Is he nice? Hart Crane, huh? What'd he write again?"

"He's a *nice boy*, Ma. Please, I have to go. I'm exhausted."

"And I'm not?"

"Listen, I have an idea I wanted to run by you," she said. "I'm thinking of going to London to work on my thesis next semester. What do you think?"

"I don't know. It seems a little extreme."

"What do you mean?" Eve challenged. *"You'd* love to go to London."

"True, true. But, it sounds expensive. Am I paying?"

"No, I can take out another student loan."

"What do you need to go to London *for?*"

"I want to concentrate on my thesis. I don't want to teach. I'm applying for some fellowships. And, there is a professor at London University I'd like to talk to about my research."

"So? Don't they deliver mail there? Oh, forget about going to England! Unless you get back with Graham and he pays for your trip. That's what you want, right? For me to pay for it. How much do you need? I can't afford to entirely support you, you know. . . ."

"Nice talking with you, Ma."

Once they'd hung up, Eve looked out her window at the dull gray sky—victim of an early setting sun—the bare trees and the paper brown apartment buildings with empty fire escapes. She was sitting on her white wicker armchair with a shawl of beige lace sprawled over the back and gazing out onto the bay windows covered by makeshift curtains she'd rigged up from swatches of thrift shop gingham. My life will go on like this, Eve thought, until I'm seventy-seven and my mother's ninety-nine and lying in a nursing home, drooling out of one side of her mouth as she lists eight decades of maternal sacrifices.

Grandma Henrietta had told her the story about visiting her mother-in-law on that awful old woman's one-hundred-year-old birthday. They had arrived at noon with a choco-late layer cake and French vanilla ice cream from Schrafft's.

Great-grandma Esther—all 89 pounds of her—was hoisted up in her bed with the support of two lace-covered pillows on either side of her. She'd worked for more than half a century as a seamstress, listening to Mozart as she'd sewed; the pillow covers were her last work of art. She'd had a stroke while standing on her head, part of her morning yoga ritual. On her birthday, Grandpa Isaac placed the needle of her victrola—which sat on one of the tea carts next to her bed—on her record of Mozart's String Quartet in D Minor. Even with the music, the cake and the ice cream, Esther managed to say, "Isaac, remember the egg-creams at Hertzman's coffee shop? We never had the money for them, but somehow, I always managed to squeeze it out. Never mind your father. He was always useless."

And, Henrietta, standing in the corner with a bag of Esther's laundry to take home, heard Isaac, her eighty-two-year-old husband say, "Ma, nothing anyone did was ever enough. Why was it never enough to please you?"

"Because," Esther had said, "That's how it should be. No one can ever make up for all the sacrifices I've made. Not if you live till my age. It'll never be repaid."

That afternoon, Eve attacked her dissertation proposal with her usual zeal. It was not an easy feat: to try and organize her ideas for such a long work with a fountain pen on reams of legal paper. She began to structure the information in her notes; she cut, pasted, and avoided chaos by tediously using white out to rewrite sentences. When the cooking timer rang promptly at five o'clock, she was having serious doubts that saving her loan money for London was more important than buying a computer.

Eve felt that whale of anger towards Graham as she faced another evening alone, no sex, no intelligent conversation. While nibbling on some almonds, she skimmed through *The Chronicle of Higher Education* for academic jobs in towns she couldn't even locate on the map. "This is pathetic. I'm infatuated with fictional characters like Mr. Darcy, and then, there's Graham," she thought, realizing that she was fantasizing about the first time she and her ex

FI

had made love. In a stern voice, she declared: "I've got to concentrate on other things besides *boys*." But, it had been such a bleak, cold day at the onset of the lonely holiday season; and she found herself unable to grade another paper, or organize another thought. Resigned, Eve foraged through her desk drawer for Hart's number. Luckily, the telephone's ring saved her.

"What're you doing tomorrow morning?" Annie asked.

Eve yawned, flopped down on her bed and rolled over accidentally onto Mr. Knightley who meowed and jumped off, disgruntled. "Exploring the sado-masochistic tendencies of the women in Postmodern British fiction in an attempt to justify that Austen's irony is a stronger form of feminism than late-twentieth-century female anger."

"I'm going shopping for a food processor. Wanna come?"

Eve pulled all her covers around her in a cocoon. Under the white blankets, phone in hand, she felt wrapped in gauze, protected. "I had a date with a guy named Hart a few nights ago. Dee set us up."

"You didn't tell me, you sneak. Was he wonderful?"

"No. He's obsessed with women *artistes*. He talked about his ex-girlfriend for half the meal."

"So it was love at first sight."

"He was . . . sort of interesting looking and nice, but not my type. I think his favorite novel had the word 'intergalactic' in it."

"Ummm, and why, again, is that a problem?" her friend asked smugly; Eve imagined her playing the role of "Knowledge" in a medieval morality play.

"I have to go work. We can't *all* spend our days skipping through town arranging for our bridal registries."

After five hours of being wrapped in the world of her dissertation, Eve took a break. She stood in front of her floor-length mirror, assuming the expression of a ballet dancer: chic unconcern. She patted the soft underside of her hair which curved up over her ears in a snail-like curl. Lately, she'd taken up the old habit of wearing her hair pulled into a bun, as if exposing her neck would recapture that thrilling sense of immediacy: the challenge of performing for an audience. Over the past year, her aging Russian ballet teacher had been reappearing in her dreams in his familiar garb: knee length pants, woolly socks, and a red tee shirt pulled tightly over a muscular chest. He'd place one hand upon the barre and lift his opposite leg remarkably high, up to his ear. A miracle for a man about to die. He could still will his body to perform that stretch the summer right before his death, the summer Eve was sixteen. Discipline, he preached, was the secret to the dancer's life.

The same held true for a scholar. For Eve.

It was a lovely but chilly afternoon; in spite of the cold, Hart's olive face had streaks of rose suffused down his long cheekbones. He was wearing an old Burberry coat with black leather gloves, as if he'd been clothed by Edith Head.

He rubbed his hands together vigorously and smiled widely; he was so excited, he seemed to be percolating. "Guess what I did last night?" he asked. Eve flinched as he leaned over until she realized that he was making sure she was safely belted into the car. "They get stuck sometimes," he explained. After a moment, he said, "I rented your movies and watched them both. Well, I did start to nod off during *Pride and Prejudice,* but it was late. Tell me what you like so much about it. Tell me about Jane Austen. I'm afraid I don't know anything about her."

Eve rarely explained why she loved that world, the beauty of its precision, the natural order of things falling into place, the balance of love and morality, so different from the tortured concepts of passion from the Middle Ages or the seventeenth century. So different from the ideas espoused in modern society and in her family, the very things from which she was running: bare your soul in therapy, joint counseling, in the pages of a memoir. During her freshman year of college, Eve had briefly considered minoring in creative writing; she'd taken some courses in the Program of the Arts department and had fared extremely well. And she was scribbling obsessively in her journal, as usual.

Then one day—when a balmy wind drifted through the open window of Farnall Hall—Professor Beckworth uncharacteristically pronounced how blessed he was to be able to spend his days paying tribute to Shakespeare. Imagine, he'd said, how lucky he was to be able to endlessly study, and pontificate on, the greatest writer who ever lived. *And* to get paid for it. His point was well taken. Eve had instantly dropped the notion of minoring in any artistic field—what she perceived to be her failure as a dancer still an ache she'd awakened to most days—and got down to the business of converting herself into an academic. She'd wanted her path to possess a framework, to be as tangible as the formula to pi. It was crazy to try to be Jane Austen; but she could live in her world.

"Jane Austen was both a genius at delighting her audience and at creating poetry out of the language; also, her novels are the perfect wish fulfillment fantasy," she told Hart. "Reading them is a way to really pamper yourself."

"So then, they're frivolous, aren't they?" Her date glanced at Eve and before she could respond, laughed, "Don't bite my head off."

"Only if you think comedy and grace are frivolous. Suffering and rage are far too overrated."

"What about passion? I remember all those love poems I read in college. Someone was always pining away for someone else. 'I am two fooles, I know, /For loving, and for saying so/ In whining Poetry.'" He grinned.

"John Donne," she said, staring, not bothering to cover up her amazement. "Didn't you say that you don't like to read?"

"Yes," he answered, his grin widening. "I took a course on seventeenth-century poetry in college and always remembered the beginning of that poem because it reminded me of how stupid I felt pouring my heart out to Sally Miles in a love letter."

"Sally Miles," she repeated, as if it were an incantation.

"You're not jealous, are you?" Hart smiled. When Eve didn't answer, he asked, "What were you saying so eloquently, before I got you off track? About passion being overrated?"

"All I was saying was that humor lasts longer than passion." A sharp wind was blowing from Hart's open window but Eve didn't mind; it suddenly filled her with a great energy.

Neither of them said anything for at least five minutes. Then Hart took her hand, gazed in her eyes, and said, "Whatever you're feeling right now, I feel happy."

"Me too," Eve blurted out.

The thing about skating, she decided—once she'd actually gotten on her feet at last, Hart's arm reaching out periodically to steady her—is that you are so busy moving, you can hardly think.

Hart was looking at Eve with those huge eyes, and laughing, weaving in and out, around her, a truly good skater. "Let's get some hot cocoa and big chocolate donuts. Whatayousay?" he'd asked.

"Sounds great," she said, feeling luxurious. When was the last time she'd felt luxurious?

"So," Hart asked, between his sips of cocoa. "What are we doing tonight?"

"Would you like to come over for dinner? Although, I'm not a great cook."

"That's okay, because I am."

They had been skating for three hours and Eve had hardly realized it. In the car, Hart paused before turning the key in the ignition.

"Anything the matter?" Eve asked.

"No. Nothing. That's what's so funny. You're not at all what I expected. I probably wouldn't have asked you out if Dee had told me more than that you were 'pretty and lonely.' You're not my usual type."

"I'm really very sorry," she said in a tight voice.

"I would have been intimidated by you."

"Well," she softened, "you put it so bluntly."

"I'm sorry. I have a tendency to be tactless when I'm nervous." He lifted her hand and kissed it. "Let's not argue." He put his hand beneath Eve's hair, causing her neck to tingle. "They'll be plenty of time for that later."

Two nights later, Eve went to a stag party Dee was throwing to celebrate her most recent breakup. "Bring Hart," Dee suggested.

"Don't be silly. I'm not getting into anything serious right after Graham," she insisted. Joe—an old friend of Dee's—cornered Eve around the deli spread and chips, and monopolized her attention for the entire evening. His thick black hair was uncombed and a long curl hung over one eye; he was smoking a skinny cigarette without a filter. Even as her skin began to heat up, she thought, "Of course he's all wrong; he has that dark, tortured, look that makes him infinitely sexy and means he just got out of Bellevue." Dee had made it quite clear that he was "limited," at the present moment. "He's just coming out of a crazy relationship and is considering intensive Freudian analysis. He wants to be a screenwriter and hasn't worked a real job in two years."

Eve ignored her friend's warnings as well as the clear message printed on Joe's shirt: *The Man who Women Hate to Love is Standing inside this Shirt*. She agreed to let him walk her home and they circled the five block radius, aimlessly, for over an hour, without talking. "Well," she said.

"Yes, well. Great company I am. It was probably a bad idea to come out tonight. I've been going through this bad scene with my father. He's a real son-of-a bitch, but he owns me. A real rich, powerful, scary son-of-a-bitch eking out the allowance to the pathetic fuckup he calls Son. Listen, you want to rent a movie?"

"Okay," she heard herself say, wondering if Joe was reciting from a movie script he'd written and memorized. Despite herself, she could smell desire rising off her skin like perfume.

Joe suggested renting a movie about a boy who shoots and kills his abusive father, but Eve drew the line at sitting through two hours of such self-indulgence. Instead, they settled on *Arsenic and Old Lace,* which she'd seen at least a dozen times. Before Cary Grant discovered the dead bodies in the basement, Eve found this naked man lying in her bed. He was tall and lean like a long-distance runner, with perfectly smooth, hairless, cashew-colored skin. Inside her head a voice was shouting, "Self-abuse alert!" But it didn't matter much as, moments later, he'd taken his hand off her breast and rolled over, his spine straight and formal, as inaccessible as a tree. Eve opened her mouth, but could think of nothing to say; a short time later Joe was asleep.

The next day, when she woke up alone, contempt crept through her like the mercury in a thermometer. She called Dee, but her friend interrupted her before she had a chance to rant about her "date."

"Guess who called me this morning? Gorgeous, fucked-up Joe. The guy who walked you home from my party. Question. Are you into him? Cause, out of nowhere, he asked me to hang out with him this afternoon. I've been into him forever."

"He's yours," Eve said.

Without stopping to analyze, Eve dialed Hart's number; he picked up after the first ring. "Where've you been?" he asked. "I miss you."

"Come over," she said.

Hart's body was long and sleek and slow. Always with Graham there was a great awakening in Eve's body; he would sweat and smile, but would not allow himself that final unleashing of his self. The first time with Hart, he graciously turned the sheets down, spending long moments touching her neck; he did not talk as they made love but cried out in the dark in a way Graham never would. It seemed, to Eve, impossible to take it in, what this meant, staring at this naked man's body; it was like standing much too close to a painting and trying to discern a pattern. Eve loved the sharp bones in his face, his curly dark hair—the color of mussel shells—showing above the V of his crimson sweater, his coarse hands. He touched her eyelids with his lips and they huddled in her sagging double bed, holding each other, tossing, kissing. Eve nuzzled her nose into his neck and traced a heart on his chest; he kissed her and they rolled together, over and over, all motion and no thought. But, once unclasped, she wanted to keep moving and so sprung from the bed into the bathroom where she doused herself with cold tap, waiting to wake up.

"My God," she said aloud to her startled expression. "This is more than I bargained for."

"How can I woo you, if you hate to ski?" Hart asked, two months after they'd met.

"If I can sit in the inn and read my French feminist criticism, I'll go."

"How unromantic," Hart sighed on the other end of the phone; but, Eve could tell he was happy she'd agreed to accompany him upstate that weekend. "Not to sound like a salesman, but," he switched into his imitation of a lower-east side Jew, "for you, daw-ling, I will throw in one free lesson in cross country skiing, which, I might add, is nothing like that *meshugeneh* downhill nonsense." In his own low calm voice, he added, "And, I'm nothing like Graham."

"Yes," she said, "I know." Eve had told Hart how the one skiing experience she'd had with her ex was too dreadful to repeat. After breakfast, Graham had dumped her on the beginner slope with a bunch of ten-year-olds and an instructor that he'd paid for; he spent the day on the advanced slope, racing away from her, over and over. And, in fact, he could have won a medal for creating distance between them: he did so swiftly, with perfect concentration, his gaze never leaving some future, finer destination down the mountain.

"We'll go real slow," Hart said, "so you can fall and bump into trees."

"How entertaining."

"Just call me Gene Kelly on skis."

The night before they left, Eve insisted on staying at her

apartment, even though Hart wanted her with him—in his five room "palace" in Brooklyn—all the time now. But, there was something she felt compelled to do.

She opened her file cabinet and reached for all her crumpled papers under "Pathetic Musings About Graham"; then, she dug out three years worth of journals from her desk drawer. Among all the neatly copied Yeats and Auden poetry were her own scribbled musings about love's allusive qualities. Flipping through her entries, Eve could see how lust had turned her into an emotional diabetic who constantly yearned for all things chocolate. Eve dragged her one big suitcase out of the closet and filled it with her "Graham Papers." It was comforting to imagine herself dressed in all black, including gloves, stuffing a huge piece of luggage with her old lover's body parts.

After dumping the evidence in the garbage room, she called Hart. "I miss you," she said, shocking herself.

"I'll be right there," was his answer. And, as she was learning, there he was. Always. As promised.

In the morning, they loaded his green Honda Civic with their suitcases and two pairs of skis. The second pair was his ex-girlfriend's, Diana's, who had left them at his apartment before departing for her *marvelous* new life with the St. Louis orchestra.

"I can't wait to fill her shoes," Eve said, as she buckled herself into the front seat.

"Okay, maybe it was a mistake bringing them. But, you're not 'filling her shoes,' and they're not haunted or anything. They're just skis, Eve. And, I knew you'd fit into them."

"What a great cliché. Were you aware of what a great cliché this is?"

"Eve, are you still thinking about that ancient comment I made?" Hart asked, jabbing her in the ribs with his elbow.

"Yes," she replied. He was referring to the pronouncement he'd made after the first time they'd slept together: "I loved the whole idea of Diana being a musician, an artist. So what? I'm over her and with you now. Even if I don't quite understand what you do." This was said after much wine drinking and pressuring on Eve's part. She needed answers; was he still obsessed with Diana (the way she was with Graham)?

"I apologize for my stupid, tactless comment for the ten millionth time," he said now. "You know I only said that because I understood her passions better; they were just more familiar to me. You know how truly ignorant and uneducated I am compared to all your worldly, academic friends. *And* Graham."

"Very funny. You seemed to do fairly worldly things with Miss Mozart."

"Did Mozart write flute music? See! I don't know anything about classical music."

"You know what I mean," Eve snapped and stared out the window. Why am I so pissed off, she wondered; because I'm getting too attached, she scolded herself. She couldn't stop her anger—even though it was aimed at herself—now a separate force, like a gust of wind knocking over garbage cans and scattering debris all over the sidewalks.

"I don't think I do," Hart answered, getting into her mood.

"All those arty, black-and-white films you saw with her and all those chamber music things you sat through for her benefit."

"First, of all, it wasn't all for her benefit. I happen to like chamber music. What's with you, anyway? You're only a snob about the culture you happen to approve of? They were documentaries, not arty films. You make it sound like we were into soft-core porn. We took one adult-ed course together and it was on documentaries. I'm sorry if adult-ed isn't as sophisticated as doctoral seminars. And, yes, it was my idea. She didn't even seem to like it. Which, I wouldn't know for sure, since, unlike you, she didn't easily speak her mind."

"Right, right, I know. Diana was *demure*. Too delicate, artistic, and graceful to communicate through mere speech."

Hart pulled the car over, right there on Tenth Avenue. Well, Eve thought, now I've done it. Now, he will turn back and deliver me home, to my solitude, which I obviously deserve.

"Hey, what's wrong? Why are you being so mean?" he asked instead.

Eve shook her head, but refused to turn around. She tried not to cry; but it was an impossible feat, keeping it in, like squeezing too much flesh into a tiny girdle.

"I think I know what's wrong," he said. She peeked at him, at his smiling, knowing face.

Eve thought—looking at him from the side—he is classically handsome; but from the front, an exaggeration of a handsome man, off-centered, a reflection in a carnival mirror: face too large, eyes too big. Despite herself, she longed to throw herself against him, to smell his skin, to feel its warmth. He was warm in all weather. "What?" was all she managed to say.

"You're just jealous of Diana. But, you don't have to be. She's gone and I don't care." He reached for her hand and covered it entirely with his own. She slumped a bit in her seat.

"You're jealous of Diana for one reason."

"Oh, yeah, what?" she asked.

"You feel the way I do."

"I feel like I don't want to be compared to your ex-girlfriends. It's . . . rude."

"You're right, you're right," he said, leaning his face closer to hers. "But, if that's the only reason, then why are you crying?"

Eve shrugged.

"I think I know why. Because you're falling in love with me," he whispered. "That's the reason, isn't it."

She didn't say a word. It mortified her that he might be right. It was too sudden, too unexpected, not what she'd wanted or planned.

"I say that because I know. Because I'm falling in love with you, too."

If it wasn't for the tears in her eyes, Eve would have been hard at work studying the fascinating brown carpeting on the floor of Hart's car. As it was, all she could make out was a beige blur.

"I'd kiss you," Hart said, resting his head on her shoulder, "but I wouldn't want to interfere with the Marcel Marceau look you've created for yourself."

She pulled down her visor; sure enough, there were two long, black streaks running from her eyes to either cheek. "How symmetrical," she said.

"Uncannily so," Hart answered.

The inn in New Paltz was appropriately quaint; there were colonial furniture, a quilt wall hanging, two fireplaces, and bowls of popcorn on several tables in the large sitting room. Karen and Tom Fisher greeted them at the door: she in a denim smock dress with pears and apples embroidered on the front pockets, he in a green checked flannel shirt and khaki pants. Another couple—in identical faded jean overalls and old sneakers—sat on rocking chairs across from each other, reading paperback crime novels.

"It's perfect," Eve said.

Hart smiled his crooked, half-smile and there was a faint blush to his cheeks which told Eve how much this weekend truly meant to him.

"Would you like the tour of our place?" Karen asked, as she handed Hart his credit card back. "Tom can run your bags up to your room."

"Sure," Eve answered, although what she wanted was to be in bed with Hart.

Karen led them into her enormous kitchen—two rooms, really—with its Victorian coal stove and myriad of pots and pans hanging from the ceiling. She offered them fudge from a tray of chocolates and then gestured that they should sit at the pine kitchen table.

"How do you find the time for all this?" Hart asked. Karen and Tom were professors at the college in town. Hart had deliberately chosen this place for that reason and then fed Eve this information with great pride, the way you'd feed your lover an unusually delicious cream soup you'd spent hours preparing. "He's more anxious to please than a puppy," Eve had confessed to Annie. "And what's so bad about that for a change?" her friend had tossed back at her.

"It's busy," Karen admitted. "Between the kids, the inn, and teaching." She sighed and added, in what Eve knew, at once, was her professorial voice, "We need to compartmentalize."

"What do you teach?" Eve asked, taking tiny bits of her marvelously rich fudge and gazing out her window at the chunks of snow crusted on the branches of the pine trees, weighing them down.

"Chemistry."

"What a great life," Eve said.

"It looks more seductive than it actually is," Karen said; the tiny wrinkles at the corners of her eyes were creased like the folds in a miniature accordion. She did look very worn out, despite her toothy smile.

Upstairs, later, in their cozy, pine-scented room, Eve questioned Hart as they unpacked. "Didn't she seem unhappy? Well I, for one, would be *thrilled* to get a job like this. It's exactly what I want. I wonder why she bothers running this place? I mean it's lovely, but it has to interfere with her real work."

"Tom told me that he is paying alimony for his two kids from a first marriage. It's been hard, financially, since the divorce. He said his first wife hated it here; she really missed the city." Hart strained to remember, knowing how Eve craved intricate details, as if they could be copied like a dress pattern and recreated. "She was in finance. I think that's what he said. Anyway, she agreed to move upstate for his career. But, she couldn't take not working and couldn't get anything good in her field, so eventually they split up."

"When did you learn all that?"

"We chatted for a couple of minutes on the stairs after I left you two to your 'girl talk.'"

"Jeez, you got all of that out of him in the course of a few minutes? All Karen told me was she wishes she had

44

more time to try out new recipes, how cooking is her true vocation. Ever consider a career as a counselor or a spy?"

He winked at Eve and grabbed her around the waist, drawing her close. "I didn't want to tell you, but I might as well. I'm C.I.A. Counselor for Irate Academics."

"Very clever," she laughed.

"It just came to me. See what you do for me? Seriously. You cause me to discover untapped resources, true intelligence that no one could have guessed existed."

"I guessed," Eve whispered into his ear, then gently bit the lobe.

In the morning, Hart's skin tone was decidedly greener. He lay on the patchwork quilt, dramatically still, eyes open. The lights were off and the red gingham curtains closed. Eve walked over to the bed.

"Hey? Are you okay?" she asked and touched his back, tentatively.

At first he didn't answer, then he rolled over on his side, facing away from her and coiled up into a fetus position. Eve gently pushed the hair off his forehead. "Hart, what is it? I hope it's not your appendix," she said, frightened to find him clutching his arms into his body, quivering.

He shook his head, but still didn't speak. Eve felt his forehead again; "Did you throw up?"

When he nodded, she said, "I'm going to get you some Tylenol from my bag in the bathroom. For the fever. It'll just take a second."

After he dutifully took his pills, Eve sat on the bed next to Hart for close to half an hour, and stroked his hair. He breathed deeply, not speaking, and she assumed that he'd fallen asleep. But, suddenly, he said, "I've ruined everything." He rubbed a clenched fist to his eye, roughly.

"Don't be silly," Eve said, lifting his hand away and holding it, its warmth penetrating into her own cool hand.

"I'm just so pissed at myself."

"What for? For catching a virus? That's ridiculous."

"It's just so typical of me. I plan our first romantic weekend away and I get sick. Stay away from me, Eve. I'm afraid I'll jinx you, all your wonderful, lofty goals . . . ."

"How can you jinx me?" Eve laughed, "you're just feverish." But a shiver ran through her as well.

He rolled over, circling his arms around her waist. "I wanted this weekend to be special."

"It is. And, there will be other chances. Unless you're not telling me something. Like you're prone to rare tropical diseases." She edged in so close to him, her nose touched his. His whole body generated heat.

"Umm . . ." he murmured. "No. I never get sick. This is just so odd," and he nuzzled his face into her neck. Within seconds, he was out.

Eve had a muffin and coffee sent up to the room and spent the morning reading a used copy of Barbara Pym's *Excellent Women* which she'd bought from a street vendor just the day before. She'd promised herself: no work on this trip and, for once, she'd been true to her word. Even though she had a pile of papers waiting to be graded for Monday's class, she'd left them at home; her book, *Circular Constructs in a Phallocentric World,* lay unopened in the bottom of her carry-along bag. For lunch, she drove to a bar and grill with old wood tables and benches, shot-guns hanging on the wall for decoration and sawdust on the ground. Eve sat and leafed through her novel, then picked up a copy of the local paper. She scanned two right-wing editorials which she was tempted to go through, circling bad grammar with her lavender pen. After skimming the second essay, in which the columnist pontificated about the immorality of distributing condoms in the local high school, she rolled the paper up into a ball and stared out the window at all the snow-topped trees. Although bored, she wasn't lonely—for the first time in months, maybe even years.

In the afternoon, Eve walked briskly through the one main street in town, stopping in almost every store to survey the endlessly quaint merchandise and to get out of the appalling cold. She felt compelled to buy Hart something special, a new desire for her. Graham had been rich and, like many people who can buy themselves anything, had neither required nor amply appreciated gifts. Their first Christmas together, she'd bought him an old leather bound edition of *War and Peace* which, she later found out, he'd exchanged for some paperbacks by his favorite contemporary writers, the two Johnnys: Updike and Cheever. Graham loved stories of traditional, middle-class American families who screwed up in the privacy of their own homes; and, they'd had several arguments about what Eve insisted was one of Graham's major philosophical flaws: he found the mediocre man "heroic." For Hart, she chose a small clock, set in a lovely redwood frame. He was always complaining about getting a late start in life, having only begun working for himself a year ago and not having saved much money.

That evening, his fever dropped to 99 degrees and he was sitting up, attempting to sip some clear broth out of Karen's state university mug.

"I'll make it up to you," he said forlornly, but with more strength in his voice.

"Stop saying that! There's nothing to make up. Look, I got you something." Eve reached into her backpack for the clock, wrapped in coral pink tissue paper.

"What's this for?" Hart asked, genuinely shocked.

"You're sick and you treated me to this wonderful place. It's a combination get well and thank you gift."

Hart wriggled around, throwing off the sheets and blankets. "I'm not used to this. I feel weird."

"Why? Didn't your parents always get you stuff when you were sick?"

"No. My mother cooked."

"No magazines, comics, gum, candy, books?" These being the comforts from her own childhood.

"No. Just chicken soup and crackers."

"Pathetic."

Hart was busy tearing the paper off his gift with happy impatience. He lifted the clock out of its box, gingerly, as if he were handling an exquisitely rare fossil. "This is beautiful," he said.

"Thanks," Eve answered, embarrassed at his emotion; there were tears at the corners of his eyes. It struck her, suddenly, that his parents may have neglected him in some crucial way. It was easy to imagine him as a boy: sad, round eyes, all that lovely blackish hair, smooth dark skin, sitting by himself in a dimly lit apartment, fiddling with his shirt buttons while his mother was out shopping for her trinkets of choice: cameo pins, thick rings, a silver cigarette lighter.

"This is the nicest present," Hart said now.

"Give me a break," Eve laughed. "That *is* truly pathetic."

"What can I say. I'm a truly pathetic sort of guy."

"Well, you're definitely easy to please."

"A four-pack of white socks from 14th Street is a great gift in my book."

"Personally, I prefer airline tickets, but what the hell!"

Hart's fever shot back up to 101 degrees later that night; Eve stayed up reading while he dozed with his head on her chest. At one point, she bent down to kiss his forehead and heard Hart mumbling.

"What's that?" Eve asked.

"I knew it," he said. "I've always had good instincts, a sixth sense about emotional things."

"Knew what? What emotional things?" He snored in response. "Knew what, Hart?" she whispered into his ear.

A few minutes later, he threw one arm across her waist and she kissed the top of his head in reply. "You'll see," he predicted. "Leave it to me, the one with the intuition in this relationship."

"See what?" she asked, still engrossed in the safe world of Miss Pym's spinsters.

"I'm right. You're the one."

"What *one?* Hart?"

He opened his eyes and looked straight up at her for a second, then closed them and said, "The one to bring home to Mom and Dad, although not necessarily *my* mom and dad! But, that's another story . . . . The girl next door. The girl of my dreams. You know." And he sang, weakly but on key, "The girl I marry . . ."

Eve sat very still. Her stomach started fluttering as if she'd swallowed a sparrow. "I need to finish my degree first. I simply can't fall in love right now," she thought, imagining the only copy of her dissertation bobbing on a thin shaky raft, so far out in the ocean, that the line where the sky met the water was the only other sight for miles. But she knew—with the giddiness that comes with envisioning your prescribed fate—that Ph. D. or no Ph. D., she'd met her husband.

In the morning, Eve did not mention Hart's confession. Instead, she treated him like a man who, in a drunken moment, had revealed some great state secret. For months, she carried this secret around, a rabbit's foot, the augur of her future life.

In the air on route to England
November 30, 1996

Dear Hart,

I should have told you I'd sent my proposal to the conference; but, honestly, none of this was premeditated. I left because I had to, because I felt annihilated. Hopefully, spending time here will erase the last two months of disappointments and betrayals, the sense that I was straphanging through my life, and finally the train stopped short, throwing me to the floor. Can't you imagine what it's like to wake up one day and feel as if you are living someone else's life? The panic that sets in?

After hours of traveling, I've finally sunk into a quiet white oblivion, my mind soft, like pudding. From the plane, I have a view of the hills of England rolling into one another as if they are giving birth. (See, birth images still haunt me. But, here, at least, they're peaceful). It's so beautiful; I wish that you could see it too.

London
December 1, 1996

I have landed safely in this "Vanilla" country. Physically safe and am staying in a cheap, ugly hotel. It's raining and the air is frigid.

Hart, will you let me know how Gemma is doing? Write or call me at the hotel. I didn't abandon the two of you forever, despite what you think, and I *need* to know that my daughter is okay. Of course, I trust your judgment implicitly when it comes to Gemma. You're a wonderful father, a much finer parent than I am.

You think I'm a coward. I probably am. But, you are the opposite, foolishly brave. It's already clear to me that you'd stay put through anything, *anything*, even self-nullification.

And is that so good: being able to endure such deprivation? Yeats wrote, "Too long a sacrifice ... makes a stone of the heart." Are you wondering what kind of person would take time to quote poetry from across the Atlantic when so much is at stake? But that's just the point! Don't you see? That's who I am.

Before we met and—without a moment to ourselves—had Gemma, I used to scribble volumes of poetry into my journals. For reference. For comfort. Then, I stopped, caught up in that other world, of round-the-clock feedings, of my mother's sudden, mounting success, of days spent away from my thesis, and I got lost.

But, I won't be lost for good, Hart. I won't. I can't be.

Kiss Gemma for me a hundred times and tell her that I love her. I do. Just writing these words makes my heart feel split in pieces, an apple whose core is divided.

Yours Always (whether you'll have me or not),

Eve

"'There is safety in reserve, but no attraction.'"

—*Emma* (Mr. Knightley to Emma).

HART WAS BRAVE. He had agreed to meet Maxie and Eve alone for a late lunch. They were at a new restaurant—with a Caribbean motif—near Union Square; there was a live band playing and on each table, in black vases, Jack-in-the-pulpit flowers bowed seductively to their customers.

Eve had been listening to the same tales of woe—about her mother's former dissertation advisor Alexandra Kimball (*Alexandra the Horrible*)—since she was eighteen years old. Unfortunately, Maxine weaved her way onto the topic again, today, in between their spinach and taco salads, and the coffee. Hart grinned a bit shyly and asked, "So, do all the Sterling women get their doctorates?"

"*Well*," Maxie began with dramatic emphasis, "I almost *didn't.*"

Eve glanced at their waitress, a girl with reddish blond wispy hair and a sugar white face with just the suggestion of pink in her cheeks. Turned full face, her ears stuck out a bit, making her look elfish. "Dancer," Eve thought, with a momentary pang of nostalgia as she watched the girl's self-conscious duck walk: toes out, calves tight as piano wires.

The summer after her freshman year of college, when Eve gave up ballet, she'd stuffed herself with chocolate-covered cherries, buttered popcorn, and mocha ice cream with whipped cream. Acts of defiance after all those years of starving.

"God, remember how crazy Alexandra the Horrible made me, Eve?"

"Yes," Eve said, on cue. At the same time that Maxie, suddenly, was preoccupied with her life—in a way she'd never been before—her oldest daughter began losing track of her own. As those searingly hot July days had turned into night, Eve could almost hear a faint wind in her ears to accompany the relentless feeling of falling through space. The determination, strong as a cast-iron pot, that gave her back definition had transferred over to her mother. In exchange, she was briefly given her mother's gift of sleep; Eve had begun falling off at the oddest times of day. She'd dream, inevitably, of the dance hall: the smell of chalk and mildew, the sound of an unmelodious tune being plunked out on chipped, yellow-stained piano keys, the sight of the dancers with their serious eyes and calloused feet, and, of course, Mr. Denosvitch—the old Russian tyrant—with his cane and his back slightly arched in his cocky manner.

"This is going to sound crazy, Hart," Maxie was saying now, "but I think God—whoever SHE is—put Alexandra, that *lunatic,* into my path to teach me that I could stand up to people. Before that everyone thought, 'Oh Maxine, she's so easy-going, nothing fazes her.' Of course, I always stuck up for my *children,* but not myself. Remember Eve, I used to give dinner parties and forget to put my shoes on. I'd be wearing my pink bunny slippers when the psychiatrists and their tennis-playing wives would arrive, that's how—oh, I don't know—*casual* I was about life."

Maxie gazed, for a moment, into the gray March day, past the rain dripping down the window like sentimental tears, and looked straight at a memory of her pink bunny slippers. "I honestly didn't know—before Alexandra got in my way—how much my own life meant to me." She directed her attention back to Hart and sighed, "Oh, well, I guess I believed I'd always be that young girl in braids and knee socks wandering happily, unconsciously, from day to day."

The blithe idiot, Eve thought, but said, "Well, you certainly made it look like you could whistle through *school.* You always slept before tests. You wrote papers the night before, just whipping them out. You made everything look easy."

"Easy!" Maxine guffawed. "When I get overloaded I nod off in chairs, cars, over piles of laundry. You were always the opposite, such a perfectionist. Remember how, in junior high, you always wrote your term papers a week before they were due? You've been more conscientious than I am ever since you pushed your way down the birth canal. *Okay,* so your standards are impossible, you didn't get that from me. I firmly believe that genes skip a generation because you were born with my mother's sense of discipline. Of course, back when you and Livy were little, nothing was considered genetic; *everything* was the mother's fault. But, honestly, I always tried to get you to have more fun. Remember how I wanted you to go on a teen tour instead of ballet camp? You know what *my* secret is? I'll tell you: I never cared as much as you! Honestly. Now that I've gotten myself off the hook for whatever I might have done to make you so hard on yourself." She sighed, "As if I *ever* could."

"So," Hart interjected, a half-smile on his face. "What did Alexandra do to . . . uhh, change you?"

Maxie lifted her spoon like a gavel and pounded the table with it. "I'll tell you what she *did:* she humiliated me! She tried to discredit my research—three years' worth—with my colleagues at the hospital, *and* with my committee. She told me—and I will never forget this, *never!*—that it shouldn't be too much of a burden on me to have to start over since I had a husband who made good money to support me! Can you believe it, the nerve of that woman!"

"Sounds sexist," Hart nodded, and Eve smiled at him.

When Maxie spoke of her former advisor, her metabolic rate suddenly accelerated. Her words were pointed with venom; she'd all but spit when she talked. "Of course she was sexist *and* bitter *and* threatened by me and my research. But her *psychodynamics* were not my problem, understand. *I* was the student. *I* was the vulnerable one! Was it *my* problem that she was a widow whose children never called her?" She waved her spoon at both her daughter and Hart. "Could you blame them? Who would visit that witch? *Let me tell you,* I mobilized myself in a way I never dreamed I was capable of! Before I left that department, the chairman,

54

my committee members, they all thought she was the *devil!"*

"Ma!" Eve said, "Don't be so melodramatic."

The sugar-faced waitress had finally made it with their drinks; they sipped their coffees in silence, mulling over their private thoughts. Eve's was: she hoped her mother didn't launch into her comparison of their respective dissertation advisors. Eve was twisting her paper napkin around the ring of her coffee cup, obviously nervous, so that Maxie sighed, "Oh, well, I get carried away when I talk about my doctoral experience. But not everyone has a bad one. Granted, no one just *sails* through. But plenty of people just work hard and finish. It looks like that might happen in Eve's case. Although, I *am* worried about that Maud Forster . . . there's more there than meets the eye . . . "

"Mom," Eve protested, "You've never even *seen* the woman!"

"No, I know," Maxie said, swatting the air with her spoon as she dismissed her daughter's objection.

Hart reached out for Eve's hand, disengaging it from its busy work with the now-shredded napkin. "Whatever happens, she'll do fine."

Maxie smiled at him with a territorial look in her eye which read: don't presume to know her better than *I do,* even if you're right. She said, "Of course she will."

Eve gave a little wave as if to say: "Hey folks, I'm here." But, she needn't have bothered. They were both grinning now. What had she missed? In some fraction of time that couldn't be measured—regardless of Maxie's opinion on the matter—Hart had joined the small clan of people who were in a pact to protect Eve.

"Eve?" Hart whispered in the dark, as they lay in his bed that night. It was just past midnight, the sky lit up by the Brooklyn street lamps was finally clear, a deep grape, nearly black, with a few discernible stars.

"Umm?" Eve answered, rubbing her foot up and down over his.

"Do you think your mom approves of me?" His voice sounded funny; it made her think of a bruised pear, all tender and fleshy inside.

"Of course. She likes you a lot," Eve fibbed; in truth, she questioned whether Maxine found Hart suitable boyfriend material. She curled herself closer to him, rested her head on his chest, listened to him breathe.

"I guess I can't help feeling that she'd be a lot happier if I were a . . . research scientist or a civil rights lawyer or a professor of . . . I don't know . . . social theory or something. I mean, she knows we're getting serious . . . we are, right?"

"Yes," Eve whispered, the muscles in her stomach clenching.

"Okay, then she must be worried. That's all I mean."

"Worried about what?" Eve propped herself up on her elbow and gazed down, into Hart's face, all angles and shadows in the dark, trying to see if there was evidence of fear in his eyes.

"That I'm not good enough for you," he said gruffly.

"Hart," she nuzzled her face against his, "that's ridiculous. You can't really believe that! You're more than good enough for me; you're *too* good! Let's look closely at this: you've already stayed awake through the *Persuasion* video—twice—against all odds, and put up with me quizzing you on the gender of George Eliot and George Sands in the middle of the sex act." She was able to joke even as anxiety flickered, like a candle deep within her. Who was she kidding anyway? Didn't she have doubts— not about Hart's worthiness, but that she'd someday crave a man whose very scent reeked of brilliance, who tantalized her with his extraordinary brain matter? Impossible standards was the family curse—passed down through the maternal line—of which Eve was alternately proud and deeply ashamed. Dee's voice echoed in her mind: "Why bother dating? Just find out the GRE scores from Princeton and have your mom arrange the marriage with the guy who gets the highest results."

"You're right, I'm too good for you!" he laughed and kissed her quickly. "But, the question is: will your mom realize my true worthiness?"

"Of course. And what if she doesn't? Who cares?"

"God, Eve. *You* do."

"Hart, honey." Eve said, and rubbed his chest to get his mind off Maxine Sterling. It was more than a little unsettling to discover her lover's vision of her as a baby kangaroo cushioned in her big mother's pouch—his recognition of her greatest character flaw. "What's the difference? You know how I feel about you."

"I just want things to work out for us. And, I'm not judging you; I have my own deal, being the *boychik* to a mother for whom the definition of love is finishing all your pot roast and never *ever* moving out of the neighborhood— just in case she needs you to move some furniture around on short notice."

Neither of them said another thing. All Eve wanted was to make love, without a word, with the acts of their bodies pushing all their thoughts away. If they didn't send their demons scurrying for other psyches to invade, at least they lay, afterwards, entangled, conspirators. In some, as yet indiscernible way—she knew—they were working together, in silence, to separate themselves from their pasts.

It was Passover and they had decided to split their time between their two families; Eve's on the first night, Hart's on the second. Night number one had arrived and Eve was more excited than nervous at the prospect of introducing her new boyfriend to the Sterling tribe.

"I can't wait to dazzle the octogenarian crew with my charm," Hart said, as they rode the elevator to Eve's Great Aunt and Uncle's apartment, cloistered from the loud vulnerability of Manhattan, in Tudor City. Walking nearly to the East River, Hart gazed up at their building and said, "Who needs the British Isles when you can get castles right here on Manhattan Island."

Now, Eve gushed, "You'll love them. They're great people. I just adore my Uncle Bernie; he's sweet, even-tempered, brilliant—better versed in literature than I am—and a wonderful husband."

"Impressive résumé. Should I ask for a job cleaning his shoes?"

"C'mon Hart. You can't help but love Uncle Bernie. He's truly the kindest man I know. Women have been falling in love with him all his life."

"I don't know if I can take the competition."

Eve kissed him to quiet his nerves. "No competition. I'm just excited about your meeting everyone. My mom's family is crazy, but I love them all." Eve had spent every summer of her childhood with her mother's family, vacationing in Maine: cabins lining the boardwalk—good soldiers all in a row—the moss green lake, the dock, soggy and dipping in and out of the water like a soup crouton. These relatives felt as crucial to her identity as her DNA. "I really just want you to feel comfortable, to fit in."

"Nothing like a little pressure to make a man lose his erection," Hart said and squeezed her hand.

"Stop it," Eve kissed his cheek, and before she could check herself, said, "I love you."

But Hart took the confession in stride. "Love, shmove," he answered in his Yiddish accent, "I'm just a merchant class Jew from the wrong side of Delancey Street. You smarty-pants Jews—with your big degrees and fancy addresses—always making us feel like real Yids."

"Ring the buzzer, Moishe."

Aunt Hannah, four foot, ten inches in her orthopedic shoes, answered the door; she looked a little older and grayer than when Eve had last seen her a few months ago but basically the same: buxom, with a hook nose, thick black-rimmed glasses, and stiff white hair. She smiled the minute she saw her grandniece. "Evie girl!" she exclaimed, "Hey, Bern, your girlfriend is here."

They stepped into the blue and yellow sunlit apartment, cluttered with too many heavy pieces of furniture, relics from thirty years in a sprawling floor-through on Jerome Avenue in the Bronx. The Schullers finally moved, in 1972, after Aunt Hannah was mugged at gunpoint in the vestibule of their building. As she always boasted, she could take the two times that a knife had been pulled on her, but the gun really shook her up. Now, their place resembled a pleasant storage room: there were too many flourishing hanging plants, too many small glass trinkets and porcelain statues of miniature figures in Swiss outfits, too many pictures of the family mounted on cardboard and dried flowers inside gold frames.

"If it isn't Helen of Troy herself," Uncle Bernie joked, traveling slowly across the room, cane in hand. "How'a doing, your highness?" Bernie kissed Eve's cheek and, in exchange, she patted him on the top of his bald head, part of their ritual.

"How are *you* doing, Bernie?"

"Aaahh, can't complain, can't complain."

"That's good, Bern. It's wonderful to see you. I want you to meet my friend, Hart."

Bernie shook Hart's hand; "Good to meet you, good to meet you," he said. "Hey, folks, come say hello to your daughter and her handsome new boyfriend."

Eve's father approached in his slow, deliberate way, gently stroking his salt and pepper clipped beard. Despite Maxie's pleading, Daniel had worn his 1970s yellow jacket with the wide lapels, a pale yellow shirt and an orangy brown tie with a slight coffee stain on its tail. "Hi Evie," he said in the nearly imperceptibly quiet voice he used at social gatherings. Once Hart had wandered off with Bernie, he draped one arm around his daughter's shoulder. "I just wanted to tell you that I like your new friend. I mean I haven't gotten much of an opportunity to get to know him very well, but he seems like a very nice fella."

Eve couldn't help smiling at her father's description, the 1940s *It's a Wonderful Life* sound of it. "He is, he is."

Eve kissed his dry cheek and waved to her mom who was sitting at the dining room table talking loudly to her Aunt Eileen, a childless widow who'd worked her entire adult life as an editor at Random House.

"Come say hello to Eileen," Maxie nearly shouted. From the kitchen, Eve could see her younger sister, Olivia—who was preparing cut vegetables and dip—roll her eyes in response to the volume of their mother's voice.

"How are you, Eileen?" Eve asked.

Tiny, plump Eileen, with piano legs and a hairy mole on her chin, shook her head. "Oh, well . . . old age is no picnic, honey. Don't let anyone tell you it is. My bowel functioning is not great but Dr. Tyler says—and I quote—'Eileen, at your age, it's a goddamn miracle that you ever reach the toilet at all.'"

"I'm sorry to hear that."

Eileen removed her eyeglasses and let them hang from the silver chain around her neck; she squinted closer. "So, how ya doing, honey?" She lifted the young woman's hand into her own brittle, square one. "Still working on that *damned* degree?"

"I'm afraid I am," Eve admitted. Remarkable, she thought, that ancient Aunt Eileen—with her unreliable intestines—could still count family achievements like beads on an abacus.

"When are they going to let you out of that hellhole? You know my grandniece, Lisa? She was going for her doctorate in biophysics at Harvard. She just finished this January, I think it was. What a smart girl, that Lisa . . . ."

Eve imagined a senior citizens' Olympics and all the members of her mother's brood lined up to throw javelins they couldn't lift, each one marked with the name of some stellar grandchild.

"Would you like some carrots and onion dip?" Olivia intervened, platter in hand.

"Oh, no thank you honey. I'm afraid this old battle-ax can't handle roughage anymore. It wrecks havoc on the bowels. I'd be holed up on Bernie's toilet until next Christmas."

Breaking free, Eve hooked arms with Hart and led him into the bedroom. Her "genius" younger cousin, David—a former history teacher at the Dalton school, turned law student at Yale—was lying on the blue reclining chair, watching a baseball game.

"Hi, Coz!" he exclaimed, elbowing his way out of the chair.

"Hi, Coz. What's new?"

Still eyeing the television—which was propped up on Bernie's dresser—he responded, "Not much. Looks like you can't say the same. Are you going to introduce me to your beau?" Dave asked, giving Eve a snide glance.

"Cousin Dave, this is Hart Orbach, my *beau*. Hart, this is my cousin Dave; he's Bernie's grandson and formidable Scrabble partner."

Hart shook his hand. "I've heard much about your excellent game skills."

"Don't be too impressed. You should see Bernie play. Razor sharp at 85 years old. Yes!" he shouted in response to the noise from the game.

"You another Harvard grad along with granddaughter Lisa?"

"Hart!" Eve nudged him in the ribs.

"No," Dave laughed, "Princeton. You must have been talking to Aunt Eileen; she's an incessant complainer, but her mind is like a Rolodex when it comes to other people's achievements, speaking of which, what do you do, Hart?"

"I'm just a humble photographer."

"Hey, don't be modest. You know, back in my youth, I had my own visions of grandeur; I won a photography contest in eighth grade."

"Back when you still had the potential to be a hip guy," Eve said.

"Hey, I think I'm quite debonair," Dave said, bowing awkwardly, Japanese style.

"I was just about to say that about you," Hart offered.

Dave laughed. "Big improvement, Coz. I hope you don't mind my saying it, but that last beau of yours was a bit lacking in the sense of humor department. His eyes used to twitch when Gramps and I were winning at the 'Game.'"

"Sounds like the style and conduct of my Scrabble playing carries a lot of weight in this family."

Her cousin patted Hart on the shoulder; "It's the one true gauge of a man's worth around here." Once they were all squeezed into the dining room for the buffet style passover dinner, Dave whispered, "We don't believe in superficial, religious rituals in this family. We are a strictly Ethical Culture, Godless bunch."

"Fine by me," Eve's 'beau' whispered back. "I've had enough hypocritical, once a year, yarmulke-toting Jews to last my lifetime. My relatives think the meaning of 'good Jews' is pulling out the electric Menorah once a year and cleaning your mink for the High Holidays."

"Big change from that around here," Eve said, as, amazingly, her Aunt Hannah—helped by Maxie—carried out a silver platter on top of which sat an enormous ham.

"You're not kidding about the casual attitude," Hart laughed.

"I think Hannah got confused between Easter and Passover in her old age," Eve said. "No one will say anything. Or care. My mom's family is composed of all WASP wannabees. I'd better go help or I'll never hear the end of it from my mother."

Eve eased her way around Aunt Eileen—who, thank God, was lecturing a sheepish-looking Uncle Bernie on the devastating repercussions of eating spicy food—into the kitchen. Olivia was by the sink, nibbling on matzo. She looked sleek and beautiful in a sienna shirtdress and black scarf snaked around her neck. Always visually artistic, Eve's sister had adopted a chic bohemian style since beginning her job, a few months ago, as an assistant for a feminist documentary maker. "Did you see Aunt Hannah bring a HAM out!" she exclaimed, nearly choking on the matzo. "Oh, my God. Do you think she's senile?"

"Ssshhh," Eve warned her, laughing. "Do you think they hid Easter eggs?"

"Maybe we should have dressed in Laura Ashley pastel smocks and stood around drinking gin and tonics. Oh, my God," she added, peering into the refrigerator, "there are deviled eggs in here. Isn't that goy food?"

"No, I don't think so. Actually, I have no idea. Is there any gefilte fish? Any macaroons? Well . . . at least they did get some matzo."

Eve touched her sister's thick chestnut hair, recently styled in an elegant, short cut: sharp lines parallel to her cheek bones. "Looks great," she said.

"Thanks," Olivia said, peering into the oven.

"So, where are Grandma and Grandpa? I want Henrietta to meet Hart."

She shrugged. "Late. Hey, look what I found." She reached in and lifted a large, silver soup tureen out of the oven, "matzo ball soup! Hints of tribal impulses after all."

Eve's grandparents made their entrance after the company had all grabbed their plates and found themselves seats, some at the dining-room table, others scattered throughout the apartment. Grandma Henrietta was the matriarch of the family, a schoolteacher of the old guard, a great grammarian, having earned her Masters from Columbia's Teacher's College in 1942. She was famous for her long, left-wing lectures, proclaimed in the commanding tone of a Victorian pedagogue, and for the fact that she had published a biography a long time ago, when she was star-tlingly young. The book was entitled *The Arbitrator of her Destiny: Elizabeth Cady Stanton*. Eve had read it for the first time when she was only ten and found it powerful, magical; later, when she reread it as an adult, she thought it—not surprisingly—a bit too didactic.

While Eve's friends envisioned their grandmothers as warm, domestic creatures, who fed them ethnic dinners and held conservative values from a simpler time, she always pictured Grandmother Henrietta outdoors, walking faster than any of her grandchildren, in her cushiony shoes, espousing the politics of Eleanor Roosevelt and reciting from Dickens' *A Tale of Two Cities*. Henrietta's home was dotted with passages, taped to the walls, clipped from books or written in her sturdy, bold hand. For thirty years, a yellowing newspaper quote of Einstein's remained on her refrigerator: "I want to know how God created the world. I am not interested in this or that phenomenon, in the spectrum of this or that element; I want to know his thoughts; the rest are details."

Eve remembered a story Maxine had recounted about her grandmother: Henrietta Goodman, biographer and teacher. As a girl, her mother wished nothing more than to have a "normal mother," someone who showed up for open house at school in a flowered dress, sturdy shoes and her hair in a bun. Instead, Henrietta made her entrance into a classroom, Katharine Hepburn-style: beige trousers, a tweed blazer, her sleek auburn hair angled close to her cheekbones. "Isn't that woman some kind of famous author?" a child would whisper and Maxie would slouch in her seat, cursing that her mother didn't have an ordinary job, a salesgirl at Macy's. Eve knew exactly how Maxie Goodman had felt.

As usual, Eve's grandma looked beautiful: she had few streaks of gray in her auburn hair and her large, hazel eyes were clear and sharp. Next to her, grouchy old Grandpa Isaac—with his bad hip and talk of the stock market—could never shine. "The goddamn Cross Bronx Expressway was jammed again," he pronounced now, struggling to remove his London Fog raincoat. "They've been doing construction on that road since 1980. Help me with this thing, will you Nettie?"

"Hello, darling," Grandma addressed Eve, after Daniel rushed in to help both her and his father-in-law with their coats. "Who is this lovely-looking young man?" she asked, smiling. She winked at Hart.

Within moments, Henrietta had whisked him off for a private conversation, leaving Eve to get a plate for Grandpa Isaac. "The roast beef looks too tough and dry," he complained. "I bet that ham's just loaded with salt. Give me some of it, anyway, would ya?"

Eve overheard Grandma Henrietta laugh flirtatiously. "It's just as well," she said loudly, "You're just *too smart* to stay in school so long. The most successful people often *are*." She poked him in the chest, "Don't forget that." This coming from the woman who had threatened to disown her daughter when she wanted to try out for dinner theater rather than apply to City College.

Hart loved her instantly. "Let me get you some dinner," he said, nearly tripping over a coffee table so that Henrietta didn't have to move.

He spent the rest of the evening attending to her needs with the solicitousness of an old family servant.

"Promise me you and your young man will visit soon," the old woman ordered Eve, kissing her goodbye at the end of the night.

"We'll be in Connecticut to see you in two weeks. Promise," Hart said, leaning down to gently plant a kiss on her upturned cheek.

"He's a good one, Eve," Grandma Henrietta pronounced. "Don't let him get away."

Just before she left, a breath on the back of Eve's neck caused her to turn around. Maxie had one hand on her hip and the other holding up her chin. She smiled at her daughter and said, "Hart seems to have made a friend for life. God, my mother still tries to be such a coquette, doesn't she?"

"Yeah," Eve said, feeling slighted. Wasn't it possible that her grandmother had simply recognized Hart's intrinsic value?

That night, they lay in spoon position on Hart's bed; Eve's nose was nestled in the warm, musk of his chest. "Hart?"

"Ummm?" he answered, in his drugged voice of near sleep.

"You were so taken with my grandmother. Was it because she's such a flirt? She is, you know. She's always loved men."

"And I hoped it was just me. In fact, I was thinking of dumping you for her." Hart yawned and mumbled in a barely audible voice. "But, it *was* nice to be accepted so easily."

"You mean, unlike how you feel with my mother?"

He shifted his hips a bit, so that they were no longer snuggled into her stomach. "I thought it was obvious why I liked your grandmother," he whispered. "She reminds me of you." And he rolled over to face her, his lips finding their way to Eve's.

Manny Orbach opened the door to his apartment, peeked his head out, pinched his son's cheek, and exclaimed, "Got ya!"

"Hi ya, dad. This is Eve."

"Of course, naturally, we're expecting you. So, what are you standing in the hall for? Come in, kids, come in."

Manny backed out of the way and Eve could see that he was dressed in jeans, a brushed denim shirt, and a skinny red tie. Hart had told her stories about his father's craving for the good life and how it conflicted with his basic cheapness: he would arrive at a sale of Italian designer clothes, at dawn, with the determination of a teenager waiting for concert tickets; he tried bargaining salesmen down on everything from Barney's sportswear to black Cadillacs; he only ate at restaurants that participated in a special discount plan through his credit card. For thirty years, he and Norma had taken their vacations in the Catskills, emptying their plates and wrapping rolls in napkins to hoard back in their room. Most significant (Eve deduced), he never *ever* lent his children money. Even college had been an expense they'd had to figure out on their own.

They walked into the foyer and heard Norma's voice belt out, "Welcome, daw-lings!" Then, entering the room, she shrieked, "My gorgeous ones! I'd kiss you but my hands are so sticky from rolling matzo balls." She kissed Hart's cheek and left a perfect red lip mark on it.

Norma wore a huge, gold turban around her head that made her look as if she were trying to hide the effects of chemotherapy (when, in fact, she was in excellent health). Immediately, upon seeing Eve, she clenched her hand; the older woman's nails were done in sparkling silver with heavy silver rings on six fingers. Her eyes were watering as she puckered her blood red lips, "Daw-ling, how won-da-

ful it is to finally meet you. We are going to be so *so close*."
With those words, she hugged her son's girlfriend, an
octopus' squeeze; Eve was amazed at how her gestures
were so perfectly choreographed to match her words. She
wondered if one could really swoon from the rich, fruity
smell of perfume. "Family means everything to me,"
Norma pronounced, actual tears running down one cheek.

Eve took this declaration as a warning.

Her first impression of the Orbach home was that it
reminded her of a museum display on Louis XIV.
Everything was done in busy black, blood red, and gold
patterns and none of the styles or fabrics quite matched each
other. There were footstools, a love seat, and a floor-length
tapestry of a huge-busted, black-haired peasant woman
sitting in front of a bowl of apples. A formidable chandelier
hung over the dining-room table surrounded by eight gold-
cushioned chairs. Every wall was covered with ornately
framed oils; the pictures were peopled by—what appeared
to be—French aristocracy, in various stilted poses. Hart had
explained that, in better financial times—before his father's
retail business had folded—his parents had frequented
auctions. And, although money had been tight for two
decades, Norma continued to behave as if she were a lead
character on her favorite T. V. show of all time: *Dynasty.*

"Shaineh maidel," Norma said to Eve. "Come help me
in the kitchen." Hart's family began arriving, all at once and
in pairs: Aunt Sheila—tall, orange haired, gangly—and
Uncle Arnie with his bad toupee; Elyse and her husband,
Joel, both in black leather, sleek as seals; scowling Vivian
and her "friend," a slender man with small eyes and a tight
line for a mouth.

"Hi," said Elyse—Hart's younger sister—pushing her
way into the kitchen. "Let me be the one to say: we're all
very happy to finally be introduced to a girlfriend of Hart's.
We were beginning to wonder about him." She struck Eve,
immediately, as a thin, younger version of Norma; in her
black miniskirt, sheer black stockings and imitation pearls,
she almost could have passed for elegant. But the grape

color on her wide mouth gave her a vampire look. Her bald, skinny, leather-clad husband looked as if he could pass for her pimp. In truth, he worked in the garment district, importing—what else?—leather goods.

"Nice to meet you," Eve said, distracted by the clank of Elyse's pearl and diamond bracelet as they shook hands.

"So you're an English teacher," Elyse said and smacked her lips. "Do you know Irene Goldfarb? She teaches at P. S. . . . something or other, on the Upper East Side."

Eve took a deep breath; but, before, she could answer, Norma had slipped her arm around the young woman's waist and exclaimed, "What a skinny girl you are. You might need more hips to bear children. Oh, well. Here we are, my favorite people, snug as a bug in a rug. Shall we chow down, my daw-lings?"

Eve nodded, wanting direly to tear out of the apartment and retreat into the quiet, civilized world of books.

When they were all seated at the table, Manny used his fork as a gavel. "So, should we do the short Seder or the long one?"

On cue, Hart and his two sisters shouted, "SHORT."

"Okay. Here we go. Why is this night different from all other nights? Hart?"

"Because on this night, we get to eat Matzo ball soup, Dad."

"Right. Now, for the prayer. God, thanks for the grub. Okay, let's eat."

Eve had the urge to elbow or pinch Hart, but restrained herself.

"So," Manny said, through a mouthfull of gefilte fish, "Norma tells me you teach in a city school. Tell me, how do you deal with all the *shvartzers?*"

"Do they threaten you, if they don't like their grades?" Norma asked.

"Mother, really," Viv exclaimed, raising a full glass of wine. "Give the girl a break." Her face was red as if she had scrubbed it with a harsh cleanser; her eyes were a sharp, oddly chlorinated blue. Contact lenses? Alcohol? Eve wondered.

"I'm *asking* an honest question," Norma proclaimed in a sepulchral voice. "My friend works in the office at the junior high in Flushing and let me tell you, it's the same story. The Jews and yellow kids are good, smart, study all the time. But a lot of the colored kids are loud, every other word out of their mouth, a curse. I never used to consider myself prejudiced. No *really!* Honest to Gawd! But, lately . . . with all the violence in the schools, it's just *so* frightening. Isn't that right, Shelia?"

Manny leaned in Eve's direction and challenged her, "Are they literate? Do they write as good as they speak in— what's that new so-called language called . . . Ebonics!— 'Yo, Miz Sterling, I be coming to class, but my Eng-lash just ain't getting better. Guess, I be going back to my old job: selling crack at the school yard.'"

Everyone snickered but Hart and Eve.

"That's enough, Dad," Hart said.

The moment Eve walked in her front door, she called Annie, "How could he do this to me?" she screeched.

"The in-laws from hell, huh?"

"Don't use that word."

"Which one?"

"*In-laws.* I mean Hart's related to these people. Is vulgarity genetic? I read somewhere about a study that said intelligence often skips a generation. Oh, where did I read that?" The only thing that popped into her head was a line from her thesis: "Every generation has its improvements." She said, "Maybe, my mom told me. I certainly can't tell *her* about this evening."

"Don't start with your mother," Annie commanded in her warning tone. "Well, let's see: maybe, you can arrange for a late-in-life adoption for Hart. Where is he, by the way?"

"Out parking the car," Eve said, pacing the old wood floors, listening to them creak. "I *do* really care about him, so why do I feel like serving him his walking papers right this minute?"

"Does commitment-phobia mean anything to you? They're his parents, not his children. You're not obligated to spend all weekend with them due to some joint custody deal."

"God, what was I thinking? I'm not prepared to get so involved with anyone. I need to finish my degree before getting serious. Maybe I should end things, nice and clean," Eve suggested, shoving Mr. Knightley off of her bed and collapsing on it in his place.

"Don't you dare! Do you even know yourself? Call me tomorrow when Hart's not around."

After hanging up, Eve waited for Hart; fear kept creeping up and then abating, like motion sickness. She tried to imagine twenty years of holidays and weekends at Norma and Manny's; it would be like suffering from a chronic allergy that plagued her during all seasons. Maybe, she'd be lucky and get an academic job overseas.

Hart kissed her fast, absent-mindedly, as he came in the door. Aiming for her mouth, he hit her nostrils. "Ooops. Sorry. How are you recuperating from your shock? Listen, I'm sorry about what my Dad said about your students. The weird part is that he doesn't even mean it. He does it for shock value."

"Well, it worked then. I *was* shocked, " she said, trying to temper her feelings. "I wish you had tried to stop him."

"How?"

"Haven't you ever confronted them? Told them that you find those remarks offensive?"

Hart plunked himself down on her bed, rubbing his hands, like a washcloth, over his face. "I used to, but what's the point? They're never going to change. Did I ever tell you that when I was a teenager, my parents used to have these conferences about me, to figure out what was wrong with me? They'd pretend to be secretive but, since my mother's voice carries across continents, I always heard. They were worried that I wasn't macho enough because I was too easy on people. With her indomitable reasoning skills, my mom concluded I must be: 'a ho-mo,'" he enunciated in his best Norma imitation.

"What? Christ, Hart."

He shrugged, trying to make light of his confession. "They figured their kid spends a lot of time alone and never talks to them about girls: must be because he's gay! The summer I worked as a camp counselor at a sleep away, I was fifteen. I'd never gone to any kind of camp before; my dad was always too cheap to send me. Right before I left for the bus, he stuffed condoms into my wallet, and made a big production out of it. Guess, it was a test of my manhood. When I said I didn't want them, he asked if Mom was right, I was 'a little queer.' It took me months to forgive him." He sighed. "But, you grow up and realize that people have their limitations. I came to terms with them: basically, they're just very ignorant."

"You're rationalizing." Eve thought it sad that he draped an excuse—"ignorant"—around his parents' cruelty, like plastic on furniture, a protection from all permanent stains. "I don't know how you can just sit there, passively, and let them fling around their vulgar prejudices without protesting. The way they insulted my students tonight was wrong, Hart."

"You know," he said slowly, shaping each word as carefully as ice sculpture. "you're talking about intolerant people but you sound pretty intolerant yourself."

"Hart," she said, softening. "I'm sorry. It's just that I'm freaked out. People tend to turn into their parents, after all."

"Are you going to turn into your mother?"

"There's no comparison."

"No?"

"My mother would never discuss my students in that way."

"You're right. But, your mother has other prejudices. Anyone without a graduate degree is a lower life form to her."

"That's not true," she said, knowing he was right. "My mother *helps* people."

He exhaled slowly, his body sagging in rhythm with the air he emitted. "Look, you win. You have nothing to worry about. I've spent my whole life feeling like I was born into the wrong family." Then, after a pause, "Eve, this isn't how I wanted the night to go."

"Why?" she asked, heading for the kitchen, to forage around, for distraction's sake. "You knew we were going to your parents. Didn't you think I'd be upset by their prejudices?"

"I'm not talking about that part of the night." Hart's whine was plaintive. "I had other things planned."

Eve stopped rummaging through the refrigerator and turned to face him. "What other things?"

"Forget it, now. The mood's all wrong."

"What mood? What are you talking about?"

"Just forget it," he said, closing his eyes.

"Why?" she insisted. "Why? Don't do this, Hart. Is something *else* wrong?" She bent down in front of him and put her face near his. "Do you want to break up?"

Hart refused to look at her. "I just don't feel like talking about this now."

"Talking about what, Hart? I don't even know what we're talking about."

"We're talking about something I no longer want to talk about. I will bring it up again when we're both in the mood."

"Hart," Eve snapped, walking close to him, "Stop this!"

"It's in the closet," he said, standing up so slowly she could see him physically fighting the inertia. "That's where I hid it before we left for my parents and you saw what a different world I came from."

"Sounds like?" she said, but already knew.

"Sounds like a bad idea?" he asked tentatively. "Just kidding. Wait here." He returned with a blue velvet box in his hand.

"What's that?" Eve asked, in her stern teacher voice, but her hands were shaking. "Are you going to give it to me, for God's sake?"

"I don't know. Do you think you could stand the idea of being married to a man who is the son of Neanderthals?"

"Hart? Are you asking me to marry you?" she asked. Eve retreated to the bed and stared at her lace-covered pillows.

"Yes."

Without opening the box, she said, "I accept. Neanderthals and all."

"Well, then," he said. "I suppose you should take this."

Eve nodded, staring at her bed sheet, refusing to look Hart in the eye.

Neither one of them moved for what seemed like a very long time. Finally, Eve said, "Let's go for a walk around the block, okay? This is just too weird. We're supposed to be happy now, right?"

"Yes. Okay, let's walk," Hart said. "Don't you want the ring?"

"When we get back. Now, let's just walk and not say anything."

So, they walked, hand in hand, without saying a word, like two planes circling around in foggy weather, prepared—but not yet able—to land.

Letters

From the Desk of Maxine Sterling, D.S.W.

Woodmere, Long Island
December 3, 1996

Dear Eve,

I, for one, am very proud of you for speaking at this conference of yours, although I wish you had told me about your plans for going overseas so that I could have arranged to take off from work to care for Gemma. When exactly is the conference? I think Hart's confused, for some reason. He seems to think that you won't be home for a couple of months which, of course, I told him made no sense. You would never leave Gemma for so long.

Your husband doesn't seem to understand how important this is to you, and I must say, I'm worried about his ability to take care of my granddaughter at the moment. He won't call me for help (he hasn't even cashed the check I overnighted him!) Okay, so he's furious at me, he even blames me for your leaving. He seems to think that I'm the reason why you went to London so abruptly. (That's not true, is it? Didn't you go to meet Professor Wellington? Now, I'm confused). I tried to convince him that your trip had nothing to do with me, but better to blame the mother, I guess. I *am* genuinely sorry if my show upset you. Of course, my intention was never to hurt you, Evie.

Good luck with your paper. (Although, you don't need luck, you always perform *brilliantly* under pressure.) Please call home right after your presentation and just check on Gemma. And, for God's sake, call Dad and me and let us know that everyone is all right. You can call collect, of course. Do you have enough money? Should I send you some?

Love, Mom

London
December 6, 1996

Dear Hart,

I spent the morning in the London Library, with the good intention of doing research for my thesis. But, I ended up reading about the dangers of childbirth in the 18th and 19th centuries, about the high incidences of women who suffered irreversible damage or simply died. The one disease I can't get out of my head is called vesico-vaginal fistulae: the severing of the walls between the vagina and bladder that occurred during childbirth, causing continual leakage from the bladder, accompanied by an unbearable, incurable stench.

At the turn of the nineteenth century, I would have died delivering Gemma. No doubt in my mind.

Jane Austen called her niece—who also had aspirations to be a published novelist—a "Poor animal," after she suffered three painful pregnancies within only three years of marriage. "Animal" is the perfect word for that aching, spread-open, liquefied thing you become. The truth is I felt like an animal the whole time I was nursing Gemma, even though I wasn't supposed to admit that now that everything "natural" is back in style. But, it was as if Gemma was still an extension of me; I was swollen and sore, unsexual (as you know . . but so were you), and tired out from such excessive intimacy. I longed for privacy. My feelings had nothing to do with love, the immense love I have for both you and Gemma.

I can't get the irony out of my head: my mother, the fertility specialist, her fame built on helping women achieve the one thing in my life—conception—that came *too* easily for me, before I was ready. My mother's face welled up in front of me as I read about all the disgusting, disfiguring things that happened to women's bodies throughout history. All because they *could* reproduce. And, here my mother is aiding and abetting in this act of both joy and pain, of "breeding," as Ms. A. says. What she isn't doing is dealing with the real work, the part that isn't glorified, that is long and arduous and for the rest of your life. Being a family. The part that isn't coming easily for me.

In the booth next to me at this coffee shop, there are two adorable children with fine, sun-colored hair. The little girl—she can't be more than two—is fidgeting with a pink and yellow ribbon, to keep it from falling off. That one action—her small hands trying to perform what they aren't quite ready to do—pierces me with sadness. Waking up to full consciousness of what I've done will be painful; I know that. I'm not as callous as you think.

Please call or write and let me know how you and Gemma are.

I love you,
Eve

Four

1995

> "'I consider everybody as having a right to marry once in their lives for love. . . .'"
>
> Jane Austen, December, 1808 (to Cassandra).
> —*Emma*

IT WAS A DISMAL morning, in late summer, when the sky was blue-gray and raindrops slid like tears down the windows. Eve had placed two potted gingkos on the ridge of the bay windows in her and Hart's Park Slope apartment, the only living thing they planned to add to their already populated home: a newly engaged couple, a cat that had scratched his identity into Hart's pine rocking chair, and a dog that—from the day Eve had moved in—took to howling whenever her key turned in the lock. Plants and two animals: these required more than enough caretaking for now. Since the engagement, Eve felt more pressure to finish her degree and aggressively search out a position within the boundaries of civilization. Yet, while avoiding pregnancy had once motivated her to map out her menstrual cycle with a cartographer's vigilant attention, lately, Eve had simply, stupidly, stopped noticing. She'd grown lackadaisical once Hart's proposal had popped into the startled air. The day Eve held that plastic stick with the tip so pink there was no second of doubt, morning was just poking its head into an ashen sky.

"I can handle this," she whispered to Mr. Knightley who had followed her into the bathroom and settled on the toilet seat, smug as a Buddha. But, if this were true, why—when she briefly glanced at her desk with her Jane Austen manuscript stacked on it—did Eve suddenly feel a strange mix of awe and sadness?

Hart had stayed up watching all three *Star Wars* videos in a row, arm wrestling sleep until sleep won. It was after three when he flopped into bed, waking Eve, who lay in bed worrying. Now, she touched Hart's shoulder and he grumbled, rolling over. Looking at the wall his back created, realizing how hard she'd have to shake it for a response, she picked up the phone. Even though it was Saturday and she knew that her parents would still be in bed, Maxie—the fertility specialist—was the only other person whom she felt compelled to tell.

"Ma?" Eve whispered. That one word seemed to fly on the tips of butterfly wings before it landed.

"Eve? Are you okay?" Maxie asked in a groggy voice.

"I'm pregnant," she blurted out. The truth was, what she did best in front of her mother was complain or make witty insights into other people's characters. Despite their easy repartee and intellectual dives into people's emotional pathologies, they thankfully managed to avoid the most piercing of intimacies.

Maxie's breathing sounded forced. "Eve? Really?" she asked. Then, as if she suddenly grasped the punch line to a joke, she exclaimed, "Oh, my God, are you sure? Okay, okay, this is not a catastrophe; let me think a minute. . . . Okay, Daddy'll *just* have to take Saturday off for once in thirty years, so we can *finally* plan this wedding. And, not a minute too soon, wouldn't you say? We'll be over this afternoon to talk. Oh wait, I forgot, I was supposed to meet your sister today to go shopping for a computer—sort of a pre-law-school present. Which, by the way, I'd be glad to get you now that it doesn't look like you'll be scooting off to London anytime soon." She took a huge breath, exhaled loudly. "Let's meet for brunch in the city, at Livy's place. I'm calling her right now and will call you back."

Eve, feeling as if her esophagus were closing up, could say nothing.

"Oh, my God, Eve, I'm too young to be a grandmother!"

Eve should have guessed that the vomiting was more than P. M. S. gone awry. For two weeks, she'd lain on the couch, feeling peculiarly drained, in a way she'd never experienced before. She'd free associate about what was causing her wretched inertia, theories involving immune system diseases, cancers that had seeped into all her glands, and a hodgepodge of mental illnesses reconstructed from conversations overheard in her childhood. Ironically, Eve never suspected the true case of her malaise until after dark the previous evening.

She'd been sacked out on the couch with Mr. Knightley, staring at the electromagnetic glow of the television; suddenly, her stomach felt like when the seat lurches forward just as the ferris wheel begins to move. "I think we should invest fifteen dollars in one of those home pregnancy tests," she'd said in a hoarse voice.

Hart's eyes were wide and pleading, the eyes of those illustrated animals on children's puzzle boxes and calendars. She imagined a child version of Hart wearing the same expression: curled up in his bed, itchy wool blanket over his head, listening to his parents fight over whether or not they could afford to move their three children from what was increasingly becoming a dangerous neighborhood. Hart often repeated the story: how he'd been mugged seven times on his way to and from elementary school. Yet, his mother didn't start packing her good glassware in newspaper until the evening after a man stuck a knife at her throat on the steps leading down to the D train. If her husband wanted to stay in Flatbush stuffing his pockets with dollars, Norma finally asserted, he could do so in an empty apartment.

But all the adult Hart had said was: "I'll run over to the all-night drugstore on Fifth right this minute."

Now, it was nearly impossible for Eve to restrain herself from waking him. She crept into the kitchen, a chill running up her body from her bare feet against the cold, wood floors. She was drinking herbal tea and trying to recreate the heaviness she'd felt when, once, she'd donned the body suit of a pregnant woman at a science museum. An hour later, Hart appeared with the pink-tipped plastic stick in his hand, his face remarkably pale.

"It's not as bad as that," she snapped, thinking: it's worse.

"We're not even married yet, Eve," he said. "I've never been less ready for anything in my life. How about you? You haven't once said anything about wanting a child. "

"In fact," she retorted, "we barely know one another."

For most of the morning, Hart had stood still and forbidding as Stonehenge, having transformed himself into a human monument of indignation. Finally, as they were at the door to leave for Olivia's apartment, he pulled Eve into his chest. He whispered in a gruff voice, "Explain to me, again, why we're meeting your parents and sister today instead of dealing with this ourselves?"

"To plan the wedding that we can't afford."

"We could use a Justice of the Peace."

"Then we won't make a profit. Which would help pay for this unwanted baby."

"I didn't say the baby is *unwanted,* Eve. You know I love kids. While other teenage boys were thinking of getting laid, what was your nerdy fiancé thinking about?"

His question was not without self-loathing for all the opportunities missed, all that squelched teenage lust. But it was also true what he said next: "I was thinking of how great it would be to have all this someday: a wife and a kid."

"To avoid thinking about getting laid."

"Yeah, I know," he said. Still, she didn't refuse when he took her hand. After all, wasn't she the one who had always harbored the fantasy of a child-free life? How had she now allowed herself to release the reigns of her destiny?

Eve's parents stood under the awning of her sister's apartment building, wind-blown, hands thrust in their pants pockets. Her father was hunched over slightly and his beard had, quite suddenly, turned from salt and pepper to almost all white, a strange contrast to his dark brown hair. Maxie— stout to Daniel's lean—was grimacing, rocking on her heels.

"Where's Livy?" Eve barked. The only time she could remember feeling such relentless fatigue was the summer she'd battled mono at camp. Finally, on her fourth visit to the infirmary, the doctor thought to test Eve for the virus. "My God, you must've felt lousy all this time," he'd exclaimed upon discovering her white cell count. "Why didn't you just call your parents to take you home?" Now, as then, Eve hated to quit, to surrender to the feeling that her blood was too thick to circulate around her veins, that her muscles were too weak to follow commands. "How come you're waiting outside for her?" she demanded.

"She's just taking the dogs out," Daniel said. "We didn't want to miss you."

"I *could have* rung the buzzer."

"I see that impending motherhood agrees with you," Maxie smirked.

There was nothing to say in response because, of course, it didn't. How could Eve feel anything but terrified about having to nurture a creature more demanding than herself? Luckily, Olivia turned the corner of Perry Street at that moment, her two basset hounds, Winston and Beast, waddling in the slow labored way that Eve figured was a prelude to her own future movements. When Olivia saw her sister, she began to walk briskly, pulling the animals and scolding them for not keeping up her pace. "Hey," she said when a few feet away, "Congratulations, you guys." She kissed Eve, perfunctorily on the cheek, then did the same to Hart. "Great news. I hope. Okay, let me get the dogs upstairs. C'mon, you morons," Olivia said to Beast, the older, slower one who had spread-eagled himself on the cement, sniffing.

Eve shook her head, wondering if defensive reserve might be genetic, like depression. If their parent's library had included titles such as *A Midsummer Night's Dream* and *Tom Jones*—instead of *The Meaning of Despair* and *The Psychology of Melancholy*—would the two of them be embracing, giddy with nervous laughter right now?

Once on their way, Maxie asked, "I hope you're not going to let that schmucky gynecologist deliver *my* grandchild."

"What schmucky gynecologist?" Daniel asked, shuffling behind his wife in the rubber galoshes he wore from spring to autumn.

"You mean the guy from school who smoked while he examined me?" Eve asked. "Are you kidding? I only went to him because he was on my student health plan."

"Good," Maxie said, smacking her gloved hands together. "Then we can start discussing obstetricians over brunch."

"What schmucky gynecologist?" her husband repeated.

They rode in Daniel's Oldsmobile (as opposed to Maxine's Lexus) uptown. The car lumbered like an old circus elephant still forced to do tricks. With every bump they hit, Olivia rolled her eyes or sighed; Eve kept her head down to stave off nausea. The floor of the car was littered with empty water bottles, paper bags, Kleenex, and broken pills; scrunched in the cushions between Hart and her was a piece of aluminum foil which she dug out. Eve opened it to find three intact pills with the word "Xanax" etched onto them. She passed them to her sister who, upon inspection, shook her head in disgust. "My father's as good as a drug lord," Eve sometimes joked to friends who craved tranquilizers or antidepressants during a particularly difficult stint.

The restaurant was a swank affair on the Upper East Side. They were seated at a round table covered by a white linen tablecloth and adorned with a glass vase containing one half-bloomed yellow rose. "Let's order champagne," Maxie said. "Maybe it will improve the mood."

"Fine," Eve said, "but I can't drink it."

"Well, just a token sip," her mother insisted.

Once her bacon and cheddar cheese omelet arrived, Maxie announced, "Good, now I can focus." Eve noted how her sister's top lip twitched as she restrained from commenting on how Maxie certainly wasn't lacking in nourishment. "Here's who you should see: Dr. Geronilli," their mother declared. "I know she has a new partner that no one has really heard much about. But, Carla's the best. I mean . . . Arnie Schaeffer is excellent as well, but he offends everyone. Of course, his manner is a problem—he has absolutely no social skills and little insight into human nature—but, he's a wonderful surgeon. Still, I think Carla's better, yes definitely, go to Carla. She's not the warmest person alive," she shrugged, a crisp piece of bacon hanging off her lifted fork, "but she's the best around."

"Who's Carla?" Daniel asked, as he wiped the lenses of his glasses with the hem of the tablecloth.

"The thing is, it's not always easy to get used to her abrupt manner. Sometimes women, especially when they're pregnant and vulnerable, get intimidated by her. But, I don't think she *means* it."

"Who's Carla?"

"These doctors, they're all such sorry cases when it comes to interpersonal skills. Still, Carla has performed terrifically in some very dire situations, which, *believe me,* left to your average schmucky obstetrician would have ended tragically." Maxie paused to extract some bacon fat from her back teeth with her finger.

"That's gross, Mom," Olivia said.

"Who *are you talking about?*"

"Dad, this isn't a vaudeville act," Olivia snapped.

"I *want* to know who we are talking about," Daniel shot back at her. "I think I should be allowed to ask questions since I'm *the patron.* Shouldn't I be allowed to know *who* I'm going to be patronizing?"

"Dad, what are you talking about?" Eve asked.

"Carla is Carla Geronilli, Daniel," Maxie interjected, mid-chew.

"Well . . . excuse me if I don't feel like paying for someone when I have no f-ing idea who she is!"

"For God's sakes, Daniel, she's an obstetrician at the hospital," his wife said, shaking her head. "What are you getting so agitated about?"

"Agitated, who's agitated?" Daniel mumbled almost inaudibly. "I'll tell you who *will* be agitated. Everyone at this table, that's who, when I refuse to pay for this pregnancy!"

"I'm going to the bathroom," Eve said, standing up, "before I have a miscarriage."

"Eve, sit down," Maxie commanded. "Daniel, *really,*

get hold of yourself. No one said anything about you paying for the pregnancy."

"Folks," Hart said, banging his spoon as if it were a gavel, "we're not asking you to pay for our baby. Why would you think such a thing?"

"We're sorry," Maxie said. "Daniel didn't mean to offend you. He's just so used to helping out his daughters, he just assumed."

"I can speak up for myself," her father snapped, then in a softer voice, "Sorry, Hart, my mistake. Habit. We're just always looking out for our daughter's interests." He chuckled dryly. "Financial security and all those boring parental concerns." And, he extended his hand in a peace offering.

Maxine's smile showed off her even, milky white teeth. But, a few minutes later, she snuck up behind Eve in the ladies' room as her daughter stood with her hands under the drier, palms up, as if to be paddled by the nuns. "So how much *do* you need for the pregnancy?" Maxie sighed. "Do you two have *any* real insurance? You know, it would have been better if you'd waited until you were married so that you could be on Hart's plan. Does he even have a plan? Or, any reliable source of income? God knows, Eve, we're more than happy to help support you through graduate school. But a husband and an unplanned baby? Isn't that a lot to ask of us? This baby *was* unplanned, wasn't it?"

"I probably will miscarry. It seems the most economically convenient solution to everyone's concerns."

"Oh, stop it. I don't know why you're talking like that."

"Hormones," Eve answered, wondering what it would be like to have a mother who instinctively engulfed her in soft, fleshy arms, whose scent—talcum powder mixed with rich, floral perfume—assuaged her. She pictured the Xanax, stuffed between the cushions of her father's car and thought: better to swallow pills than to expect love without constant criticism.

But Eve called the number her mother had given her. The doctor was at a conference for the rest of the week.

84

Why didn't Eve come in to see her partner for a blood test, a perky voice asked. She agreed, although suddenly there didn't seem to be any question about her condition; her body was swelling with excessive fluids like a river bloated from weeks of rainfall. In the doctor's waiting room, Eve read in a parenting magazine that there is a 25% rise in blood volume during pregnancy. She fought off images of herself turning into a gelatinous blob—much like a creature in a third rate sci-fi movie—too enormous to clothe. Certainly, she was learning quickly: there was no grace in childbearing.

Dr. Lila Chay strode into the examining room and Eve was immediately struck by the contrast between her youth and her chillingly competent manner. She had straight dark obedient hair and eyes that reflected little light. Her posture was nearly perfect. But when she extended her hand, she smiled and her face relaxed. She wore a black skirt with tiny yellow stars printed on it and black leather sandals. While Eve spoke, the doctor swung a silver teardrop pendant that hung on a mustard-colored ribbon around her neck to and fro, in a slow pendulum motion, as if it were an augur of things to come.

Eve introduced herself and thought how it was not preferable to have a beautiful woman sticking her plastic-gloved hand inside of her than a pock-marked, aging man with the dank smell of tobacco on his breath. In fact, if something that felt borderline obscene had to be done to her, better it be performed by a slimy character who Eve could resent than by a beautiful woman with whom she instantly felt rivalry.

The internal was quick and painless and as always made Eve picture herself as an oversized goose being stuffed. Dr. Chay snapped off her plastic glove mindlessly, with all her patient's internal goo on it. Eve wondered if the doctor always managed to perform the procedure automatically—as if she were merely turning on the ignition to her car—without ever feeling as if she were committing a violation.

"Okay, looks good," Dr. Chay said, "Why don't you get

dressed and then call your husband from the waiting room? The two of you can meet me in my office."

"He's not my husband," Eve murmured, after the doctor left the room.

Dr. Chay's office was small and filled with books, papers, and diplomas on the walls; there were no plants, no fish tank, no flowers to cheer it up. Eve tried to decipher the tiny script lettering on her medical degree but, from her seat, couldn't make out the name.

"Congratulations, folks," Dr. Chay said and smiled— what seemed a seductive smile—at Hart. "We'll be getting back the results of the test in a couple of days. Just give us a call at the end of the week. But, from the look of things: the softness of the cervix and the results of the home pregnancy test, I'd say, without a doubt, that Eve is at least a month pregnant."

Hart squeezed Eve's hand and, instantly, his eyes filled with tears. "Congratulations, sweetheart."

"Thanks," she answered, as she slid her hand away, numb. All she really wanted—at this moment of panic— was to inspect Dr. Chay's credentials properly. Of course, Eve knew that she had every right, as a patient, to ask the doctor directly; but, her reasons for doing so were not the appropriate ones. Life had always been a contest, for Eve, but since her hormones had kicked in, her competitive urges were soaring. Was this how a mom-to-be was supposed to feel? Maybe the doctor had made a mistake with the diagnosis, after all.

"Now, I'm going to write you a prescription for prenatal vitamins which you should start taking right away and I want to go over diet a bit. Good nutrition will really help you through your pregnancy, help you feel more balanced and able to gain a good amount of weight, but not too much."

Eve wished she could freeze frame the moment as she imagined it: Dr. Lila Chay and Hart deeply engrossed in a discussion of leafy vegetables, while she rummaged through desk drawers for proof that the doctor had been comfortably older than herself when she achieved her status as an M. D.

After their appointment, Hart needed to run downtown to finish a shoot. "I love you so much, Evie. I'm so happy. It'll work out," he said and kissed her check. She nodded mechanically and said nothing.

Eve had no summer classes to teach that day and no desire to return home to her dissertation. The now familiar nausea had overtaken her, as if she'd been stuck for hours on a bus, inhaling a rotten egg smell wafting up from the streets. What she wanted most was to call either Dee or Annie. But, since her engagement, whenever Eve told Dee anything personal, her friend scoffed and her face took on an expression which combined haughtiness with jealousy and regret. If Eve dared to utter a complaint about Hart, even the simplest thing—he could leave his underwear and tee shirt on the floor next to their bed for three days before noticing—her friend's mouth would curl into a witchy smile. "Be careful of what you wish for," she'd say. Eve ended up reporting her pregnancy to Dee's answering machine. Her friend's breathless, hoarse voice promised only: "As soon as I can, I'll call you back," to the sound of Annie Lennox singing, "No more I Love Yous." In turn, Eve received a message the next day: "Hey, pretty Freudian with your mom being a fertility specialist. Guess congrats are in order. Or, are they? Talk to you and you can fill me in on the dirt." If Eve revealed her ambivalence about the baby, Dee would grab it quickly, and feed off of it, a snake on a juicy rat.

Then there was Annie whose wedding was fast approaching; with precious little time to go, she still had decisions to make about the most inane things. Eve knew that Arthur offered little help with planning and that her own mother was at odds with Mrs. Schwartz about every detail of the event, right down to whether Annie should carry a bouquet of white roses or pink. When stressed, Annie clapped shut like a screen door attached by a spring; all of her tremendous self-discipline and that almost childlike belief in the power of one's individual will could prove daunting.

"Listen, Hart," Eve said as they walked arm-in-arm to the downtown subway. "What would you think if I went to visit my grandparents for a few days?"

"Your grandparents? Why?"

Eve shrugged. "Mini vacation; to process everything. I think I need to go on a retreat."

Visits to Henrietta meant structure: fresh squeezed orange juice and toast for breakfast, lunch at noon, a walk to the pond every afternoon before four, a dinner which included soup and crackers. There was no room in her grandmother's puritan rituals for messy emotions between people. In Henrietta's world, life was as carefully contained as her rows of refrigerated meat, packed in Tupperware, zip-locked in plastic, frozen in aluminum foil held in place by strips of masking tape.

In her mind, she plotted how she'd invite herself to their condominium, using this happy news as a carrot. Grandma would retrieve her from the bus stop and drive home— seated on a pillow in order to be able to peer over the dash-board—in her 1972 white Cadillac. Once in her home, Eve would canvass her bookshelves, all the old familiar works: Walt Whitman's *Leaves of Grass*—her grandfather's 1855 edition—next to the original Babar story written in French, John Locke's *An Essay Concerning Humane Understanding,* next to A. A. Milne's *The Christopher Robin Story Book.* Eve was already smelling the books' musty pages, envisioning Issac's light blue recliner, Henrietta's 1964 globe of a different world, when Hart's voice broke into her reverie, "Your grandmother is 84 years old and taking care of a semi-invalid, not running a spa," he said icily. "We need to deal with the situation between the two of us, like planning a wedding."

Hart was right. She could not hide behind starched sheets and a set bedtime, there would be no retreat back into safety, into childhood. Her neat, organized, goal-oriented life—a life modeled on Henrietta's—had mutated, like a cell gone bad. How had she let this happen?

"Oh God, I forgot my socks," Hart exclaimed, once they'd slowed down for yet another traffic light, on this endless journey to the Brooklyn Bridge. They were late for their wedding, or rather the photographs before the ceremony, what they'd hoped to be a sophisticated Sunday afternoon affair in a currently chic Tribeca restaurant named Ramona's. It was only a few months since Hart had proposed.

Despite all of Norma's tricks—much hand-wringing and quivering of the lips—they'd managed to stand firmly by their choices: it would be buffet style; they would use a jazz band that also played some wicked classical guitar for their walk down the aisle together; they would have a reformed service with a female rabbi officiating. They had, however, placated Eve's soon-to-be mother-in-law on three points: Olivia, Annie and Dee, in grayish lavender ballerina-length dresses of their own choosing, would be Eve's bridesmaids; she would throw a bouquet, mostly to satisfy her curiosity as to the true desperation of her friends; Eve would wear a dove-gray gown, ankle length with no train. (Norma had not been informed that her future daughter-in-law would be gestating as she walked down the aisle).

Eve was proud of her gown and smug over the fact that she had found it on her first day shopping. Her mother and she had eyed it, wedged between two red and black numbers, at an odd little store in Soho. It was handmade of Spanish lace, with seed pearls sewn into the neckline, and very delicate looking, but four sizes too big even in her puffed-up condition. They'd brought it to three seamstresses until they found one willing to cut it down to Eve's size. Still, she had to pin her bra to the inside of the dress and had already dreamed of saying her vows topless.

The morning of her wedding, Eve was jarred out of a dream by the phone's shrill ring. The first thing she felt was an ache in her neck from sitting up all night to protect her hair.

"I never should have gotten it set," Eve said to a snoring

Hart, as she touched the flattened locks in back. "Yes?" she barked into the phone.

"Listen Sterling, keep it down, would you," her friend croaked.

"Dee? What happened?" Eve turned the redwood clock around to face her. It was not yet seven in the morning. Nausea crept through her gut like a worm, and she launched for the crackers by her bedstand.

"I've been up all night; Jon and I broke up after fighting so that the whole neighborhood could hear. He's such a sick fuck, Eve."

"What's the matter?" Hart asked, groggy. "Did the restaurant double book us with a bar mitzvah?"

"Dee," Eve shouted into the phone while chewing, "I'm getting married in five hours!"

"Jesus, Sterling," Dee broke out in a hoarse, gulping sob, "Don't you think I know that? I just wanted to tell you not to worry if I'm late. I'll be there. Christ, I'm so hung over. I feel like dog shit."

"I'm sorry. But, please, Dee, I need you there." Eve hung up the phone and, without pause, dialed Annie's number.

Arthur answered. "Unless it's an emergency, I'm not here. Tax season is over."

"It's me, Arthur, Eve. It's an emergency."

"'I've got the wedding bell blues,'" Arthur sung off key. "Hold on. She's taking her temperature."

"She's sick?" Eve asked but, got no answer; he'd already put her on hold. Eve felt a growing hysteria, not unlike the moment when you realize the plane is going down.

"Oh, God, Hart," Eve cried, shaking his shoulder. "Get up. No one is coming to our wedding."

"What?" he asked, not opening his eyes. "Don't worry. My mother will be there singing 'Sunrise Sunset.'"

"Please, Hart. You were right all along. Let's just go to city hall and get married."

"Nothing you wear could possibly match those green walls." They had gone to Brooklyn's city hall to get their license and had agreed that, with its snot green, peeling walls, it should be noted in travel books as a landmark of New York's ugliness. Nevertheless, there were several couples—in various stages of disarray, speaking a variety of languages—waiting their turns to get hitched.

"Eve?" she heard Annie say. "What's wrong, Eve?"

"What's wrong with you?" she nearly shrieked. "Arthur said you were taking your temperature. Do you have the flu? Don't tell me you're not coming?"

"Of course I'm coming. I'm checking to see if I'm ovulating. Never too soon to start, I say. Wouldn't it be great to be pregnant together?"

"Oh, God, Annie. I don't even want to be pregnant *alone*. The reason I'm bothering you at this ungodly hour is that Dee just woke me up, *weeping*. I think I finally fell asleep around 4:30. She broke up with that asshole, Jon, last night. How accidental is that? I don't even know now if she's going to show up!"

Annie made tsk, tsk noises. "Don't worry, she'll be there. Even if I have to tie her to the ski rack on Arthur's car. She'll be there."

"Tell Annie to tell Dee that my cousin Kevin will be there," Hart said, sitting up now, "he's an orthodontist, a real catch."

"I have to go. I have to make a pot of tea and try to pry my eyelids open," Eve said to Annie, "Thank you. You're the best."

"One word of advice: don't drink too much. Remember, I had to pee all through my wedding ceremony. Otherwise, just relax. Everything is taken care of. You're going to have a wonderful day."

What Eve wanted to ask but, of course, couldn't was: am I making a fatal mistake? But, it was too late for that.

As they were rushing to leave the apartment, the phone rang again. "I'll get it," Eve shouted and lunged for the phone, tripping over a throw rug and nearly landing in a dish of strawberries left mistakenly on the kitchen counter.

"Mazel tov, my daw-lings," Norma said. "Just calling to let you know how thrilled and excited I am, my precious ones, and that I'll be there, with bells on. *Now,* down to business. I know I need to remind you to be early and to make sure that everything is ready. You two lovebirds, with your heads in the clouds, you think you can just put together a wedding at the last minute and it will go like clockwork. But, remember, you need to be on top of the staff at the restaurant. You can't trust anyone else to care about this. It's *your* wedding, after all."

"In the dictionary under Jewish mother, there's a picture of my mother," Hart said once she relayed the message.

In a snit, Eve emptied the breakfast berries into a plastic garbage bag, tied it and swung it over her shoulder. "If she tells me, one more time, about Kathie Lee's show on flower arrangements for weddings . . . ." She stopped herself, Maxie's complaint ringing in her ears: the Orbachs hadn't paid one penny towards the wedding, but gave advice and criticism, to whomever would listen, at every opportunity. Eve and Hart had been over his parents' lack of generosity and Norma's *chutzpa* a million times. "What else, except for her kid's lives, does my mom have to preoccupy her?" Hart asked now, pushing Eve out the door.

It was true. Manny's one-liner was, "If God could create the earth in seven days, the kids can plan a wedding in twice as many weeks" which he repeated, like a mantra, whenever his wife fretted that no one was paying proper attention to the details. Of all the family members on both sides, only Norma had the time or inclination to throw a big party and she had been forbidden to participate, except to give a list of guests to Maxie. "Left to her, it would take place in China Palace on Bell Boulevard and would have a red velvet motif," Hart warned everyone.

Eve had been timing the length of this traffic light on Court Street, in the Cobble Hill section—three minutes so far—when Hart realized he had forgotten his socks. She glanced down at his feet to, in fact, see bare ankles meeting his scuffed old loafers. "Didn't you pack them with your shoes?"

"Yes. I purposely stuffed them into your black shoes and then left them on the kitchen counter."

"Oh, well, looks like I'll have to walk down the aisle as is."

"Christ."

By the time they pulled up to the restaurant, the day had turned viciously humid. It was the end of September, but felt like July; even with the windows wide open and the car in motion, there was no breeze. People on the street were beginning to fan themselves with their newspapers and the stench of garbage—a rancid cod mixed with urine—wafted through the air. Norma, standing on spike heels outside of Ramona's, waved a silver-lined handkerchief, frantically. Next to her, Manny stood as still as one of those cardboard cutouts of political figures.

"Oh, my daw-lings," Norma exclaimed teary-eyed, once they'd parked and joined her on the curb. "I was so *very* worried." Eve couldn't help but stare. Her future mother-in-law struck her as a cross between Morticia from *The Addams Family*: skin-tight mermaid dress, a black and silver sequined thing that shined like amphibian skin and was lined at the ankles with a black lace hem, and Jo Anne Worley from her *Laugh-In* days: a thick black hair fall knotted into a ponytail and hung from ridiculously high on her head. Silver chains, one after the other, rippled down her neck, creating half-moons of wrinkled skin, and three prominent chunky rings adorned each hand. Eve wondered if, once the reception got underway, she planned on telling the guests' fortunes.

Slowly, Manny dabbed the sweat off his forehead with a tissue. "She was getting ready to call 911."

"What are you talking about, Ma?" Hart asked. "It's only 10:30. We're not due here 'till 11:00."

Morning sickness sucked the breath right out of Eve and she slapped her hand over her mouth.

"The photographer is setting up inside," Norma proclaimed in her best tragic voice.

"The end of the world is near," Manny said, beginning to unhook his bow tie. "All I know is if I don't get in there soon, I'll need to go home and shower and miss the wedding."

Hart asked,"Why are you even outside like this?"

"Where are my parents and sister?" Eve joined in the cacophony of complaints, the wave of nausea having passed.

"Not here," Norma stated and smiled so insincerely Eve could imagine her deliberately copying it from a Hollywood star preening for the camera. "We didn't want to interfere with the florist and the photographer. We wanted them to have *artistic license* to do their work."

Manny was gesturing at his wife: she did, she did, he pointed at her. "It wasn't my idea to melt out here on the streets of Calcutta."

"What are you talking about, Ma?" Hart queried. Eve realized, then, how nervous he was and that she had to get him inside and away from his parents.

On the outside, Ramona's didn't look like much; it held no architectural distinction with its huge windows which gave it the appearance of an old factory and its slightly faded sign painted in a soft bluebell color. But inside, the restaurant matched the conception Eve held in her imagination of what a Cuban nightclub would look like. It was an enormous loft space with stained dark wood floors and huge pillars. Almost prehistorically large palm trees were planted in pots, spaced near tables, so that their leaves would sweep lushly over the diners' heads. On the farthest wall from the entrance was a full-length mural, painted in vivid reds, oranges, and yellows, of dancers: shirtless men and women in layered, low-cut and sleeveless dresses, all swirling fiercely in motion. Eve fantasized Cuban jazz musicians— with swarthy complexions and slicked-back hair—playing sexy music on the stage, while rich women with their cleavages showing half-listened on the balcony of the second level which jutted out into the room. When they'd first spied the place—having taken a one day tour of the restaurants Eve had circled in a section of *New York Magazine*— she'd immediately been captivated. Maxie had given a deposit after tasting their chocolate sponge cake covered with fudge icing in the shape of a top hat.

There was no music playing now, just the swishing sound of ceiling fans and clanking of plates, as waiters in white tuxedos arranged place settings. There was such an elegant yet sensuous feel to the room that Eve began to get excited about the wedding. But within moments, chaos reigned; an eastern European accent reminded her that this was a Sterling/Orbach affair, and therefore, cause for hysteria.

"If," the voice said, managing to get *Sturm and Drang* into that one, tiny word, "if . . . your charming mother had not called me, just last night, mind you, to thank me, I would have left without a thought, without a second thought about *not* doing the arrangements."

Eve swung around to face the florist, an obese man, who was sweating profusely and wiping his face with dramatic importance. "An odd woman with a bad Zsa Zsa Gabor accent called me at seven this morning, saying she was instructed to get me here by nine o'clock sharp."

"That would be my . . . ah . . . mother-in-law."

"Well, I told her she must have gotten the wrong information, that I was certain this was a noon wedding."

"It is," Eve said now, apologetically, although her concentration was on ripping off the wrapper from her packet of saltines.

"I did figure that out for *myself*," he wiped his brow with a Shakespearean gesture. "But I was standing outside for an hour and a half in this appalling heat. No one was even here to open the doors for me."

"I'm really sorry," she said.

"I'm lucky that I didn't have a heart attack which, with my girth, would not be unlikely."

"Please sit for a while and have some water. I'm sure the waiters will get you something else to drink if you like. I'm so sorry . . . ." she trailed off, antsy to get upstairs and find a toilet she could hover over, just in case.

Already, Eve was foreseeing doom: Norma would, indeed, elbow her way on stage and belt out show tunes from *Gypsy*. Her own family—late her entire life—would end up missing the ceremony, stuck battling in her father's beat up 1980 Oldsmobile, bathed in the yellow glow of the Midtown Tunnel. During the reception, Maxie would smile graciously but avoid Eve's father who caused the delay by stealing out of the house for an early morning jog. Her sister—furious at her parents as usual—would physically disown them. Her posture would improve, sequentially, according to how angry she became, until she resembled Grace Kelly on a receiving line.

"Excuse me," Eve said to the florist. "I need to get upstairs and get ready."

Norma was in the dressing room, built for the band members the restaurant booked. She was rubbing powder on her cleavage. "Freckles can easily be mistaken for liver spots in women my age," she said.

Self-pity stuck in her windpipe like a peanut, causing her to cough and nearly gag. Here she was, on her wedding day, feeling queasy, hot, and damp, with only Norma for female companionship. Where were all the women who loved me, she thought, whose job it was to coddle and reassure me on, what was supposed to be, the most important day of my life?

"Dad's having trouble with the engine," Livy said, out of breath, hurling her way into the room and nearly throwing her gown onto the makeup table. "Mom and Dad got into another fight over his growing-up-poor complex and how he refuses to buy a new car because of it."

Olivia had just returned from a week at a dude ranch after quitting her job with Wally Dickinson, the feminist documentary maker, but had managed to return in time for the wedding. She was scurrying about Manhattan, like the white rabbit, looking for a job so as not to get evicted from her apartment.

"I'll be out of your way in a minute," Norma said, puckering her lips and reapplying the hideous red color.

Eve wanted to scream: "No you won't, not for the rest of your life."

The ceremony was short. Eve found it difficult to concentrate as she was experiencing intermittent waves of nausea which she staved off by taking quiet, deep breaths. On top of this, she felt unexpectedly shy. Getting married in front of a crowd struck her as oddly exhibitionistic, as too intimate an act to share with one hundred people. Eve shot a glance at Hart whose face was drained of color and whose eyes were teary. Did her heightened emotions and physical discomfort cause a momentary lapse of cognition? Suddenly, she wondered, panicky: who is this man? What am I doing here? And who—in this crowd—knows the truth about my condition?

Afterwards, everyone descended upon them like a flock of birds around a chunk of bread. Eve could hear her mother's loud voice, laughing as she shook guests' hands. Maxie and Norma stood on opposite ends of the receiving line, looking like bookends from two mismatched sets. Maxie was wearing a soft pearl-pink dress, no jewelry except for her thick silver wedding ring, and very little make-up. When she smiled, she looked lovely: fine white teeth, eyes bright and quick, feathery chestnut-colored hair, prominent cheekbones. The photographer snapped pictures with professional fury. Hart had encircled Eve's waist and drawn her close; he was flushed and talking much more rapidly than usual.

Finally, the reception began and people, happily, turned their attention away from the wedding couple and towards the food. With her plate of chicken in wine sauce and scalloped potatoes (none of which she planned to eat), Eve headed for her table, finally feeling giddy relief. Approaching Eve was a woman with a long horsy face, an aquiline nose, small blue eyes, and thick white hair pulled back in a tight bun. It was Maud, her dissertation advisor. Tall and angular, she wore a black velvet smock with a copper brooch pinned close to the throat. She extended her long, bony hand, "Congratulations, Eve," she said. As always, her voice resonated, making Eve think of an echo in a church, rich and cavernous. Was it paranoia or was there a hint of a sneer in the way her thin lips curved? Did she suspect the pregnancy? "Lovely wedding. Best of luck to you both."

Once Maud was out of sight, Hart shuddered. "She looks like a Calvinist preacher. Or, like someone who was reincarnated from one of the those women who was burnt at the stake in Salem." He whispered in Eve's ear, "Back for revenge."

"No, she doesn't," Eve corrected him. "She looks like Virginia Woolf, only less glamorous. I think she's sort of attractive. Anyway, it was nice of her to come." After all, this woman held great power over her life. *Her* life.

Annie—best complimented by clothes along the line of a navy pantsuit—appeared awkward and uncomfortable in her shoulderless lace dress. She smiled at Eve and Hart as she made her way across the room and puffed up her already frizzy hair. "Beautiful wedding, kids," she said and hugged Eve. "How you feeling, Evie?"

"Like I'm carsick."

Annie squeezed her friend's hand, then raised her eyebrows. "Just don't throw up on my new shoes. Oh, look, Dee's made her entrance, finally."

Dee had missed the ceremony. "I can't believe she'd do that to me," Eve kept repeating to Hart. When Dee finally slithered into Ramona's, in a slinky, satin version of her bridesmaid's dress, too late to be a bridesmaid, Eve finally knew how she felt: like a kid who's discovered that, over the summer break, her best friend has replaced her with a new buddy.

"God, she's all over that poor creature," Annie proclaimed.

"Cousin Kevin," Hart laughed.

"Is she trying to do an imitation of that actress in *Sea of Love* . . . what's her name?" Annie snapped her fingers. "Ellen Barkin. Why not just wrap her legs completely around him?"

"Well," Hart said, "Maybe we should have videotaped

the wedding, after all. A sexual act would certainly make a memorable event to show to our grandchildren."

"Get a plate and come sit with me," Eve instructed Annie. "I refuse to even say hello to her. I won't have a fight at my wedding."

"Okay, honey. Try not to feel bad. It's her problem. Oh, by the way, it looks like your mother has managed to charm her way into your professor's good graces." Sure enough, standing by the bar, glass of wine in hand, Eve's mother had fixed her "intense listening look" on the woman whose back—straight and punishing as an arrow—faced the two friends.

While sacred, the tribal rituals of Eve's family were far from conventional. For example, Passover at her aunt and uncle's. Another example was this, Eve's wedding. Daniel had, begrudgingly, agreed to let Maxie make the toast. Never a verbal person, he got especially nervous speaking in front of large groups; Maxie, on the other hand, was a natural before an audience. Once, she had taken an eighteen-hour train ride to Akron, Ohio, to give a paper at a conference. She loved travel and had never been on a long train ride. She wanted to see the countryside (later, she declared, "There is not one moment of memorable landscape between New York and Ohio"). But she quickly discovered that she'd misplaced the outline for the essay she was going "to scribble on the train." Additionally, she had forgotten to pack her wallet and another pair of shoes. Her husband had ended up wiring her money but not in time: she gave her talk—the one she'd fallen asleep writing en route—in her green Keds sneakers. Afterwards, people actually "applauded," she bragged, and an editor of a social work journal asked if she'd "honor him" with publishing her speech. It was entitled: "The Impact of Consecutive Miscarriages on a Couple's Marriage." A real show-stopper. But Maxie could still draw a crowd; she was a regular Joan Rivers of the infertile.

"For those who know me, you realize that I just wrote this the night before," Maxie began. Much laughing among her fellow workers and relatives, confused rustling among the Orbach crowd. Olivia, sitting across the table from Eve, closed her eyes quickly, an involuntary reaction. What she really wanted was to put her hands over her ears; Eve knew, because she felt the same way.

"For those of you who are mothers, you're all too familiar with how stressful having children can be, how their problems wear you out before your time." Moans of recognition. Eve grabbed onto the sides of her chair.

"How can she complain at your wedding?" Olivia hissed.

But, Maxie quickly changed tracks. "A child's wedding is one event for which we can feel unqualified happiness, especially when your daughter is marrying a man as fine as Hart." Cheers from the Orbach clan. And in a more a reminiscent tone: "Eve has always been a good daughter. Lovely; you can see that for yourself. Extremely smart. But, of course, that she gets from me." She winked at the crowd.

"Maybe we should book her in the Catskills," Hart said.

Olivia's eyes now widened and she shook her head.

Maxie was saying words like, "conscientious," and "driven." But for a minute, Eve could not listen, from that woozy, out-of-body experience she now attributed to the pregnancy.

Maxine was saying, "When she was born, she was the image of my mother and I thought: 'Oh, God, I'll have my hands full.'" She turned toward Eve's grandmother—who was seated close to the stage—and gave a little bow. "Excuse me, Ma. Henrietta and I have had our differences but no one can deny what a tremendously generous and strong woman she is. A real fighter. I think Eve has proven herself a fighter as well. To you, Hart." She glanced up; she was smiling but with tears in her eyes. "I say this. Never forget, we Sterlings are high-maintenance women. To quote a great lady—I hope the English literature crowd and Eve will appreciate this Mary Wollstonecraft, in *A Vindication of the Rights of Woman,* wrote. . . . " Here she looked down at a wrinkled file card, "'For if it be allowed that women were destined by Providence to acquire human virtues, and, by the exercise of their understandings, that stability of character which is the firmest ground to rest our future hopes upon, they must be permitted to turn to the fountain of light, and not forced to shape their course by the twinkling of a mere satellite.' Hart, dear, I know will never expect a satellite and as—excuse the poor metaphor—two, independent planets, you, Eve and Hart, should light up the sky."

"What a cool speech," Eve heard Dee say.

Truly cool. So, what was wrong with Eve? Why did she feel like a guest at her own wedding, her own life?

On the way to the bathroom, Eve heard Norma's voice, "Mrs. Orbach, Ohhhh, Mrs. Orbach." Christ, she thought, refusing to turn around until she used her proper, unchanged name, I am sandwiched between Mary Wollstonecraft and Mrs. Bennet. She wondered if her identity would start to fade, like a movie ghost, if she would become ephemeral if not quite invisible. Was this married life? Being negated by huge, matriarchal forces?

Luckily, Norma was detoured by her daughter, Elyse, who was decked out in a short black leather dress. "Mom, wait a minute. Cousin Lorraine is feeling very insulted cause no one from the wedding party stopped by her table. . . ."

"Eve," Hart pulled his wife into the ladies' room.

"What the hell are you doing in here?" she giggled.

"We may have a problem. Since your mother gave the toast, my mother thinks it's only fair that she gets to sing."

Eve peered into the mirror and watched herself scowl. "Very funny."

"I mean it, Eve," Hart said and mocked a forlorn expression. "Maybe just one verse of *"Sunrise, Sunset?"*

"Are you kidding? Ask her if she'd like to do a duet with the florist, maybe karaoke style."

Eve rushed out of the bathroom, leaving a confused husband. This, she thought contritely, is the beginning of my marriage, marked by my having a temper tantrum.

One of the first to leave, Maud approached Eve. She

said, "Your mother and I had a talk. Interesting woman. Although, I wasn't sure if her interpretation of Wollstonecraft applies to this event " Then as she edged towards the door: "I look forward to reading your next chapter. Just *keep* your focus, Eve," and she narrowed her eyes, but only for a second. "Good luck." Eve nodded, figuring her mother had slipped her advisor a fat check under the table. In a daze, she imagined Maxine and Maud in a boxing ring, battling over their respective readings of *Vindication,* without concern that Hart and she were even present at their own wedding. Eve turned around to search for her new husband, and the thought flew through her mind: would she even recognize him in a crowd?

New York, New York
November 10, 1996

Dear Eve,

A few weeks ago, I tried to contact you about a conference I'll be attending in December. The woman who answered the phone had no idea who you were. I figured you'd moved and forgot about calling (I admit). But yesterday, I ran into Sydney Anderson. (Tall, big-busted, still pretty in what you called "her tight-assed Newport WASP way." She just defended her thesis on Philip Roth's ethnocentric vision.) She'd heard through the grapevine that you'd gotten married and moved out of town. Well, I guess congratulations are in order.

I called Dee Glassman for your address. She made no attempt to mask her lack of enthusiasm at hearing from me. But, I reassured her that my intentions were purely work-related. "The 19th-Century British Literature Conference" in Bristol looks like it's right up your alley. No, I haven't come over to "the other side." I'm still an Americanist. But, I'm working on an article on expatriates—beginning with Henry James—to take my mind off the job search (and thought it might be fun to experience their pleasures abroad). I defended last fall and am relieved to finally have all that behind me. I took a year off, before embarking on looking for a teaching position, to edit my dissertation into a book. (Prospects for publication look good and my fingers are crossed.). How is your thesis coming along? Almost done, I hope.

I'm including information on the conference. I remember how much you wanted to present your work in England.

Best wishes.

Yours, Graham

London, England
December 10, 1996

Dear Professor Wellington,

I was disappointed not to hear from you in regard to my
paper on Jane Austen; I realize that other duties—teaching,
etc.—have kept you busy. I think the thesis of my essay—
Austen's subversive feminism within the parameters of her
oppressive culture, as contrasted to the masochism revealed
through twentieth-century women's fiction—went over
well.

I do hope to hear from you soon; and, I'm very much
looking forward to your arrival in England. I am hard at
work tightening up the methodology in my dissertation, at
Professor Forster's suggestion. Will you be able to spend
much time going over structure? I imagine one or two meet-
ings would suffice.

Once again, you can reach me at the phone number
and/or address at the top of this letter.

Many thanks,

Eve Sterling

"What a blessing that she never had any children! Poor little creatures, how unhappy she would have made them!" —*Emma*

THERE WERE 157 titles, in the University library, with the word "motherhood" in them. Those that weren't cataloged as fiction belonged in the women's studies section; this latter group was particularly preoccupied with the long, oppressed history of mothers or the mythology inflicted on the entire institution. Eve cross-indexed motherhood with pregnancy and discovered abstracts on childbirth practices around the world that would make a robust young man keel over with queasiness. Under the orange glow of the triangular shaded lamps, she read about complications from botched deliveries that caused her breakfast to flip over, like a fish, in her belly.

Eve was not sure what she was doing tucked away in the stacks, all through the chilly April afternoon, scuffling through texts dating from the 1940s to the present. All she could offer herself, by way of explanation, was that research held out the promise of true knowledge and knowledge would quell the odd combination of terror and anticipation battling for first place in her gut, now that she had entered her last month of pregnancy. She read psychoanalysts' excerpts from Freud to Winnicott and discovered that to be "good enough" she would need to pack up her life as neatly as a paper bag and store it in the drawer for at least a decade and a half. Of course, the feminists advocated a different track; one prominent sociologist warned Eve to make motherhood a relationship rather than a profession. That struck the right chord, but why did it sound so cool, so perfectly correct, so impossible to achieve?

Eve reached one hand around to the pain in her back and sighed. Even *she* knew that a baby could arrive like a tropical storm; you had to seal your home in preparation and wait. Still, it might come with more chaotic force than anything she ever imagined, altering the look and feel of her life irrevocably. How would one explain to such a creature that she must not consume her mother's life, that she needed to ease with grace into her designated role? Beloved, but not exclusively.

That evening Eve taught a freshman composition course at a community college in downtown Manhattan. Their assignment was the first draft of a paper—based on articles she'd frantically clipped from magazines—on "The State of Daycare in America" (her new obsession). Eve guessed that the most passionate essay would come from the insightful, enraged Felicia Henry. A willowy black teenager with hooded eyelids, Felicia was the single mother of a hyperactive one-year-old and the daughter of an alcoholic. "You should never 'ave gotten me started," her student said as she slapped her assignment on Eve's desk; she had a bitter grin on her face, exposing all her clean, straight teeth. "But, hey, you'll find out soon 'nough, I guess. Right, professor?"

When Eve had just entered her fifth month, Rosie Alvarez—the girl with a ring on every finger and fake gold earrings the size of fists—had called out, "Hey, Professor Sterling, you preggers?" It had been a few minutes before class time and kids were wandering in, slumped shoulders, listening to Walkmans or talking too loudly in their seats; Rosie's question stopped the squall of English slang and Spanish. All eyes focused on the teacher, round with wonder or narrowed in humorous expectation. The jig was up. Eve was poking through even her most oversized sweaters.

"I am," she'd said. "It's a girl." Although only thirty years old, Eve had insisted on an amnio to ensure that her baby was not suffering from severe chromosomal abnormalities. During the three long weeks that she waited for the results, Eve imagined Chinese mothers willingly handing over their infant daughters to husbands who would snuff the life out of the baby with once innocent pillows—for the crime of having been born female. The last week, she began to panic, convinced that the baby had some horrible genetic disease, a punishment for her own ambivalence. She made three visits to the Museum of Natural History and treaded through its long halls, staring at the stuffed panthers as if her destiny shone out of their soulless yellow eyes.

The reaction from her F101 students—applause, laughter and whoops of congratulations—had been the only unequivocal voice of approval Eve had received about her baby. At the next class, five female students, including Rosie and Felicia, brought their professor a store-made devil's food cake. The whole class celebrated by slicing it with a plastic fork and handing out a sliver to each of the 37 class members.

At the end of the hour, Eve collected only a half dozen papers. "The rest of you will have to hand your assignment in next time if you don't want your grade lowered," she said, sternly. She waddled to the subway, in the drizzling rain, her backpack tearing into her shoulders from the pull of all her books; she visualized her couch and a cup of herbal tea. Once in position—her feet snug under their thick, gingham quilt, her Sleepytime tea in hand—she would balance her student's work on her protruding belly and read Felicia's paper.

By the time Hart returned home that evening, the sky was dark as oblivion. Eve had established an intimate rapport with their couch in whose soft cushions she decided to make a permanent home. She was thinking about being wrenched out of her prescribed fate when she heard the sound of her husband's key in the lock. It was such an ordinary act; it revealed an implicit trust in the routine workings of the universe.

"Hey," Hart called into the darkness. "Any hugely pregnant women home?" Artificial light illuminated part of the room; the rest was shadowy. "You two okay?" he asked and patted his wife's belly. "Just exhausted?" He sat on the edge of the couch; then, slipping off the shoulder strap of his Leica, lowered his most precious object to the floor instead of securing it in the closet as usual. Eve thought how, since the wedding, both of them had been half pretending that her "condition" was nothing more than a momentary glitch in their plans, a stubborn virus that was hanging around in her system for a particularly long time. They hadn't even picked out a crib.

She grabbed his forearm and shook him. "Say goodbye to it, Hart. Just wave *au revoir, sayonara.*"

"Okay: *sayonara, ciao, arrivederci,* for that matter. Why are we having a mini-Berlitz lesson here? What are we saying adios *to?*"

"*Freedom.* You should read my student's essay. Between childcare problems, work, and school, her life's a three-ring circus. "

Hart picked out an essay from the pile of papers on the floor. "Hey, good sentence structure. Are you sure this is one of yours?" he smiled. "C'mon. Why are you comparing her situation to ours? What is she, seventeen? Unwed? Working at McD's?"

"She's nineteen and, no, she's not married but," Eve straightened the pillow under her back, "she lives with her mother who babysits. More built-in help than we have. Having an offspring sounds too exhausting. What do you say we forget the whole thing?"

"Okay. Let's just forget it."

"It's just that it's going to be impossible to get anything accomplished for awhile. Like eighteen years." Eve conjured up the image of herself kissing each and every page of her dissertation as, one by one, she flung the first half of a never-to-be-completed manuscript out the window and into the chilly Brooklyn sky. "Okay, here's the thing," she said, "we didn't want this baby. You said it the day I told you I was pregnant and then dropped it. You never actually *told* me . . . but, I knew it's what you wished for."

"Wished?" Hart nearly hissed on the "s." Eve was glad because her husband's rage would be a good distraction from her own mounting anxiety.

"That this baby may never be born. That I'd get an abortion."

Hart stood up slowly; then, he picked up his camera and carried it off to the bedroom. The few minutes he was out of the room was such a relief, Eve almost fell asleep, safe in this couch from which she'd never emerge.

"Why don't you tell me what's *really* going on," Hart said, back on the scene, a few minutes later.

"No sinister ulterior motive, Hart. It's just we aren't behaving like happy expectant parents, picking out layettes and decorating the nursery. You've been distracted and distant since the honeymoon, working all the time."

"And you've been obsessed with your thesis and talking to your mother round-the-clock. What the hell's a layette, anyway? Some kind of kiddy porn?"

"Hart! My mom's paying for the baby. I feel I owe her regular reports on her progress."

"And how do you think that makes me feel, your parents' paying for our baby?"

His use of the word "our" just knocked Eve out. She took his hand. "Have you even had your dinner yet?"

"No," he grinned, a kid caught by his mama. "I'm starving."

"Go make yourself something; I can't get up." He sighed and Eve noticed how exhausted he looked, the circles under his eyes, as if smudged by charcoal.

While Hart was rustling in the kitchen, Eve tried to sink back into that languid state, so blissfully numbing. But her senses were so acute, she could hear everything: the couple upstairs breathing heavily (they always made love early in the evening and fought after midnight); the taxis' horns beeping, their wheels squeaking as they passed other cars on Seventh Avenue. Her insides rumbling as—she imagined—her body was frantically producing extra blood and fluid by the moment.

"I guess I've been feeling left out," he said, reappearing with a peanut butter sandwich and a glass of milk balanced on a plate. (His penchant for what she called "little boy food" always struck Eve as poignantly sweet.) "I never really got a chance to be married to you. You know, just the two of us."

"You feel as if we were forced into marriage."

"Stop making me the bad guy in all this." He slid down beside her. "This is my baby too. And I've already fallen in love with it."

Eve eased her way up to a sitting position, proving to herself that she wasn't paralyzed from the neck down. "That's sweet and sentimental, Hart. But, it's easy to say before the baby is born." She was deliberately trying to start a fight and they both knew it. If he looked at Eve as if he wanted to whack her, she wouldn't have blamed him. Instead, his eyes were forlorn. Much worse.

"Evie, I'm nervous. I'd be nuts not to be. I wouldn't have chosen this time to have a baby and, as for a crib, I'm sure Amanda would be glad to share her doggie bed—just kidding. Hey, lighten up. Just because we're not buying diapers and teething rings months in advance doesn't make us bad parents. We'll be okay."

"Well, I hope you're right, Hart. Because these hormones are wreaking havoc with my emotions. I'm not the cold-hearted career woman I used to be."

"Uh-oh. Look out world, a kinder, gentler version of Eve."

Early the next morning, she awoke ravenous. After tearing to the bathroom, she engaged in what had—of late— become a ritual: pillaging the contents of her kitchen with a murderous determination only to discover she could eat very little before indigestion ensued. She gobbled breakfast in front of an open refrigerator, swallowed a slice of roast beef, a chunk of bagel with butter smeared on it with her finger, gulps of pulpy orange juice. Then, still in her sleep attire: sweatpants, plaid flannel nightshirt, and thick bushy socks, Eve padded into the living room to attack her thesis. Throughout the last trimester, she'd gotten into the habit of trying to bully herself—as she dragged her body around, bloated and slow—into approaching her work with maniacal perseverance. Only now she had three weeks left and was nowhere near completion.

Despite her great intentions, Eve found it impossible to organize her third chapter; the material was all there, but any sign of clear thinking on her part was missing. With sweaty, constantly overheated fingers, she waded through piles of paper; but her mind immediately began closing off, not able to make sense of the words presented on the page. Under the rubble of thesis notes was her journal. Eve picked up her lavender pen, ready to write her daily lament when the phone rang. "Sterling," the hoarse, breathy voice said. "It's me, Glassman. Long time no speak. Want to grab an espresso—decaf *for you*, of course—and shoot the shit?"

"How about Tallullah?" Dee said, "A la Demi Moore's kid." Eve knew that her friend identified with the actress as they shared similar voices, perfect figures, and an egocentric vision of the world.

"I don't think so. I don't want to call my daughter something that would guarantee sending her into psychotherapy even before the onset of adolescence. Too expensive."

The two women were mulling through baby name books in the huge Chelsea edition of Barnes and Noble. Dee's idea that they "check it out" translated into: let's meet on neutral territory (no trace of husband or imminent child anywhere but in Eve's womb). But, while Dee made a beeline for poetry, Eve had wandered away from critical theory into fiction and ended up where her true obsession lay these days: the infant/child-care section.

"Also if we call her Tallullah," Eve said, once her friend joined her in baby names, "then I would have to call her Bankie for short."

"So, play it safe," Dee said, glancing down at a book which she'd grabbed off the shelf, "Go the geological route and name her 'Crystal' or 'Amber.'" She pointed with one long, yellow-stained finger to the author's list of the most popular girls' names in America. "You could have a whole sort of ensemble thing going: pierce her ears at birth and give her earrings to match the name."

How could Eve mention that, in fact, the top choice on her list—Gemma—had a more geological sound to it than the three her friend already trashed? "I always thought Calamity Jane had a nice ring to it."

"Ah, *Jane*. I figured you'd get around to the old Austen motif. You *always* do."

"How about a cappuccino? Maybe it will improve your mood."

"Hey Sterling, there's nothing wrong with my mood," she said, glaring. Then, she smiled and said, in the old Dee way, "Nothing that getting laid wouldn't cure."

Seated, Dee suddenly appeared childlike in size, dwarfed by an ex-boyfriend's black leather jacket, the sleeves of which she needed to roll up in order to drink her espresso. Her silver bangle bracelets clanked against the tiny cup as she picked it up.

"So, what are you getting?" Eve asked her, reaching for the two books poking out of her new backpack, also black leather.

"Auden's collected poems," Dee said. "And this New Age book on auras and some other spiritual garbage. They're gifts for this cool guy I met a few weeks ago. He's into some weird stuff, but is an amazing poet."

"Yeah?" Eve touched her hand and, then, immediately withdrew it. Dee was so tense, Eve wanted to joke that her friend's aura neatly matched the rest of her outfit. Instead, she just asked, "Anything promising there?"

"He's got a butt worth sinking your teeth into."

"Well. There's a lot of future in yummy butts."

Eve waited for a snipe; but Dee just sat there, fiddling with her espresso cup, then rubbing the huge stone in her turquoise and silver ring, her lips curled slightly into a haughty semi-smile. "I've decided to put all my eggs into my own basket for the time being. Since the writing's going great."

Eve did not have to see *her own* aura to know it was a dark shade of green. "Great," she said, without conviction. "What's going on?"

"I found out yesterday that two of my old Joe poems were taken by *Poetry* magazine. The guy is dog shit but I managed to mold him into not-so-smelly art."

The two smiled in mutual satisfaction over the fact that this man—who prided himself on torturing women with his precious angst—could be transformed into something valuable. "That's great, " Eve said. "You're on your way to fame and fortune."

"*Success,* Eve. Knowing what I want. Speaking of which, now that you're one minute away from popping out this baby, are you going to own up to the fact that this bun-in-the-oven was planned? You're a smart girl. You knew how *not* to get knocked up. You've been doing it for thirty-one years, right? You had to want this."

"Are you saying I'm lying? Towards what end?"

"No, not consciously lying." Dee leaned forward, "But, figure it out: the Big Tamale works with the infertile. So, obviously, getting in the family way was your unconscious' way of proving your worth. I'm seriously worried about you, Eve, with all this self-delusion going on. I mean, I'm afraid you're going to flip out when you realize how hard it is to finish that tome of yours with a kid hanging onto your tit."

Eve rose up—eyes focused on the display of new books near the entrance—and said, "I have to go." In a daze, she walked out of the store, away from the single life she'd once shared with her friend.

The night before Gemma was born, Eve rented *Esther and Ruth,* a film set in 1946, about two Jewish-American sisters struggling for autonomy from their mother who was desperate for them to marry successfully. Eve had seen the movie before, which made it easier to watch, since she couldn't really concentrate on anything besides the cramping which began inside the enormous, low hanging mound that would be her daughter and burned all the way down to the back of her shins.

"It's show time," she said to Hart now. But he had fallen asleep, his mouth slightly open, his hand across his eyes, in defense, as if even his body knew instinctively: this was no time to rest.

Eve shoved his shoulder once, made her hand into a fist, but then stopped. Maybe because the glaze in his eyes had deepened in the eerie light coming from the reflection of the television and Seventh Avenue, she let him off the hook for this—what she'd learned was—the first stage of labor. The contractions were consistent and far apart, so she waited—congratulating herself on her remarkable calm—turned off the movie, and walked into the kitchen to make tea. Eve knew from Lamaze class that making tea was something all women about to deliver should do. She'd settled on some Orange Spice, when a twisting pain, like someone suddenly snapping a rope taut through her torso, forced her to slouch over. "God, this floor is dirty," she thought when the blurring cleared up.

She was mopping the ugly brown tiles—the kind with indented patterns you can never quite clean—when Hart walked in. His eyes had that red hooded look of someone doped up. "What a strange thing to be doing. At 1:00 in the morning," he said and his head bobbed slightly.

Pushing the mop with fierce stamina, Eve didn't answer; she always waited a beat to see if Hart fell back to sleep. Shortly after moving in together, she discovered his mysterious talent of dozing while standing up. Once, furious that he'd performed this trick in the middle of a fight, she'd actually tipped him over, thinking of cows stupidly slumbering on their feet. He opened his eyes in complete bewilderment before he landed on his knees. Leaning against the arch of the kitchen's entrance, he was out again and snoring; at least, he'd learned to protect himself by conking out against some sturdy, inanimate object.

Now, in a normal speaking voice, Eve said, "I'm in labor." She knew he couldn't answer, and he didn't. This was the sort of test of his love she'd begun subjecting him to since the wedding: hear me in your sleep, read my thoughts, make our lives magically fall into place. Loudly, Eve repeated her mighty declaration, "I'm in labor."

"Uhh?" he mumbled. Finally, as always, she shook him hard. "Really? Why didn't you tell me?"

Didn't she need all of her energy to achieve this feat, this remarkable trick of birthing a child? Should she really have to keep her husband awake as well?

"Why are you mopping the floor? Eve, don't you have two more weeks to go? Should we call the doctors?"

"It's the middle of the night," she said but she did return the mop to its place between the fridge and the counter, wishing she, too, was thin enough to slink into that tight space and hide. "We'll wake them."

Hart shuffled, eyes half-closed, into the kitchen. "Want the guy at the all night deli to deliver her? These are his hours."

"I love Tommy, and his wife *has* had four children." She punched her husband lightly on the arm. "He's probably a pro by now."

Lethargically, Hart scratched his fingers through his curly black hair and yawned so that you could see the back of his throat. A joke between them was that Hart was the tortoise to her hare and, now, Eve envisioned him as that huge, sluggish reptile, extending his leathery neck out one inch at a time. "Evie, I don't feel that we're prepared to have this baby on the living room floor."

"Okay, I'll have it on the bed," she answered. "Are you going to call?"

"Maybe its Dr. Geronilli's night." Dr. G., who Eve had tried to see exclusively, at her mother's prompting, was a heavy-set woman in her late forties who cracked bad jokes and cursed with a thick Brooklyn accent. Hart walked to the phone on her desk and turned on the lamp. Suddenly—in the heat of early labor—so much of their black and red furniture pleaded poverty to her. The Persian throw rug Grandmother Henrietta had given them was badly faded and the prints—some black and white ink drawings from *Harper's Weekly* that they'd bought on their honeymoon in Cape Cod—looked like cheap reproductions. Only Hart's photographs—the deserted train station in winter, and the portrait of a one-eyed Eve, the right side of her face in shadow—were worth hanging on the walls, she thought.

The attempt to do up her single woman's studio in thrift-store fineness—faded lace draped over a ratty marigold armchair, salmon pink dried flowers—had seemed silly, young, once they were married. She now wanted to live with heavy, solid objects.

Eve slunk down into the chair by her desk, an antique monster from her parents' den; to the right of it hung her favorite drawing: William Caxton demonstrating the first English printing press to Edward IV. The strain, in the laborer's neck and back, from pulling the huge lever was what Eve focused on when she sat down to write her dissertation, day after day. She gazed up at it, waiting for some sense of familiarity to console her. But she was hot, the room was starting to spin, and the picture looked like nothing more than lines and faces, devoid of any personal message.

"Okay. Thanks." Hart hung up the phone. "It was their service. I'm sorry; it's Dr. Chay's night. They're going to have her call us."

"Shit," Eve said and hunched over in her chair. For the cost, she thought, getting your favorite doctor should be as easy as putting a coin in a jukebox and pushing the buttons.

Fully alert now, Hart ran to her. He put his hand on his wife's forehead, his gesture for gauging sickness of all kinds. "What's wrong? Is it killing you?"

"No, it's her. Dr. Chay. I don't want her delivering my baby; she's a cold fish," she sighed. "Do you think she's younger than me?"

"Ambitious, even during life's most mystical moments." He shook his head but took her hand; just the warm touch of him quieted her. "Eve, look at me. We're going to have a baby."

She refused to look up. She felt tremendously ornery, flushed, and achy and as if she were transforming into some phantom creature, half human, half beast. "I'll believe it when I see it."

Hart answered the doctor's phone call which came twenty minutes later. "Dr. Chay said we really should have waited until the contractions were more regular," he reported after hanging up. "The hospital will turn us away." Eve envisioned herself circling the hospital, squatting as she reached inside and pulled a baby out, as adeptly as she would a Tampax.

"Let's lie down and wait," Hart said and yawned.

In bed, she drew her legs up and rested on her side so that the cramping would feel less intense. Surprisingly, she fell asleep and dreamed: she'd found Dee dead in her apartment, naked, her body contorted, her face covered by a scarf. Then: a newspaper clipping with a smiling picture of a young Dee—not more than twenty—in which it described an unwanted pregnancy which ended in her giving the baby up to her cousin, named Olivia. When Eve heard the news, she said, "And that's why Jane Austen never dealt with having babies in her books. Too messy."

She awoke, startled, to find herself bathed in moisture. Images from her endless graduate school days swirled through her semi-consciousness, metaphors for feminine wetness: menstruation, mother's milk, amniotic fluid. She patted the sheet underneath her, "I think my water broke," she said to her somnolent husband. "Oh," was all he managed in response. Then, his voice creaked faintly, "Let's go."

Hospital admitting was dark and cool, formidable as an Italian church. When Hart told the receptionist why they were there, the girl gave him a blank look, cracked her gum, and motioned for them to have a seat with her weapon-sharp nails. She insisted that they fill in insurance information even as the leakage from Eve's body formed rings around her feet.

Once checked in, there was no Dr. Chay in sight. A smiling nurse with an apricot complexion and a thick black braid escorted the couple to the birthing room. "My name is Susan," she said in a sing-song voice. "I'll be with you the whole time." The ache was deepening as the nurse spurted the cold jelly on the flesh above where Eve's baby was lying, waiting. Eve heard the familiar, galloping heartbeat as the nurse explained how the graph charted Gemma's response to labor. Observing her constricting flesh being translated into black marks on paper, she pictured her baby thrashing frantically, like a captured fish, down the canal, into the world. "Wow," Susan whistled. "You're dilated to six centimeters. You should be out of here in no time."

"Go call my mom and tell her," Eve instructed Hart, once she was lying on the table, her knees up, a sheet draped over her waist and legs. She was proud of her body for its efficiency. "This might be okay," she thought, "if I can do it quickly and without fuss."

"Is it okay if I leave?" Hart asked, concern rounding out his eyes like pennies.

"It's fine," Susan said. "She's doing great."

Dr. Chay—in her white coat and snapping her gum—made her entrance a half hour later. "She may make it through in here," she said to Susan. Eve knew that the doctor thought that giving birth naturally was superior to any other way, and that not too many women pulled it off. Eve had been reciting her mantra for weeks: "the more drugs the better," but now was feeling that old competitive urge. She wanted to achieve this difficult feat, just as she'd always wanted to excel, to outdo, in every aspect of her life.

An hour later, she was already pushing. Nonchalant, Dr. Chay left the room to get a candy bar. Then, without warning, Eve felt as if someone had taken a saw to her spine. She was being cut into pieces, the girl in a magician's box. She cried out, startled and betrayed; there was the taste of vomit in her throat, choking her. Panting now, instead of breathing, Eve tried to speak. "It's my back. Get her off my back. I CAN DO IT. Just get her off my back."

Hart, stroking his wife's forehead, yelled, "What's going on?"

The sawing turned more violent as another contraction began: someone was hacking Eve's backbone with an axe. She thought how the baby would no longer be leaping out, a confident gymnast with her arms outstretched. If she was lucky, Gemma was hiding—curled into a ball—like a child under her desk when the bomb hits.

"Back labor, of all the bad luck," Susan explained, having dropped the sing-song tone. "We're taking you to the delivery room and we'll see about getting you an epidural." Susan squeezed Eve's hand and looked into her eyes, bright blue lit-up eyes.

"I'm right here, Evie," Hart chanted, over and over, making absolutely no difference.

In the delivery room, the pain crystallized into a spear of glass, lodged in between two vertebrae. Each time the contraction came, the spear wedged its way further into her spine.

Dr. Chay was back, chomping on her candy bar, cool as a professional executioner. "Let's try and concentrate on pushing, Eve."

"She needs the epidural," Susan said in a voice hot with anger. "She can't do it."

"It's really late in the labor." Chomp. Chomp. "Let's try, again."

"I CAN'T," Eve screamed, the contraction blinding her from everything but moving shapes and colors. The pain was increasing in velocity and Eve felt her body traveling without her. "Do something! Just give me a C-Section! I promise not to sue!"

Eve heard Dr. Chay sigh, clearly disappointed by all the theatrics. "Okay. I'll ask the anesthesiologist what he thinks."

This time when the contraction came, Eve immediately began to wail. She had given up on any decorum or control, and knew she'd be mortified when she remembered this later. "Let's just try and breathe together. Okay, honey?" Susan's voice reached her ear like a stream of liquid. "Squeeze my hand back, if you can try."

Eve squeezed her hand. "Give me drugs!"

"The doctor's working on it. Just concentrate on me and try not to tense up before the contraction. Okay, here it comes."

Eve tried to focus on the nurse's face, her mouth making quick, eee, hyena noises. She was imitating Susan's breathing, when the face turned into a pale, then, fuzzy moon.

"She's passing out," Eve heard Susan say. A few minutes later, Eve felt a different pair of hands on her back, rolling her over. "Eve, my name is Dr. Dehlia, can you hear me?" a rich voice with an accent said. Eve must have nodded because he said, "Good. Now, I'm going to prep you with an anesthetic which will be cold, but won't hurt. Then, you'll feel me inject the epidural into your back. You have to promise not to move, dear. Good."

A contraction clenched her insides just as the needle pierced through skin; Eve's leg shot up like a peeing dog's. "Damn," the accented voice snapped. "Well, we'll just have to see what happens."

Hart, now practically hysterical, shouted, "What does that mean?"

"It's coming again," Eve cried and the pain in her back, behind her eyes, in her brain, bore down on her so hard, she was transforming into a one-dimensional creature. In some far off corner of her mind, Eve remembered a passage from her favorite children's book, *A Wrinkle In Time,* when Meg tesseracts through black time, feeling as if her insides have been flattened.

"Push," Eve heard a symphony of voices shout. But, they were no longer her concern.

She knew she was sobbing and pleading; yet, every time a contraction came, she made some feeble attempt to co-operate in good girl fashion.

There was a rustling, then a presence. "Okay what's going on here?" That deep, rough voice. Dr. Geronilli. And, a moment later, Maxine bursting into the room, knocking the swing doors into hysterics. "*What'swrongwithmydaughter? Oh, my God!*"

The doctor's hand was cool and firm on her patient's knee; "Eve? Can you hear me?"

Maxine leaned into her daughter. "I'm here now, I'm here," she said augustly. "*I'll* get to the bottom of this."

There was a buzz of voices all talking at once at an excited pitch; her mother's shrill above the rest: "You *cannot*, understand me, *cannot* allow a person, any person, but especially *my* daughter, to be tormented in this way."

Dr. Geronilli: "Mrs. Sterling, is it? Would you mind going into the waiting room? I can't work with you in here."

An indignant snort: "I'm not leaving. I'm sorry if that's a problem. You should have thought of that before my daughter's delivery was left in an amateur's hands."

"I'm outta here," Dr. Chay announced. Then, the sound of the doors slapping themselves silly.

"Okay. Let's everyone just calm down," Dr. Geronilli said. Then to Eve, "If we give you another epidural, you need to promise me that you will try to push, even if you can't feel anything. Can you do that?"

"YES," Eve swore, wild with the anticipation of relief. She had no idea what she was promising.

"Okay, prep her for another dose and then let's get her into room 106. Looks like this little one needs our help getting out into the world."

"Thank God," Maxine said, accompanied by several clucks of accusation, just as the needle penetrated Eve's spine.

Laid out on the gurney, Eve glanced up at tense faces and imagined the doctors as boatmen, racing her towards the river of death, paddling their giant oars. Then, suddenly, her body sank into the delicious exhaustion of non-pain. For a moment, she had to fight to stay awake, as Dr. Geronilli, Maxine, Dr. Dehlia, Susan, Hart, and a young balding intern with a half smile all surrounded her. She was lying on a table in a larger room with an enormous light glaring down, mortified to recognize the view her mother was privy to. When Dr. Geronilli instructed her to push, Eve commanded her body to obey and felt nothing.

"Great," the doctor said. "You must have been working out during your pregnancy. Your muscles are listening."

"I used to do ballet, " Eve croaked, awed that the compulsion to list her accomplishments was surviving anesthesia.

"Okay, now Dr. Johnson is going to lean on your belly and ease the baby along. Dr. Johnson."

On cue, Dr. Johnson moved under the light; his half-smile came into focus above Eve. Like the cheshire cat, she thought now, punchy with the exhilaration of not feeling her body. He placed his palms at the top of her ribs. "Okay," Dr. Geronilli orchestrated, her hands reaching inside of Eve. "Now, push. C'mon. What's the baby's name?"

"Gemma," Hart said, as simultaneously, Maxine proclaimed,"Gemma Isabel—Isabel after Daniel's mother."

"What?" Hart asked, startled. "Her middle name was supposed to be Sybil after my grandmother."

"Sybil? No offense but Sybil is the name of a crazy person. Come to think of it, I've always hated that name. I knew a girl once in grade school named Sybil and she definitely had more than one personality lurking behind that homely face of hers. And all of them mean. . . ."

"C'mon, Gemma, "Dr. Geronilli coached. "Let's go, Gemma."

There was a great deal of pushing and pulling. Dr. Johnson kneaded Eve's belly with two hands while she floated, gloriously, in and out of time.

"Okay, now. I see the crown of the baby's head. We're almost there."

"You can do it Eve!" her mother exclaimed. "Just push down on your diaphragm like this." She inhaled loudly to demonstrate.

The room was prickly with anticipation: Hart started breathing harder and faster; Maxine was shifting her weight from one leg to the other; Susan was giving Eve's hand quick little encouraging pats.

This was the finishing line.

And, then Gemma (Isabel or Sybil) Sterling-Orbach was born, just like that, in an anesthetized blur.

"Perfect," Dr. Geronilli pronounced, as she and the others worked on her in the corner where Eve couldn't see. The baby cried, a short, not very convincing cry, then became peacefully quiet yet alert. Just like Hart, Eve thought.

"Oh, let me see, let me see her!" Maxine gasped.

But, Dr. Geronilli, ignoring the queen's command, laid the exquisite prize down on the new mother's chest.

"My, she's small," Eve said, as she looked down at her daughter: cone-shaped head, olive skin, mouth opening and closing like a guppy's. Holding Gemma—a tiny thing clutching arms and legs into her middle—Eve saw: she had the eyes of an angel.

Letters

New York, New York
Winter, 1996

Dear Sterling,

Chances are, after everything that happened between us, you'll never answer this letter. But, hey, it's worth a try and I promised your friend Annie Sunshine that I'd try to help rescue you from yourself. Annie asked me to pitch in because, despite our differences of late, you and I have been friends a long time.

I ran into Annie in our old haunt, Telly's Place, the day after you bolted. She turned even paler than her usual pasty complexion when I asked about you. She actually figured I'd encourage you on your Fantasy Island head trip which, of course, I might have if my father hadn't left me when I was two years old. I also think she's in a state and that's another reason why she blurted out the info. Seems she's leaving for China tomorrow to adopt a baby girl. (Hasn't she been married for about five minutes? Maybe, she can't stand that her best friend had a baby first. That's a juicy piece of gossip we'll have to put off discussing until your head's on straight, but it does look like Annie's *finally* demonstrating ABERRANT COMPULSIVE BEHAVIOR!)

Listen, Sterling, this is a bad scene. It sounds as if Hart has freaked out, understandably, and isn't speaking to anyone. You were enraged with me for telling the truth in B&N, last winter. I may have been callous, but I was right. Of course you weren't ready. But, now that you have a daughter, you need to deal with that fact (in person). If women with half a brain can figure it out, you certainly can.

Annie told me what happened with your mother and that asshole advisor of yours. It sucks. I don't blame you for fleeing the scene of the crime. You do have a lot to grapple with when you get home, and I know what a control freak you are! Okay, things have spun out of control. Welcome to life! You can handle it, Sterling.

When you're home, and if and when you feel like it, give me a buzz. Regardless of the shit that happened between us, I still love you and always will.

Yours, Dee

"Had Elizabeth's opinion been drawn from her own family, she could not have formed a very pleasing picture of conjugal felicity or domestic comfort."   —*Pride and Prejudice*

FOR THE TWO days that Eve remained in the hospital after Gemma was born, she could not find herself, her face was so puffy, so distorted. She looked as if she'd been given cortisone treatments. She looked like Zelda Fitzgerald, locked away. The first evening, Eve was groggy, stumbling in and out of a place where self vanishes, fighting to reenter the world. She tried to kick, to hurl herself through the membrane of drugged sleep but failed. The morphine streamed into Eve's veins, preventing her from shaking the specters out of her brain, streaks of fog that floated into the crevices, blocking understanding. By morning, some of the fog had cleared up.

"Can you believe what she had to go through," a woman with the trace of an Irish accent said. "What a hero!"

Eve thought it must be day because the purple beneath her eyelids had turned into a whitish yellow glow.

"Of course," said another, soprano voice. "But that's Maxie for you. We should all have such mothers."

Eve's eyelids felt molded shut, as if her face were covered by a plaster-of-paris mask. She managed to peel one back so that she glimpsed the two figures hovering near her bed. She recognized the brown glossy hair and creamy complexion of Lydia Duffy, the head nurse on Maxie's unit. Next to Lydia was the plump triangular figure of Lizbeth O'Kane, the secretary. Even as they spoke in hushed voices, Eve's heart sped up with the realization: her baby had been born. Where was she?

"Did you hear the story of how Maxie sent poor Alice— that new pie-faced kid—running all through the hospital, looking for me?" Lydia asked. "It was my day off. Luckily, I was home helping Paul with a research paper on Machiavelli. I ran out of my house so fast, I didn't notice until I got here that I was still wearing my Isotoner slippers on my feet, I swear to God!"

Lizbeth's laugh was a cackle, a jarring contrast to her lilting, little girl's voice.

"Does someone think they could get me a cup of coffee?" Eve squeaked. "Real. With caffeine. I feel snowed under."

"Oh!" Lizbeth said, startled. "You're up. "I'll see what I can do."

"Breakfast should be here any minute," Lydia predicted and, in fact, just as she said this, a women carrying a plate with a metal cover entered the room. She plunked it down, mechanically, on the adjustable shelf attached to Eve's bed. Right behind her was Maxie with fortyish, bespectacled, peak-nosed Dr. Tamar, the pediatrician. He stood so close to Maxie's heels, Eve thought he was purposely playing the loyal Sancho Panza. In fact, he said, "I am your mother's obedient drone."

"Oh, shut up Kenny," Maxie laughed.

"I'm here to report that Gemma is a gem. Ha. Ha. All her parts checked out fine as of 6:30 a. m. And don't forget to thank your mom. If it wasn't for her, you'd never have this gorgeous private suite." He did a sweeping arm gesture, imitation game show host. "Enjoy your cold oatmeal and rock-hard roll. "

By noon, the room was swarming with hospital employees, all friends and fans of Maxie Sterling. The proud grandmother was standing among them, recanting Eve's birth in a stentorian voice. Hart sat next to his wife on the bed, cradling Gemma and humming "Morning has Broken" in a superb Cat Stevens imitation. Still woozy, Eve was scooping Jell-O as orange as candy corn onto her spoon, when Annie walked in. "Did I miss something?" she asked. "Did my invitation to your mom's soiree cross in the mail?"

"No," Eve said softly. "It's everyone else who's confused. They seem to think my mother had the baby."

Annie squeezed Eve's hand and whispered, barely audible, "At least you *can.*" It was the only time she'd alluded to this tension between them. Every month since her wedding, Annie had been trying to get pregnant, but to no avail. "Here," she said and presented her friend with a perfectly wrapped gift: milk white paper with a pink rosebud bow in the center. Eve opened it carefully. Inside, among crinkled tissue paper, snug as an oyster, was a tiny cotton dress; it was a plum wine color with buttons in the shape of angel wings.

"Annie, it's beautiful," Eve said. She wanted to tell her best friend so much: how her delivery was this horrendous, mythical journey down the River Styx; how her body was tender and overripe; how the first sight of her daughter was the opening of the window letting in the jewelled shock of light. But even Annie's gracious manners couldn't hide the envy in her eyes. "Has Dee come?" she asked.

"Hart left a message on her machine, but, she hasn't even called back."

"Here she is," Hart whispered and placed a sleeping Gemma in Annie's arms.

"She's gorgeous," Annie said. All three sat, mesmerized, listening to the baby's quick, shallow breaths.

"Hart," Eve asked, after a few minutes had passed. "Did you bring my book?" Hart shook his head but smiled. Then, he rummaged around his backpack and retrieved his wife's copy of *The Next Wave of Feminism.* Eve had been searching for a quote, was it, just yesterday?

"Are you nuts?" Annie exclaimed.

"I'm just going to flip through it while Gemma's napping," Eve said. "What's the harm in that?"

"Ever hear of obsessive-compulsive disorder?" Annie asked. "There's medication for these things. I could get someone to prescribe it but not if you're breastfeeding."

"Oh, here it is. 'In each of these texts, the protagonist struggles with—or attempts to ward off—madness caused by the oppression of a patriarchal society which forces women into sadomasochistic roles as wife/mother/nurturer, and, ultimately, hysteric.'"

"Talk about prophetic."

By mid-afternoon, the traffic jam in Eve's room had gotten so congested, people had to collect outside. At one point, a colleague of Maxie's—a young woman so thin even her lackluster hair appeared anorexic—stood by Eve's bed and recanted horror stories about her own birth experience in the hopeless drone of a dirge. When the woman's unblinking owlish gaze became too much for Eve, she said, "I think I need an intermission." In truth, the ache from her episiotomy was making Eve think of a show she'd seen on PBS about female genital castration.

Then, in marched Olivia, with whom a close sisterly relationship was as alien a thing as the Greek alphabet, as turtle soup. ("Jane Austen died in her sister's arms," Eve thought, "and I can't even squeak out a plea for sympathy in front of Livy.") She whisked past the congregation outside—with salad plates in plastic containers from the Korean deli on the corner—then positioned herself on the edge of the bed and began feasting on sushi. After briefly discussing Gemma (Olivia did coo appropriately as she bent down over the bassinet), Eve asked about her sister's newest venture. Employed as some executive's assistant at a small film production company, Olivia was just "marking the calendar" before going to law school. "I'd like to make more documentaries, but there's no money in that," she said, through a mouth filled with raw fish.

"Mom's been talking about how *she* should have been a lawyer since I was about seven years old," Eve said weakly, glancing in her sister's direction. She was wearing a forest green scarf around her neck, an oversized linen blazer to match—with a small pin on it that read: *Hillary Clinton for President*—and a short black skirt. Eve admired her sister's innate flair for style; she was a woman of choice words who knew how to accessorize.

"Oh please!" Olivia nodded, cracking her knuckles. "I'm *actually* going to do it. I've got to get some power and do something worthwhile. But first I need some time off. I'm trying to save money to travel in July."

"Where are you going?" Eve asked, anxiety starting to rise in her like temperature. As long as Olivia was working as a glorified secretary, at least she wasn't achieving much; after all, she was four years younger.

"I think I'm going to go for a three week tour of India, and then we'll see. I'd like to also go on this horseback riding trip through Spain, but I probably won't have the cash."

Eve nodded, imagining July with a baby: steam rising from the streets, melting the wheels of Gemma's English pram. Meanwhile, her sister would be galloping along the Spanish coast, head high—like a heroine on the cover of a trade paperback—waves from the Mediterranean Sea crescendoing in the background. "You know, you won't make any money doing anything worthwhile," she pointed out, sinking into the pillows of the hospital bed.

"I know. But, I'll get to help abused women and boss people around. I fucking hate to take orders from men screwing around on their wives and killing themselves to come up with story ideas on the level of *Beavis and Butthead.*"

"Well, good luck," Eve sighed, closing her eyes to signal a need for rest.

"Thanks, but I don't need luck. I need good LSAT scores." Olivia licked a piece of raw fish from the corner of her lips, catlike.

"If you want them, you'll get them."

"Well, thank you. It would be nice to hear such positive feedback from Mom and Dad for a change."

Before they were able to get into their "Mom and Dad Don't Take Olivia as Seriously as Eve" discussion, Norma and Manny paraded through the door. "My cue to leave," Olivia whispered. "Congratulations. She's beautiful," she said and dashed out of the room.

By this time, the nurse in charge had posted a sign outside the door: "No visitors unless cleared by R. N. on duty." With Hart sitting ever vigilant at her side, Eve had no choice but to let his parents in. But, moments later, Gemma began her soft hiccuping cry, a signal Eve already understood as her daughter's need to nurse. When she announced this, Manny grinned like a little boy who'd been found with both his hands tugging at his private parts. Daniel and Hart led him out of the room in search of coffee.

Norma had brought a huge sack of fruit in her red vinyl bag; now, she reached in and took out a banana, then began peeling it with her large fat fingers. Eve stared at the gold nail polish as she cut the banana in half.

"I read in *Prevention Magazine* that bananas help you get your strength back," she said and leaned closer to her daughter-in-law, stroking her cheek with her damp hand. Eve could see the wrinkled, brown skin of her cleavage above her tight leopard-pattern shirt. The shirt reached the thighs of her black leggings and was clutched at the waist by a black belt with a huge gold buckle in the shape of a lion's face. Hart often made fun of how his mother spent half her life lying in the sun; her skin looked shellacked and she joked how her "girl" from Brazil (meaning her fifty-year-old housekeeper) constantly remarked how she and Norma could be sisters. "They're filled with vitamins, potassium and . . . it's zinc, right?" she asked Maxie who had followed her in-laws into the room, acting as Eve's bodyguard.

"Not sure. But that sounds right, Norma. God, I could use some rest. After the morning I just had."

"Mieskeit" Maxie and Norma—finally agreeing on something—murmured near Eve's bed awhile later. Eve had dozed off but was now awake and facing the window, her eyes mere slits. It was early evening; in striking contrast to the ashen and liver-colored buildings, the sun was a ribbon of yellow and gold in the sky. The two grandmothers shook their heads and "tsked" in unison, like members of a Yiddish chorus.

"I'm awake," Eve warned them.

Maxie cupped her hand over her daughter's knee. "We went through quite an ordeal in that delivery room, didn't we? Thank God, I was there throwing my clout around, making sure you got that epidural. Oh, did I tell you how I called the ADM to get you a new nurse after they dared to assign you one of those horrible agency nurses?"

Eve shook her head.

Maxie was drawing the shades closed so that the sinking honey-blond sun wouldn't streak into the room. "I have to say: I'm quite proud of myself. Everyone looked at me like I was crazy. But I told the security guard to get the ADM on the phone and a minute later, I heard this voice over the loudspeaker, just like that: 'Mrs. Maxine Sterling, please pick up the telephone for the ADM.'"

Eve looked over at Norma; she'd gotten off the bed and was arranging a silver platter of nuts and fruit on the window ledge.

Maxie began to pace, gesturing: a pompous attorney embellishing a closing argument. "I got on the phone and the nurse—this new gal that I didn't know, *just our luck*—had a soothing, quiet voice like Aunt Kay has . . . you know, that reassuring Protestant tone: don't get too excited, now. I said, *forcefully*, my daughter had a terrible labor and needs rest. I said that it was obscene that a hospital with this reputation should be employing clearly *unqualified* nurses."

"You said that?" Eve asked, feeding her mother the right line: Abbott to Costello.

"Yes, I did," Maxie nodded, vigorously. "All these visitors looked at me like I was crazy and sort of skulked away. Even Dad, who's used to me, got embarrassed and quiet, 'like, you're being too brazen again, Maxie.' I didn't care. The nurse started asking me questions in her don't-get-excited voice and I cut her off. I said, 'Listen, listen,' I said." Maxie pointed her finger at Eve emphatically; she shifted her weight as she settled into the story. "'I know almost all the nurses in this hospital and they're wonderful. I have no idea why it should happen that my daughter, *of all people,* should get the one incompetent idiot that your department had the misfortune of hiring. But, I will give you five minutes to get Lydia Duffy into my daughter's room or I will begin a lawsuit against my own place of employment.'" She stopped pacing and shot her audience a grin. "Well, what do you think?" she asked, "It worked."

"Thanks mom," Eve said, halfheartedly.

"I've cut up some delicious kiwi. Try a piece," Norma said with arched pronunciation, as if she'd been studying with Henry Higgins. "Manny swears it helps him move his bowels."

Hart and Eve moved out of Brooklyn exactly one week after Gemma was born. Since the second trimester of Eve's pregnancy, Hart had spent hours by their bedroom window, glaring out at the indigo night, punctured by as many street lights as stars. He'd shuffle an egg from one hand to the other, waiting. All it took was the wail of an ambulance, a fire truck, or one police siren to make him practice pitching. Before any eggs left his hand, he warned, they needed a plan to leave the city. It was his paternal instinct; after their daughter was born, they'd be gone.

Eve's ankles were still swollen. She lay on the floor with her daughter wrapped in a blanket while Hart and the movers carried out their belongings. "This is crazy," she chanted over and over, glancing down at her old lady fat feet, snug in yellow rabbit slippers. In the mirror, the face reflected back at her was boneless, pale as an egg. "Where am I?" Eve whispered, sucking in her checks.

Their new destination was a two-family hundred-year-old colonial with tiny rooms and slanted ceilings, located in suburban New Jersey. Wandering Jews crept down from the front bay windows. Wisteria with white flowers clung to the house; yellow and pink tulips lined the walkway, their heads dipped as if in prayer. It was an experiment, Hart said; if his wife couldn't adjust to the Garden State, how was she going to pack up and relocate to Big Sky country (if her career so dictated)? When Eve voiced her anxiety over this plan,

Annie said, "I never thought you were the academic nun you claimed to be, willing to go anywhere for the sake of your mission."

Eve felt like a pioneer, covered wagon packed with supplies: Gemma, Amanda, and Mr. Knightley, crossing the frontier. For her, the border was the Lincoln Tunnel with its dull yellow walls, the undiluted stench of urine wafting through the car vent and the clopping noise of the car as it trotted over bumps in the road. Eve had lived in the city for twelve years. Now she was entering a new world, hormones out of whack.

Maybe, it was the hormones that caused her mind to reel with negative images; one constantly replayed over and over that first week of Gemma's life. Eve was seated on a stool in a dark damp room, nursing her in that sweaty, milky, weepy haze that had become the instant tedium of her new life. Voices, confident and clear as clarinet music, played on her phone machine, reporting scholarly coups: grants won, plum jobs found. Eve wondered if her buzzing hormones had tapped into some well of spiritual power gone awry; she cried all the way to this other, inferior state.

When they got to the house, the movers had already begun hauling their furniture up the stairs. Maxie, in beige burlap-looking pants and blazer, stood on the lawn supervising in loud, clear, and consoling tones. Olivia, wearing a tee shirt with Thurgood Marshall's face drawn on it and a black cotton mini, stood at the door and rolled her eyes in her mother's direction.

"What are you guys doing here?" Eve asked, too fatigued to deal with her anger at this invasion of the Sterlings.

"Mom figured you could use the help, considering that you chose to relocate while still bleeding from childbirth."

"Don't look at me," Eve said, glaring at her husband who was busy with the movers. "It was *his* idea."

For months, Hart been following the case of a child molester who'd already attacked four toddlers in their Park Slope neighborhood. Eve had struggled to persuade him to wait until Gemma was out of infancy; but, for the first time since she'd known him, her husband had stood firm. They'd made all the plans during her third trimester, before the acknowledgement of their mistake erupted like a bad case of hives.

"Let me see the little munchkin," Olivia insisted.

"Hi," Hart said, walking by with Gemma in her car seat. He was peeved—Eve knew—that the Sterling women felt entitled to show up uninvited. "Decided to join our little party?"

The three of them shuffled into the narrow hallway and up the stairs, carpeted in a mustard yellow shag, to the apartment. They walked to the back of the house, to the dining room. With their table and chairs in it, the room—with its sloping ceilings and century-old, warped wood floor—seemed to have shrunk to dollhouse proportions. Eve felt like the giant Alice, slouched over in the Rabbit's cottage.

"So, Eve, you going to ask me about my LSAT scores?" Olivia challenged when they had all finally sat down. Gemma—head lobbed to one side of her car seat—had been placed in the middle of the table like a wedding centerpiece.

"What did you put in this, Miss, rocks?" a gangly, unshaven mover asked, a box of Eve's books in his arms. "Where do they go, please?"

Hart rose in slow motion, nearly sleepwalking. "I'll show you. You stay here and rest, Eve."

"Good thing we showed up. You two look like you just finished a round of chemo," Olivia commented, running her fingers through her hair.

"Thanks so much," Eve said. "No cancer patient looks this fat and bloated. Gemma refuses to go to sleep before three a.m." She rested her head—which felt dense as a bowling ball—on her folded arms.

Olivia leaned over and gazed at Gemma's tiny round dark face; her eyelashes were black and straight, reaching her cheeks. "Can't you just keep her awake during the day?"

Eve sighed, "She's too little for that." She stared at her daughter, stunned by motherhood.

"So. . . . Don't you want to ask me my scores?" Olivia asked, an edge to her voice. When she got no response, she peered. "Do you have post-partum depression? Well, do you want some coffee?"

"If you can find it."

"Don't worry. Of course, I brought my own. So," she began again, rummaging through a cardboard box in the adjoining kitchen. "Here's the Mister Coffee. *So*. . . I did great."

"Is that the real reason you're here? To show off?" Eve began to gently rub Gemma's toes which reminded her of corn niblets. She'd already learned that her daughter wouldn't stir if Eve touched her while napping.

"Don't be a bitch. Couldn't you try for a little enthusiasm?" Olivia asked. She turned to the half-century-old stove which was now sputtering, like the little engine that could, to keep the flame from dying out.

"Hip hip hooray!" Eve flung her arms in the air with mock enthusiasm. But she knew if her head wasn't reeling, she'd have been grateful for any help they could get with the move.

"Well," Maxie said, out of breath, "these stairs *certainly* are rickety." She stood at the arch to the dining room. "This place must be 200 years old. I just can't understand it, when I was your age, all I wanted was to move back *into* the city. Your father insisted we live in Long Island; he wanted to own trees. Well, he has his trees, but I still miss the city. I know you will too."

"Any more criticism while I'm up?" Eve asked.

"Noooo," Maxie sighed. "Except, couldn't you have found an apartment with a bit more elegance? Or at least one that had been dusted after the last tenants moved out? This place is incredibly dirty. It'll take me *days* to clean." She heaved her body into a chair the way you would throw down a bundle of laundry.

"What exactly are you doing here, Ma?"

"Don't be ridiculous." She waved the question away. "Didn't you know I'd take time off from work to help you out? For God's sake, Eve, what possessed you to agree to move one week after having a baby, anyway? It's absolutely insane. Don't you think I was worried? Besides." Big sigh. "Someone has to be here to organize things."

"That's Hart's job, Ma. He put his projects on hold for two weeks."

Maxine clucked. "And, who's paying for that?"

Olivia asked briskly, "Coffee?"

"Thanks." Maxie reached for the mug she'd bought with the stick figure of a woman pulling out her hair and the words streaked in red: *"A Mother's Work is Never Done."*

"Why not open a clinic for chronic fatigue sufferers?" her sister mumbled.

Eve glared at her, ready for the explosion. All her life Olivia had been standing up to their mother in a way Eve never could. Once when she was only five years old, Olivia refused to put on her winter coat before leaving to pick up their Chicken Delight dinner. Lips pursed, eyes glaring, arms stiffly at her side, she was an expert at the silent tantrum. Maxie—fed up with her daughter's daily battles for control—left the house with Eve, the easy child. They drove around the same few blocks four times before returning home. Olivia was standing by the window in the same eerily still position in which they'd left her; she never broke down in tears of fright the way Eve would have. Even at that young age, she seemed to value independence more than she feared abandonment.

Maxie said, "Hey, I work hard. I'm allowed to be tired."

"Listen, I've been working full time *and* studying for the LSATs the last two months," Olivia snapped back. "But, I don't walk around like I'm the only one carrying the weight of the world on my shoulders."

"Excuse me. What kind of thing is that to say to me? Who do you think paid for that prep course?" Maxie slammed her hand on the table. "Even though I'm not convinced law school is the answer for you, that you're serious about it."

"Oh great. Here we go with the Olivia-can't-take anything seriously speech."

"I didn't say *that.*"

"I'll pay you back," her youngest daughter said, barely opening her mouth, "Just don't offer if you don't mean it."

"Now, wait a minute." Maxie rose slowly.

"Is this what you two planned? To show up and fight at my new, ugly house? Do you think you could stop this before you wake the baby up? Or take it outside. I'd like to spare Gemma from family trauma for her first month, at least."

"You're right. It's not fair to you guys. I'll go," Olivia said, addressing her sister. "Unless, there is something you need me to do?"

"No, stay," Eve said. "But, we won't get to unpacking until tomorrow." She glanced at their mother who was sitting again and sipping her coffee, eyes fastened on the scraped up butcherblock table. "We could order dinner. Although I have no idea from where."

"No thanks, I'm meeting Terry in the city." Her new lawyer boyfriend of two months. She kissed the tuft of black hair on the very top of the baby's head. Then, looking down, she grabbed her jean jacket off the back of her chair. "Take it easy, Eve. This place will be okay." She turned to leave without saying goodbye to her mother.

"See ya. Thanks. Sorry I was such a grouch," Eve said. "Congratulations on your scores."

"Goodbye, Olivia," Maxie said to her younger child's unyielding back.

At six a.m., Eve woke for the fourth time since midnight. Engorged, she frantically scoured through boxes of utensils in search of her breast pump, a blue plastic contraption which reminded her of the bongs that had floated from one slow motion hand to the next at college parties. "I can't stand it," she cried, feeling the panic lodged in her chest like an appalling case of indigestion. As it turned out, she had a body built for maternity, Eve, the once aspiring dancer, skinny from childhood.

"Jump in the shower," Hart suggested, in his new weary voice.

Too sore to nurse—the main activity of her blurred-together days and nights—she ripped off her tee shirt and ran to the bathroom. She watched milk stream from her breasts as the hot water hit them, then ran her fingers over the thick patches under her skin; they resembled the remaining sheets of ice in a thawing pond. "Let's try and imagine this scene in a Jane Austen novel," she instructed an imaginary class, punchy. "Fanny was way too fragile," she began. "She'd have died in childbirth. Elizabeth might have pulled it off with all her robust energy. But it's just so *hard* to picture Darcy without clothes on."

By ten o'clock, her daughter strapped in her Snugli, Eve set out for her first walk in the dreaded suburbs while Maxie and Hart began the arduous task of unpacking. The street was fragrant, pollen dripped from the trees like silver strings with baby pearls strung through them. Eve felt stuffed up, hazy but light. "I never had allergies in the city," she thought. She knew that the town was a few blocks south and that there was a park close to the railroad tracks, so she headed in that direction. Gemma cried softly as Eve tried to construct a viable scenario for her life, in this place. "I need to get down to work before I completely lose it," she thought. But how? She never slept; she hadn't had a coherent thought since her eighth month of pregnancy.

At Hugo's deli, Eve bought a giant lemon muffin and a lemonade as her second breakfast, having eaten two pancakes at 3:30 a.m. She was feeling enormous, still starving, bargaining with herself about starting a diet. "I'll just eat half of it," Eve pretended as she dug into the paper bag and scraped off the thick, crusty top of the muffin. By the time she got to the park, she'd finished the whole thing.

"Hey, little Bee," she whispered to her finally dozing daughter, "promise you won't see me as a bad role model if I'm forced to wear stretch pants for the rest of my life, and watch reruns of *Thirtysomething* on *Lifetime* all day." Seated on a peeling green bench next to a paved, circular path, she took out a book from Gemma's baby bag, *Jane Austen: The Comedy of Economics*. Two minutes later, she dove back into the pink and black sack and pulled out *Mirabella* magazine. "Oh, God," Eve exclaimed. "They're showing midriffs!"

"It's too rude to have 15-year-olds modeling fashion for what is supposed to be a 'woman's' magazine, don't you think?"

Eve looked up into the freckled, sunlit face—broad white smile, eyes hidden by blue tinted glasses, brown curls reaching to her elbows—of a women about her own age. She was leaning on a stroller in which a girl slept with her arms around a ratty Big Bird doll. "You must be new to these parts; I know all the mommies in this park. I'm Jo," she said, "and this is Abby."

Shielding her eyes from the vibrant April sun, Eve gazed up in the other woman's direction. "Eve and Gemma. Hi."

"Upper West Side, right? You have the same twang that all the former urbanites here have. Mind?" She motioned to the bench.

"Go ahead," Eve said as she shuffled herself over, awkwardly trying to cradle Gemma under the harness attached to her body without waking her. "Park Slope, actually. I thought everyone in this town was a displaced New Yorker. That's why we moved."

Jo popped a handful of fish crackers in her mouth. "Want some?"

"No, thanks. I just finished my second breakfast."

"Welcome to mommyhood. Are you sure? They're pizza flavored, my fave." At Eve's refusal, Jo stuffed them in the net pouch attached to her daughter's stroller. "Most are Manhattanites, but Park Slope and Hoboken are copacetic. Just don't say you're from the other Jersey burbs. I'm from Los Angeles" she said.

"Do you like it here?"

Jo took all of her hair in her hands, spun it around into a knot on the top of her head, and then let it unravel over her shoulders. "I hate it," she said, head tilted in Eve's direction, fingers in her hair, busy twisting it back up into a bun. "There is something so *fundamentally* depressing about the east coast, don't you think? Everybody running around, neurotically, like little rats in their cages."

"I don't know . . . I've never lived anywhere else."

"California is definitely the answer. All that gorgeous beach, healthy people, no one keeling over of *karoshi.*" She kicked her legs out in front of her. She was wearing cherry-red sandals, black leggings, and a red and white, wide striped, knee-length, polo shirt.

"I love your outfit."

"I don't have *outfits,*" Jo turned to face Eve as she removed her sunglasses, revealing soft brown eyes. "I have mommy *shlep* clothes. Is she your first?" She eyed Gemma.

"Yes," Eve said, and kissed the top of her daughter's sweet-smelling head, a mixture of shampoo and infant sweat from being stuffed in the sling like a baby kangaroo.

"So you're still making an attempt to be a grown-up woman with clothes and places to go. You'll figure it out," Jo promised, ominously. "Are you hightailing it back to work after the standard six-weeks of adjustment?"

"Yes. No. Well, actually, I'm in graduate school. I'm working on my dissertation." There it was again: panic entrenched in her esophagus like a plum pit.

"Good luck with cutie over here." She stared at Eve as if she needed a straightjacket. Then, twirling her sunglasses around, she said, "My big sis is a prof at UCLA."

"Wow. A dream job. What field?"

"Linguistics. The history of the English language." Jo gently ran her hand through her daughter's fine curls, then kissed her round cheek which was flushed with sleep. "Her husband, Tor, is Swedish and teaches 'Western Cultural Folklore,' or something equally obnoxious."

"That sounds wonderful to me."

"Yeah, well, Alice is the genius of the family. I just got the good looks and the rich husband." Jo patted Eve on the shoulder. "I get to hang out in the park all day with Abby

141

and carpool Sam and his friends home from science camp. Then, after making my famous cornflake chicken dinner, I ruminate on how to actually refurnish my three-floor colonial. It's a great life."

"You don't work?"

"No, I'm just a suburban JAP. In my former life, I co-owned a restaurant in L. A. The Rainforest. It was like the name sounds: cool, upscale, natural eating and all that—seaweed and alfalfa sprouts—but endangered. Running a restaurant is on par with raising kids, workwise. But, at least, I hung out with interesting people and partied." Jo gazed at her child and sighed, "Now, it doesn't even seem like it happened in my lifetime."

Ardently, Eve said, "I spent my entire twenties in the stacks of the Columbia library so that I'd end up with a job like your sister's."

"Well," again, she patted Eve's forearm. "We're in the same club now."

"Do you ever think of going back to work?"

"Only twenty-five hours a day. But I have two tootsies to think of who need mommy karma around the house while the sun is still shining. And besides, what would I do? I can't go back into the restaurant business, it's too crazy; it takes all your time. If I weren't such a great screw, my husband would probably have left me by now. All I do is whine about my existential boredom."

Eve laughed, nervously. "Thanks for cheering me up. Is everyone in this town as upbeat as you?"

"Are you kidding? Let me lay it out for you." Fiddling with her sunglasses, Jo launched into an obviously seasoned monologue. "Those in Joan and David shoes: corporate lawyers, editors, saleswomen, the ones whose kids are raised by the Jamaican nannies; there's the espadrille crowd: those 'I've got to be me' freelance artists and writers who volunteer endlessly at the elementary schools. Then we have the sneaker crowd: the stay-home mommies whose husbands are never home, who play tennis all day—when not volunteering at the elementary schools—and fuck the tennis instructor, when they aren't redecorating their houses; then they fuck the decorator. Then there are the earth shoe crowd: they are too busy breastfeeding their children until their bar mitzvahs to care about anything else except saving the whales."

Laughing, Eve said, "God, you should do stand-up."

"Nah. I just have a lot of time on my hands to assess my environment."

"Any thoughts on what you're going to do, workwise?"

"Some idea," Jo said. "But with kiddles, everything is in slow mo."

Her little girl shifted in her stroller, dropping her doll. "Mommy, pick Bird up," Abby demanded, eyes still closed. "I need a juice pack."

"Hi, precious," Jo leaned down and kissed her daughter on the nose.

"Yuck. Don't do that, mommy," the little girl whined.

"Okay, cranky. One juice pack coming up." Jo reached into her net pouch and came out with a box of pineapple-grape juice with a white plastic straw attached to it.

After a long sip, Abby looked up at Eve with wide brown eyes; she had her mother's freckles, but dirty-blond hair and darker skin.

"Hi. I'm Eve. And, this is my baby, Gemma."

"I'm not a baby," Abby scowled.

"No, I can see that," Eve smiled at her indignation: furrowed brow, lips pursed together in sheer stubbornness. "How old are you?"

"Six," Abby answered, then sucked greedily on her straw.

"She's two-and-a-half," Jo said. "Her brother's six. Right, pumpkin?"

"I'm not a pumpkin," she said, now trying to wiggle out of the stroller's seat belt. "I'm a girl."

"That's true," Jo said. "Well, I better be heading home before Miss Abigail has her post-nap shitfit."

"I guess I'll go home and help my husband and Mom unpack."

"God, you really *did* just move; you must be exhausted. That puppy of yours looks just hatched."

"She's a week old."

Jo squeezed Eve's leg hard and glared straight in her eyes. "Are you an *actual* crazy person? Tell me before we become better acquainted. I mean, I come across weird but that's just because I'm an actual riot. I have no energy for true crazies."

"No. Just a little overly ambitious." She shook her head, thinking again how her old life had mutinied, and she was alone without a map of this odd terrain. "The move was actually my husband's idea."

"Don't you two believe in recuperation?"

"I don't think we were entirely prepared; we sort of plunged right in."

"Listen," Jo said, "I have to go get my car before they ticket me. They love giving tickets in the suburbs; it gives the state employees something to do. It makes one nostalgic for real crime. You want a ride home?"

"No, thanks," Eve smiled. "I'll just keep walking until I lose about twenty pounds."

"Okay. I'll give you my number and you can call me. We'll get together and go to yard sales."

"Sounds great."

"You'll love it here. Suburban living is a hoot," Jo said, scribbling down her phone number on the back of a drugstore receipt. She didn't ask for Eve's telephone number in return. "Don't hang out in parks too often. You'll start to feel like you did when you were single, going to bars, hoping someone will talk to you, feeling like crap when none of the other mommies give you the time of day."

"Oh, I won't have time for that. I have a ton of work to do."

"Yeah? Well, *ciao,*" Jo said and waved as she pushed Abby towards a row of stalwart cars—hearse-size station wagons and hefty jeeps with gigantic tires—that lined the park like medieval soldiers surrounding the moat.

When Eve returned home, Hart was in the living room, hooking up her computer on the desk near the bay window.

"I tried to maximize the light," he said, huffing as he turned the desk slightly, looking for an outlet. "Your mother's in the back, on the phone with some cable television show. And has been for about an hour. How's my little girl?" He walked over, rubbing the sweat from his forehead, under the long curl of his black hair.

"Out cold, although she should be up screaming any minute. I met this really funny woman at the park, sort of the town's welcome wagon lady for cynics. Why has my mom been talking so long to the cable company? And, what do we need cable for right away anyway? Is that your grand plan, Hart? To get me out here in no-man's-land and hook me up to a hundred channels immediately?"

"No," Hart kissed Eve quickly on the mouth. "There is no conspiracy afoot to lobotomize you. And, she's not talking to the cable company, but some assistant producer. I didn't get the whole story but, your dad called and gave her the message. Remember that show she was on last year?"

"The Paula Whiteman Show?" she asked, gesturing for her husband to begin the arduous task of untying and unbuckling the baby sling.

"Whatever. Well, it seems that they got a new producer and she's had a lifetime of infertility problems or something. Anyway, she saw the show on tape and got obsessed with your mom."

"Oh, that," she said, sitting down on the couch. Gemma, now in Hart's arms, was starting to stir which meant she had to immediately begin unhooking her nursing bra. "So she's giving this woman counseling long-distance on our phone bill?"

"I don't think she wants counseling, Eve," Hart said. "I think she's interested in giving your mother her own show." Hart lifted the now crying Gemma into the air as his wife undressed. "Hi Little Bee. Don't worry, the mommy milk machine is coming," he cooed.

Eve sat there stunned and bare-breasted. "Her own show? That's ridiculous. What's she going to do for an hour, every week, make infertility jokes?"

"I don't know," Hart said and handed Gemma back to her. "From what I could hear, I think they want her to give advice, and run her group in front of an audience."

"Who would want to discuss their frustration and grief in front of millions of people? Don't answer that," she said, sliding Gemma into feeding position. "I know who. The same people who confess that their husbands are having sex with their dogs on *Jerry Springer.*"

"I doubt they'll be marketing themselves to the same audience as the *Springer* groupies. Why don't you ask your mom?" he motioned to the door with his head.

Maxie stood in the entranceway in black stretch pants and a huge, butter-yellow tee shirt, hands on hips, large and arrogant as a bouncer. "I'm going to be famous," she laughed and slapped her thigh. "What do you think of this as a title. . . ?" She spread the palms of her hands apart until she was transformed from bouncer into traffic cop halting cars on both sides of her. "*Mornings with Maxie!* My new T. V. series every Saturday at 8:00 a. m. Start out local, then see about syndication. So, what do you think? *Mornings with Maxie.* Can you believe it? Maxie! That's me!"

Letters

Brookfield, Connecticut
USA
December 9, 1996

Dear Eve Jael,

Sometimes old people have extra insights into things. I'm not referring to anything unnatural. It's just that because our own lives are winding down, we're more attuned to . . . . Oh, what am I talking about? I can just see you shaking your head, saying, "Grandma, you've lost your mind." But, I haven't, Sweetheart. All I meant was that Grandpa and I knew, the night we met Hart at Hannah and Bernie's, that you were going to marry him. Both of us had the same thought: "He's the one for our Eve."

Honey, I spoke with your mother last night and kept saying how confused and concerned I was about you. I finally wangled some semblance of the truth out of her, although she was still too damn vague. Well, I'm furious at her. How dare she even mention your name on that show of hers! If other people want to parade their private tragedies in front of millions, that's their business. But, I know that you would never want your dirty laundry hung out for the world to see, and I told her so in no uncertain terms. She was very contrite, but I refused to back down and got off the phone, still angry. On this issue, I'm on your side one-hundred-and-ten percent!

I'm so sorry this nonsense went on. I don't know what got into your mother! Please feel free to call me anytime, night or day. Don't think twice about the time change. It just would be so wonderful to hear your voice. I'm so proud of you, Eve. You've accomplished so much, already, in that damned-awful program of yours (I blame that horrible woman professor for *all the crap* that's happened to you, I really do). But, you're just too hard on yourself, you always have been. Now, I know that you've always been impressed by my achievements and considered me hard as steel (in a good way). Someday, I'll tell you a story about me. But, you have to come home to hear it. It's a bribe, if you couldn't tell!

All my love,
Grandma

On route to Guangzhou, China
December 11,1996

Dear Eve,

Your mother gave me your address in England, right
before we left. Things happened quite unexpectedly (I'm
writing this on an airplane taking us to the Chinese
consulate to pick up medical forms for our new daughter).
All of a sudden, we were told by the agency, China had
"opened up" again. This was our chance! We were also told
that it would probably only take two weeks, altogether, so
Arthur could stay the entire time. You can imagine how
happy that made me!

The trip was more exhausting than I'd anticipated. We
flew to Japan, stayed overnight, then took a morning flight
to Shanghai. Luckily, we were with a group of four couples
who were from New York, so we had some American
company with whom to share our happiness and our
concerns. We stayed in a bleak hotel with no heat. There has
been no time to explore, and, frankly, I didn't have the
energy. After a night of broken sleep, we ate a "western
breakfast" of runny eggs and weak coffee, and vowed to eat
only "Chinese food" until we reached Hong Kong on our
way home. We then met up with our facilitator, Zheng, and
took a train headed northwest to Nanjing, four hours away.

During the ride, I got my first migraine. I took the
Clomid for the last time this week (trying for two babies at
the same time, am I crazy?) and wonder if my body just
can't handle the combination of travel and upset hormones.
By Nanjing, my head was throbbing so badly, I was worried
that I wouldn't be able to keep going. Zheng took us to sign
papers and meet with provincial officials and a representative from the orphanage, and, I was so angry that I had such
an awful headache, I had trouble focusing on this incredible
event.

We met our daughter that same day; the director of the orphanage brought her to the hotel. He didn't suggest a "tour" of the orphanage, and, honestly, I was afraid to see it. I know, intellectually, that I'm going to have to deal with my daughter's past. But while waiting for her to arrive, my adrenaline was pumping so fast, I thought my heart was going to come out of my chest. And, the truth is, all that matters, for now, is that our baby is young—not yet three months old—healthy, and beautiful. I'm enclosing a picture of her: Sage Louise (Louise after Arthur's grandmother). Isn't she incredible? It's hard to describe exactly how I feel: enchanted, blessed, frightened. That next night, we stayed up for hours just watching Sage sleep, wondering what her life had been up until that moment. It feels unreal, that she is really ours. I don't know if she quite believes it either, she is so quiet and has yet to look us in the eyes.

Once, I dozed off and dreamed I was in your mother's hospital—having given birth—and when the nurse brought me the baby to breastfeed, I realized I had no milk, that there had been a mistake. And she took the baby away. Apparently, from what I've read, my "maternal anxiety" is very common. I woke up, crying, but didn't want to wake Arthur. The poor man is exhausted (he fell out almost as soon as the plane took off, with his baby daughter in his arms!) Sage was in a crib the hotel provided (I worry about this, also, certain that the safety standards aren't as stringent as in the United States) and when I first gazed down at her, I panicked. There is such a stillness about her, and, she never makes a sound when she sleeps. I had to open the shades to let the street lights in, then stare at her chest to make sure she was breathing.

We waited five hours in the freezing Nanjing airport before, finally, our flight was ready. The delays here can get you crazy, and, make you incredibly homesick. The entire time, Sage did not cry. I'm sure that, at some point, I'll have more to report about China itself, but for now, all I can do is stare at my daughter.

Eve, I hesitate to write this but, don't you miss Gemma? I am hoping that by the time I get home, you will be there too. Then, we can really talk. Please forgive *my own* self-involvement; it seems I am in love.

Yours,

Annie

" . . . for a very narrow income has a tendency to contract the mind, and sour the temper."   *—Emma*

"I LOOK LIKE the before picture on a Jenny Craig commercial," Maxie moaned on the telephone. But even a storyteller of Homer's talent couldn't create a tale of woe from hearing this woman's voice.

Hart and Eve sat in front of the television, blurry-eyed, having watched a fully alert, fussy Gemma for most of the July night, a night as rich and sweet as blackberries, starless and warm. Finally, their eyelids aching to shut, they had laid their daughter down in their bed between them, careful to position her away from pillows and the bulk of their bodies. Maxie's phone call woke them before eight. "Shit, is your Mom ever going to give us some breathing room?" Hart mumbled as he lifted the baby, carefully, as if she were a porcelain doll; he delivered her safely into her crib, still unconscious.

Having just finished taping her first show an hour earlier, Maxie sounded as happy and astonished as if her lucky numbers matched those tiny white balls that rolled in the lotto reading. Now, she was babbling, as the beginning credits ran: "All anyone at the hospital could talk about, yesterday, was what I should wear. Okay, I know black is thinning but, as Jane, the lactation specialist said, 'Black will send the wrong message, will scare viewers away.' Of course, she's right. I associate infertility with death; I don't want confused, first-time viewers to think I'm a funeral director. But, there *is* my own vanity at stake here; I have to choose 'slimming' colors. That's the word Adrienne, the producer, used, 'slimming.' Honestly, Eve, do you think that navy and red suit is 'slimming?' I look like Babar, the elephant!"

"Celeste," Eve interrupted the monologue, which might have continued throughout the half-hour program, otherwise. "Babar is a male elephant."

"Right. Oh Eve, listen to me. I sound like an idiot, don't I?"

At this moment, her mother's television double was announcing the theme of today's show to her "actual group" composed of six women and one man. In a kindergarten teacher's voice, the screen Maxine annunciated, "In-fer-til-ity as Met-a-phor."

"Hey," Eve said. "That title was my idea!"

"I know," her real mom answered. "Adrienne loved the title. I told her my genius daughter—the Ph. D. student in English—gave it to me."

"And? Do I get any compensation for my genius?"

"Yes," Maxie boasted. "You get to be the first born child of *a soon—to—be celebrity.*"

"Great."

"Oh, here's the part where Danielle is going to start cursing out her husband for not sticking up for her with her mother-in-law. What a story poor Danielle has. First baby: twins, stillborn. Second baby: second trimester miscarriage. She's had so many losses in her life, I *can't* take it. And that mother-in-law, I'm telling you, the warmth of Hitler."

"Ma," Eve demanded, "are you going to let us watch?"

"Oh my God, look at this. They didn't edit this out of the program. Oh, *God.*"

On the screen, Danielle let out a loud "Damn it," breaking the somber mood of the group. Maxie's television double leaned over and gently placed her hand on the other woman's arm. "Did this bring up particularly bad feelings for you, Danielle?" she asked.

"No, oh no," this skinny, sharp-featured, person trumpeted. "No. Oh, no." She jumped from her seat with a pole-vaulter's energy. "I just got my period."

In unison, the four remaining women on the television chanted, "Are you sure?" Their heads all nodded in her direction, one at a time, creating a domino effect. "C'mon," said one chubby woman with curly hair, "let's go check." The women all stood up at once. "Is there a bathroom on this set?" another one addressed Eve's mother.

Hart couldn't stop laughing.

"I can't believe this," she said. "Was this planned for comic relief?" she asked her mother.

"No. I swear to God. I was panicked. But, naturally, I gathered my resources and performed *brilliantly.* See, I'm explaining the limits of stress that you're pushed to when you've had so many problems conceiving or bringing a child to term."

Television Maxie was completing this sentence: "so many problems conceiving or bringing a child to term."

"Do they follow her to the bathroom and watch her pull her pants down?" Eve asked.

"No, Adrienne thought it best to take a commercial break here."

"Oh, this is sensitive," she said, laughing along with her husband. "A commercial for *Pampers!"*

When the show was finally over and she was able to hang up the phone, Hart pulled his wife closer to him on the couch. After a few minutes had passed, he whispered, "So, how do you feel?"

"Embarrassed. Weird. Proud of her. Jealous."

Annie and Arthur lived in one of those enormous pre-World War II apartments, on Riverside Drive, that had been in Arthur's family for over 30 years. At Annie's wedding, in an elegant but staid New York hotel, Arthur's father presented the newlyweds with a formidable gift: their home for good. He and his wife were retiring to Sarasota, Florida right after his son's honeymoon. Arthur came from a wealthy Jewish family with the quiet manners of Mayflower descendents. His father had owned his own accounting firm which he left in Arthur's capable hands, but much of his mother's family lived in England and France, working as such things as barristers and wine merchants. Excellent furniture and china, from Copenhagen and Paris, adorned the Schwartz's house; all of it, they'd left for Annie and Arthur. Eve knew that Annie adored, was intimidated by, and felt beholden to the Schwartzs.

Arthur had a long, lanky, 6'4" body in which he moved through life in a stiff and uncomfortable way. His only attractive feature was his almond-shaped blue eyes, but they were usually hidden by his glasses: small, round, tortoise-shell frames perched low on the bridge of his nose. When he opened the door, that Sunday afternoon, he looked more exhausted than Eve had ever seen him. "Hi, kids," he whispered. "Annie's just getting ready. Come in, come in."

He hurried them in and they sat on matching wing chairs with light blue tapestry which the senior Schwartzs had brought home from one of their European shopping jaunts. Hart unhooked the Snugli and, gingerly, laid the sleeping Gemma on the oriental rug at his feet.

"Drinks anyone? I know Annie prepared lunch. She'll be right out." He fiddled with his watch with exaggerated concentration, uneasy, as always, around *"the artistes"* (his label for Eve and Hart). For the next few minutes, they sat still as stones. When Annie entered the room, they reshuffled themselves in their seats.

Eve had never seen Annie so unpresentable when "company" was over; she was wearing a wrinkled sleeveless denim dress and her hair, which she had piled on top of her head, had started to unravel down her neck. Her face was blanched and the circles under her eyes had a bluish tinge to them. Annie had reported the facts to Eve: how she had been trying, without success, to get pregnant for the last year; how after the first twelve tortuous cycles of waiting, she was now pumping her body full of hormones and watching her face swell into a mess of pale doughy skin splattered with tiny red dots; how her energy ping-ponged from manic to lethargic; how she was seriously weighing other options, such as taking a month off from work in order to spend it in China, where a baby daughter could be hers. Eve had considered questioning her friend: wasn't the decision premature? Wasn't she overreacting? But, there was no tactful way of approaching the subject, not when the fact of Gemma—magically conceived, it seemed, and unplanned—was already a bruise on their friendship.

When Annie ran to kiss her, Eve realized how truly isolated she'd been feeling. She hadn't seen her best friend since Gemma's birth, two months before; she and Dee hadn't spoken seen the incident in Barnes and Noble. How intensely Eve yearned for her life in the city; here, she would be surrounded by movement and light—like Saturn by its magical rings—protected from boredom, inertia, lack of purpose.

"It's so great to see you," Annie said, flinging one arm around her friend's waist. "I'm really sorry I haven't come out to visit for so long."

"It's okay. I haven't come in," Eve said, reciprocating the gesture so that they were linked, like two high school girls sharing a secret.

"Yeah," Annie shrugged. "But you have a baby."

"And you have a job and a doctorate."

"She's due to defend at the end of the summer," Arthur preened. "Her advisor said it's amazing how quickly she's raced through it, considering her job is so demanding."

Annie unhooked her arm and walked over to the window. "I want it over with as soon as possible so that I can arrange for things in China." She faced the street, and stared down with the concentration of an anthropologist studying the scurrying people for new clues about mankind.

"I think that's great, Annie, I really do," Eve said, beseechingly. But, she was thinking: why rush things? Give yourself time to enjoy earning your doctorate. Be with your husband. You can still get pregnant.

"Oh God," Annie cried out, "I'm such a pig. I haven't even taken a good look at Gemma! I'm so self-involved! Have you ever known me to be so self-involved? Let's chalk it up to my crazy reaction to the hormones."

"It's okay. She's out. She's a great napper," Eve said. "It's nighttime we need to work on." She bent down to nuzzle her daughter. Gemma lay with her arms flung above her head, her face crunched up into a pout, her skin, a rich smooth amber from the sun.

For a moment, Annie just stared, then she turned to her husband and reprimanded him in a feverish voice. "Arthur, why is she on the floor when we have a crib, for God's sake?"

"I didn't know if you'd want me to . . . you know."

"I'm sorry, folks," Annie swung around towards her company. "We haven't been very gracious. Come, Eve. You can put Gemma in here."

The room was three times the size of Gemma's and flooded with southern light. The crib and matching rocking chair were a lovely, varnished pine with tiny pink and lavender flowers painted on them. Annie had hired a painter to transform the walls into a light shade of lavender with a hint of gray in it, and on the floor, she had put down a shag white rug. Eve thought of Gemma's stark room with its utilitarian crib and unpolished wood floors and felt a pang of envy. Arthur had always struck Eve as a kind-hearted bore whose money had simply made him more palatable. Now, she appreciated how sensuous, how seductive, his money could be: it bought better wood, prettier colors, and a more prized piece of the sun. But, it hadn't yet produced a baby, Eve reminded herself.

Hart set Gemma gently in the crib; she howled once, pounded her small fat fist into the mattress, then rolled over and relaxed back into sleep.

After a few moments, the four adults tiptoed out of the room. Annie closed the door and exclaimed, "Oh, she's precious. I'm so happy for you two. Let's go into the kitchen, Eve. I bought all kinds of delicious things for brunch."

They sat on chairs whose backs were adorned with a braided wood design in the shape of a flower; they ate bread and lox, three kinds of cheeses and huge juicy strawberries, drank a rich blend of coffee and smelled the fragrance of pink and yellow roses placed in a glass vase as centerpiece. Annie talked about Beijing, about how exotic Asia was supposed to be (the sights and smells, the language barrier), about how she'd heard the streets were always crowded and that people spit everywhere. She'd been warned, by the adoption agency, about delays with paperwork, and about how the orphanages were desolate and cruel places, like Victorian asylums. She was frightened at the prospect of having to stay in China by herself, once Arthur returned home; it seemed inevitable that she'd be forced to wait for the paperwork to be completed. "I'd kill Hart if he did that to me," Eve thought. But, Annie could put it into perspective: her husband's work pressures took precedence over her own terror at being abandoned—on the other side of the world—with an infant so small her heart still raced as quickly as a sparrow's.

After rattling on, Annie said. "You know, I spoke with your mother yesterday."

"She told me. It was nice of you to watch her show," Eve said, tentatively.

"I was surprised. The show was . . . I don't know, intelligent, warm. Your mom *is* warm, you know. I mean she's always been. But, she was accessible, unlike all those cold creepy doctors Arthur and I saw."

"She's a good person," Eve said. She ran a small knife down a hunk of Gouda cheese and sliced hard. "I'll tell her you said so." The weird sensation Eve had been experiencing, intermittently since her wedding, was back: she was fading in stages. In her novels, Jane Austen's heroines were promised a happier inclusion into society through marriage. But, in reality, the author knew how suffocating motherhood could be, how as a "spinster" she could remain the keen-eyed spectator, blissfully alone with her work. The irony of life astounded Eve: right after the birth of Gemma—a glorious event which hampered her ability to work in unexpected and immeasurable ways—Maxine had accelerated her career into a whole new dimension of success.

"Did you speak to your mom about me?" Annie asked.

"Well . . ." Eve paused, as if it were imperative that she sip her coffee. "She just told me that you called and that she really likes you."

"Oh, that. She's known me forever," Annie said, standing up and beginning to collect her guests' plates. "I got a great German cheesecake for dessert. I'll be right out."

Once she'd left the room, Arthur leaned over in Eve's direction and said in a loud stage whisper, "I don't mean to spill the beans but, what's the big deal? You girls tell each other everything, anyway." Then, in a normal voice, he said, "Personally, I'm not thrilled about this, but my wife says it might do her some good to be a guest on your mom's show. She insists it's nothing like those talk shows with illiterate guests revealing their trivial, vulgar lives just for notoriety's sake."

Annie shouted from the kitchen, "Arthur! I wanted to tell her myself."

Eve felt lifeless, like Daphne transformed into wood.

"Listen," Annie explained, reentering the room with the perfect-looking cheesecake on a Lenox platter. With Arthur's help, she slid the plate down onto the table. "I feel sort of funny about this."

"Are you sure you want to do it?" Eve found her tongue to ask.

"See, she agrees with me, honey," Arthur pronounced, suddenly animated, gesturing with his long, fleshy hands. "I keep telling my wife to relax and calm down, to stop focusing on getting pregnant. If she just relaxes, it'll happen."

"Arthur!" Annie exclaimed, glaring at her husband.

"No, that's not what I meant," Eve said. "I'm only questioning the idea of going on television. It just doesn't sound like you, Annie. You're such a private person."

"That's normally true. But, your mom reminded me that I have nothing to be ashamed of. I'm just worried that I'm imposing on the relationship between you and her."

"Don't be ridiculous," Eve said, pouring herself more coffee, then staring at the cake with great concentration.

"I know how things are between you two, all the competition issues. It's tricky. You get along so well but, she *always* upstages you. To be fair, Maxie upstages *everyone.*"

"That's certainly true!" Hart said and reached, under the table, for his wife's hand.

"Look, I guess I'm doing this because I thought it might be . . . cathartic for me. But, it's important to me that you feel okay about it. Women are very territorial about their mothers."

"For God's sake, Annie, you make it sound as bad as if you wanted to have sex with my husband."

"Oh, no," Annie laughed and Hart joined in. "I'm not even allowed to have sex with mine, except on designated nights." And they segued into an animated discussion of the direct correlation between lowered libidos and babydom.

For Eve—as always—it was a relief to drop the subject of Maxine's omnipresence in her life, a subject as complex and intricate as the workings of one's own mind.

The summer began to drag like a bored, exhausted toddler traipsing through the park, watching her feet. The heat and the pollen seeped together, as if in a thick muddy stew, so that on some days just leaving the house was intolerable. Eve would watch Hart get dressed in the morning and think, "Soon, I won't talk to another adult, except for my mother, for ten hours." As a girl, she used to sing, soulfully—"Over the Rainbow"—along with Dorothy, as if she, too, wanted to go to that magical elusive place. But sometimes she would wonder how, logistically, one arrived at such an odd destination and, if once there, she would be lonely. Now, Eve felt that, like Dorothy, she had woken up in a strange land in which the customs were nothing like those at home.

Finally, midway through July, she broke down and called Jo—the only soul she knew in the town—and invited her for lunch. "Sure, toots," the other woman said. "I remember you. Hard to go from *The Life of the Mind* to diapers and nips isn't it? I'll be happy to come to lunch. Sounds like you could use some cheering up."

Both of Jo's children were in school until 12:30 and Gemma was taking her early nap. They had been given this gift of time, right smack in the middle of the morning, like one tiny precious jewel encased in a heavy brass setting.

"It's remarkable," Eve declared, handing Jo her mug of Mocha Java, "how claustrophobic it feels."

"That's motherhood for you," Jo said, crossing her long legs and encircling the mug with her slender white fingers. She was dressed in a sleeveless black tee, black leggings, and white tennis sneakers. She wore no makeup and her hair was a mass of uncombed curls, loosely held from her forehead by a tortoise-shell headband.

"It isn't really about Gemma herself. She's such a wonderful, easy baby except for the not sleeping part. It's everything in my life. It's all slowed down and I have so little control over it." Eve stopped herself; she didn't know Jo and refused—on principle—to indulge in an inappropriate confession. "Parenthood puts joy in one's heartsand shackles on one's feet," she laughed.

"Look, toots," Jo said, spreading raspberry jam on her walnut orange scone. "You're nursing, correct? Okay. That means, in effect, that you're still in that hormonal weepy stage. Nursing is just an extension of pregnancy. You're not going to feel like a whole separate person until you stop. I nursed Abby for six months and, then, *had* to stop. I used to have prison dreams, every night. Anyway, what about that *engaging* thesis you're writing? Do you have time for that? A major advantage of working at home is you don't have to wear a shirt."

Eve smiled, flattered that Jo remembered. "I'm almost finished. Soon, it will be in my advisor's hands and I'll really be in limbo."

"Well, you could always meet the locals and make some extra pennies ringing up purchases on a cash register. I'm just kidding; don't get insulted! Anyway, I didn't mean at ShopRite. Didn't I tell you? I'm buying a boutique."

"Really? Congratulations."

"Well, I can't just pack lunch boxes and backpacks for the rest of my life. Beside, Richard—my long-suffering husband—is beginning to think I'm a real bitch. All I do is complain all day; I'm hell to live with. I thought of seeking employment but self-employment seems much groovier. Here's the thing: I couldn't decide between books and teddies, which is a better bet, you know? I mean this bookstore craze is really in and this town thrives on writers. But I like the idea of lingerie. Maybe as a reminder of my youth, when I actually still flipped through a Victoria's Secret catalogue, on occasion. So, the store's gonna be both. A combination woman's bookstore and lingerie shop with a sexy name. I've been playing around with Armour and Lace."

"I can just see the window layout," Eve said. "You could have mannequins in lacy purple bras and underwear holding copies of *The Second Sex* in their hands."

Jo ran her finger around the rim of the coffee mug, "No joke: I like that idea. And, I think the store might work. God knows, it cost a little fortune just to open a place down on Laurel Court."

"Wow! I'm impressed." Laurel Court was a long, cobblestone street filled with overpriced stores: antique furniture, hand designed jewelry, gourmet coffee, South American pottery, along with two upscale restaurants which served such Yuppie delights as mochaccinos and potato kale soup.

"I actually thought about you the other day . . . ."

"Gee thanks," Eve laughed.

"In *context* with the store. I thought you, of all people, would know everything about women's books."

"I do. If you look me up in *Who's Who*, it says: 'Eve Sterling international authority on *all* women's literature."

"Well, if you need a job, let me know. Maybe we could work something out."

"I will," Eve said, almost meaning it, almost intrigued.

"Welcome couples everywhere," a television Maxie mouthed while a monotone voice translated the words into dubbed Spanish.

Hart laughed, "When do the Japanese dinosaurs come on?"

Eve and Hart were sitting in the living room, in their sweatpants and tee shirts, balancing plates of quickly congealing eggs and buttered bagels with cups of lukewarm coffee on their laps. Gemma was finally lying in her playpen, after having interrupted the breakfast meal with squeals of hunger of her own. Now, she was gurgling with contentment, the sounds that followed a good half-hour of nursing. Eve was trying hard to ignore the burning sensation coming from her dried, itchy nipples. But, in fact, she'd never concentrated so much on her breasts before and yet, paradoxically, had so little interest in sex. Even in adolescence, Eve's only reaction to her changing body was thankfulness that she never developed past an "A" size cup. At the time, it boded well for her aspirations to be a dancer. Now, being a milk machine did not make her feel more in touch with her true femininity and ultimate purpose in the cosmos—like the books and articles promised—just brainless and teary-teated: a pathetic beast.

"God," Eve exclaimed and pressed a button on the remote, "What possible audience do they expect to get for this version?" *Mornings with Maxie* was now offered, simultaneously, on two cable channels. On channel 35—the woman's network—Maxie was annunciating in her deliberate stage voice, as if needing to reach the back of the house. "Soooo, the infertility, for you, was in-ten-sif-ied by the sense that you had failed in some way?"

The person to whom she was addressing her comment was none other than Eve's best friend of twenty-odd years: Sarah Anne Kushner Schwartz. Annie was dolled up in a silk burgundy suit with black shell buttons. Someone had applied lipstick in the same color as her outfit as well as a smoky eye shadow, thus transforming Annie into an exotic version of herself. She looked like a casting director or the head of a woman's magazine, not the cotton and denim, shrink and social advocate who Eve knew and loved.

In a tight voice, Annie said, "Intellectually, I've always understood that infertility should not be equated with failure. I know that women are often misguided into feeling guilty; they are told by family members, friends, sometimes even doctors, that they can take control of their reproduction, if they just 'relax.' But, that's just not true. I know all this and yet, emotionally, I still wrestle with the sense that I've let down my husband, and even my parents."

"I know just how you feel," a strident voice piped in. The camera panned the room, settling on the face of Danielle, the woman who—on the first show—had declared that she'd begun to menstruate in front of an audience. "You just want to avoid your family like the plague. All those nephews and nieces at every family event and your sister-in-law always there with some helpful advice, like 'Have you tried standing on your head after, you know, doing it? It worked for a friend of mine.' Of course, your sister-in-law didn't have to resort to any tricks since she's a fertility goddess who gets pregnant just by looking at her husband."

"Right," chimed in a tall, frizzy-haired woman in a plaid pants suit. "And, why is it that everyone—friends, relatives—suddenly feel compelled, I mean *compelled*, to discuss their copulation habits with you. 'Lily was conceived in two months; Matthew took a bit longer, four months.' God, it's like this competitive thing with women: who takes the least amount of cycles before giving birth."

Maxie touched Annie's forearm in an encouraging pat, a gesture Eve had already discerned from previous *Mornings* was aimed at getting a hesitant guest to participate. Annie was a talk show junkie, but Eve could see that she was becoming disoriented; from a distance, these shows were entertainment to Annie, as far away from real life as Shakespeare in the Park. Now, suddenly, she had been cast in a live production and was supposed to use her most intimate problems as script.

"For me, competition has been less of an issue," her friend said. "I guess I've just felt terribly sad that a baby hasn't come naturally, easily. Like a lot of woman, I assumed that I'd just stop using protection and . . . voila!" She laughed, self-consciously.

"Do you want to talk about what saddened you, what troubled you, the most?" Maxie coached, psychiatrically.

Annie looked up into the camera with a pained but unwavering gaze. "Not being able to have my husband's baby . . . and disappointing all that family, his and mine." Her eyes welled with tears and Eve squirmed in her seat. "This is terrible!" she said.

"It *is* weird," Hart agreed, "to be sitting in on someone's therapy session. It's freaky when it's someone you know, like walking in on Annie and Arthur having sex." He bit into a bagel and chewed on the thought. "Ugh, can you imagine Arthur in coitus interruptus?"

"Seriously. I can't believe my mother's doing this. It's so disturbingly intrusive. I can't understand it; my mom used to be so big on privacy." She was ripe for a conversation in which she'd peel away at her mother's personality the way a dentist scrapes plaque off your teeth. "Olivia's right. Success has completely corrupted her," she said.

"Well, it's not as if she had to bribe Annie to go on the show," Hart replied as he lifted up Gemma who—after dozing for all of fifteen minutes—had begun to fuss. "It was Annie's decision. She wanted to go."

"Still, she's my friend, you know. I feel protective of her."

"Don't feel so protective. She'll probably come out of this with thousands of adoring fans and a book contract for half a million dollars," her husband grumbled. "As if Arthur and his family don't have enough money."

Eve felt a tightening in her chest, her heart clenching. All summer, Hart had been arriving home from work with a distracted look on his face, as if he'd heard warnings of an impending civil unrest on the radio, but didn't want to disturb "mother and child." Somewhere behind the blurred, milky screen that had been erected between Eve and her life, she knew: her husband's work wasn't going well; money was scarce; he was suddenly worried about lack of security. "Maybe you could write a book about your famous mother-in-law," she said. *"The Inside Dirt on Maxie."*

"Maybe. And, I could point to her daughter and son-in-law, a couple with no fertility problems whatsoever, who simply can't support their baby daughter without her help and constant interference."

In that one moment, Hart's eyes were glossed over with defeat, but the expression on his face was so acerbic, Eve had the urge to slap him. Then, instantly, this other mean face was gone, as thoroughly as you erase an Etch-O-Sketch drawing. "Sorry. Sorry to interrupt your mom's show."

"Forget that. Talk to me Hart."

"What's to say?"

"You tell me. You certainly don't talk to me about what you're thinking or feeling these days. Not since the baby was born, in fact."

It was as if a new weather front had swept in from the North, the air was just brewing with bad feeling. Gemma, sensitive to the sudden chill, began to whine. Eve picked her up and unhooked her bra, resentful that she had to quarrel with her husband in this half-naked, vulnerable state. It was hard to be an effective debater and someone's foodstuff at the same time. In the background, her television mom was saying, "And is considering adoption putting any of these negative emotions to rest?"

Hart, standing now, with his plate full of crumbs, looked down at the stained carpet, not of their choosing. "I don't tell you things because I don't want to worry you," he said. "You have enough to deal with trying to finish your dissertation for Maud and taking care of Gemma."

"And what are these things you haven't been telling me?"

"Eve, she can't possibly be hungry, again. Look, as I've been saying since Gemma's birth, I didn't want to have to go over the bills with you all the time because I want you to focus as best as you can. We're not getting any rest. Maybe, if I'd been thinking clearly, I'd have told you. Listen, I'm going to take Gemma out for a walk in the park. We'll talk later."

She would have insisted that he needed to stay and explain himself, rather than let uncertainty fester in her, but the phone rang. Hart picked it up and—without even saying hello—he handed it to his wife. "It's for you, of course. It always is. Say hi to Maxie for me."

Eve hung up without saying a word to her omniscient mother, then scampered down the stairs after them. They were already outside; Hart was strapping Gemma into her stroller. "Hey," she said, opening the screen door and stepping onto the slate walkway in her bare feet. "Don't you even say goodbye?"

"I didn't want to keep you from talking to your *real* family," Hart said into their daughter's lap, as he buckled the belt around her soft, round middle.

"You're my family. Wait. I'll come along. We can talk." Eve looked down at a patch of clover near her feet and thought, "If I find a four-leaf one right now, everything will be okay."

"Discussing our finances is not my idea of a pleasant morning. Go talk to your mother. Call your sister. Then, call Annie. Run up the phone bill! Indulge!"

Debilitated, Eve headed to bed for a much needed nap. She hoped her dreams would provide insight into her increasing feeling of disassociation from her life. But if the answer to her quest appeared like an augury—a great black crow flying purposely through her unconscious—there was no sign of it upon awakening. Instead, she woke with a thumping headache to the sound of Gemma whimpering. Hart was kissing the top of her head, over and over, crooning: "Mommy's coming; Mommy's coming." He looked at his wife dispassionately, as if, in fact, she really was just the milk dispenser, and handed Eve her daughter.

As soon as Gemma latched onto Eve's breast and began to nurse—without shame over her greedy, gnawing sucks—Hart sank into a chair and said, simply, "Our financial life is in ruin."

"Ruin?" she asked. "Aren't you being melodramatic?"

"Not if you feel strongly about paying the bills."

"God, I knew we were having problems. I mean, the constant calls about late bills makes me crazy. But, I figured we were paying our rent and putting food on the table, right?"

"There's something else: I asked Viv for a loan—I didn't want to tell you about that either—but, of course, she refused, so it doesn't matter." He clasped his hands together and squeezed so that his knuckles, on one hand, turned white. "I don't know what I was thinking asking someone from *my* family."

"You asked your sister for a loan without talking to me first?" she exclaimed. "Of course it matters! I'm your wife; she's your sister. You're supposed to talk to me about such things."

"What's the difference? You ask your mom for lots of things without discussing them with me first."

Gemma, who was feeling the tension, had turned from her mother's breast and was droning in complaint. Tomorrow, Eve promised herself, she would start the baby on bottles.

"What's happened to the wedding money we put in the money market?"

"Gone. Used up. I've been using it while trying to save my dying career."

A shiver ran through Eve, quick and startling as glass cutting skin. If marriage was the slow unpeeling of an exotic fruit, what happened when—under one layer—you discovered mold festering instead of fresh, glistening pulp? "You used up ten thousand dollars? It's all gone?"

"It's not as much to go through as you think. And, then, I wanted to spare you from my problems with work," he said. "My parents are completely untouchable, but I was so desperate, I almost called them. Instead, I called Viv, hoping that I might be able to stave off disaster until I drummed up enough work to keep myself self-employed. But, no such luck. As it turns out, that's no longer an option."

Hart was capable of presenting both an empty bank account and the end of his aspirations with the resolve of the Grim Reaper. But, Eve felt flooded with confusion and anxiety. "What are you saying? That you're not going to work as a photographer anymore? How could you make such a momentous decision without discussing it with me first?"

Gemma began to howl.

Her husband—this man with a secret life—shrugged. "What's to discuss? I have no choice. I've been looking for a full-time job, at ad agencies, with benefits. Eve, let me take her." He lifted their daughter out of his wife's folded arms, exposing her poor, sad breast, drizzling milk.

"Nothing to discuss? You're right. It's just our life," she screamed in accusation, quickly draping her tee shirt over her body. As if Hart emitted magical rays from his finger-tips, his touch quieted the wellspring of their daughter's unhappiness. Gemma's face changed from crimson to her own olive skin tone within seconds. Safe from her madwoman of a mother, she could begin the murmuring chant that lulled her back to sleep. "I can't believe this. How could you go through all our money without telling me?"

"I don't know what I thought, " Hart said, desolation in his voice. As he left the room to put Gemma in her crib, he said, "You should have married Graham. We both should have."

The notion that romance needed to co-exist with economics had always been as foreign to Eve as swallowing swords. Economics was a concept, a theory, the name of a college course. She had tried to live her life like a chess game—calculated, civilized, a brilliant strategic plan—but, somewhere along the line, had failed to follow the Goodman women's rules.

Although she would fervently deny it, Maxie viewed the world with the same snobbish sensibilities as did her own mother, Henrietta: she respected firemen, policeman and the man who put up your wallpaper, because they all served some understandable and necessary function, like the characters on *Mr. Roger's Neighborhood*. Jobs Maxie didn't accept as true careers were "Sales Rep," "Account Executive," "Financial Analyst;" she had been known to say, "Works in business? But what does that *mean?*" Her children, she had convinced herself, would always have money, effortlessly, as if earning a fine living occurred in nature to those who were morally good. During their childhoods, lessons in practicality were as scarce to Eve and Olivia as fresh fruit is to the London market in winter. Instead, money was assigned a symbolic value as is everything in fairy tales.

Now, Eve felt desperate for a new plan to replace the old: magically, thoroughly, and with a moderate dose of pain. Her first instinct, as always, was to call her mother. But, the thought of having to withstand Maxine's reproach was finally more than she could take. "Maybe Hart is right," she thought, "I can't keep turning to my mother."

That afternoon, she called Jo.

"So, what's the *tsuris* today?"

Eve thought, this is how she perceives me: woman with a complaint, like a figure painted in oil, forever labeled by her epithet: woman with a parasol, a comb, a rose. *A complaint.* She needed to redefine their relationship in different terms. "No *tsuris*. Just wondering if you were serious about your offer the other day?"

"About working in the store? Absolutely. Are you really interested? Because, you know, it might take awhile to get the show on the road. My target date is mid-autumn. But, I've never opened a store before so my estimates aren't worth much. But, you know, I could use your help with inventory, books not bras. I'm sure we could come up with a workable salary. Whatdoyasay?"

"Great," Eve responded, trying to thrust a note of cheer into her voice. "Could I bring Gemma with me?"

"Where else would she be? *The Executive Mum's Babysitting Service? Please.*"

"In that case, any amount of money you offer me is more than I'm making now."

"Things that good, huh? Listen, I don't know you well, it's true. But, I can sniff out post-partum a mile away. After both my children, I had a year of pure torture. I started seeing this shrink around that time who told me to write down all my dreams in order to discover why I was angry. But I couldn't figure out what I was paying her for. Give me $80 an hour and I could come up with that little journal writing assignment myself."

"How did you get your momentum back?"

"Momentum?" She laughed. "You *never* get it back. Not in the same way. You wait. They grow up a bit; you gain little increments of your independence back. But, basically, it's a life sentence."

"But now you're getting back into the swing of things, opening up your own business."

"Sure. Hopefully. But, it's all this enormously exhausting juggling: of time, energy, schedules, emotion. It's probably more of a blow to you because you're so directed, which, frankly—as my well-dressed therapist pointed out—I'm not. Okay, listen. I will definitely call you when the time gets closer. In the meantime, hook your bra up and get out of the house, sweetie. You sound as if you've been locked in San Quentin for a good, long time."

"I'll just be happy when this summer is over with, that's all," Eve said. "Then, I'll hear from my advisor and Gemma will sleep more at night. And I'll feel like the old me again."

"Oh, summer will be over sooner than you think," Jo exclaimed. "And then the freezing, sleeting, East Coast winter will set in so that all the nice mommies end up housebound and alone, quietly going crazy. But, for now, perk up and let's meet for lunch next week. Okay, I have to run. Abby wants me to play Princess Leia."

"Oh, I have to go, too."

But, in fact, there was nowhere in the world Eve had to be. The urgency that a young, childless, working woman feels had left her body. The metabolism of her existence had changed so entirely that she felt ghoulish, as if she were haunting her life rather than living it. Autumn would be better, she kept telling herself, when Maud was back. But a new voice—Jo as prophet—now chanted in response: Worse will follow. Freezing, sleeting winter. The winter of your discontent.

Letters

London, England
December 20, 1996

Dear Professor Wellington,

As Christmas break is fast approaching, I thought we might arrange a meeting. The secretary at the English department informed me of your office hours; unfortunately, I was unable to catch you either Tuesday or Thursday.

I'm sending this letter, overnight express, and would very much appreciate it if you could call me collect as soon as it arrives so that we can set up a time to get together when you get to England.

Thank you very much.

Sincerely,

Eve Sterling

Sometime in the Gray of Winter
London

Dear Hart,

This is not my city. I miss everything, even New York's grid, the ease with which I could get where I wanted to go. All day, I wandered, in and out of stores—not bookstores, too painful—but can't recall a thing I saw. I want to tell you all that's happened to me, but am afraid it's too late, that you'll never forgive me.

How did we manage to create so much chaos in the first year of marriage, Hart? Isn't it ironic that a person like me—someone who thought she craved a graceful life above everything—has been living this mess? When I left, I was falling faster than Alice down the rabbit's hole. It felt as if there were only Gemma left. And—I don't know if you'll believe this— I honestly felt as if my rage was some dark and evil malignancy festering inside of me. I was afraid to be her mother.

If it's any consolation to you, I'm discovering that there is no exile from my life.

I miss Gemma. I miss you. What am I going to do if you don't take me back? I'm sorry it took me so long to realize what is most important. Forgive me.

Love,
Eve

"Of all respectable professions for young women literature is the most uncertain, the most heartbreaking, and the most dangerous."
—Trollope, "Mary Gresley"

ALL THE WINDOWS were open, yet the hypnotic late September sun could not find Eve, as she was hidden under two sheets, in her perpetually damp nun's cell of a room. Observing the palms of both her hands, she noted how, in one place or another, all the lines were fragmented. Gemma was in her crib taking a nap and Hart was on his way home. Eve lay in fetal position, on the bed, prickly with anxiety, wishing that there was a trap door on the top of her head that she could open, to toss out all the waste that was floating inside her mind.

Had it just been this morning that Eve had dressed in her "all black power suit," and stepped up on a bus bound for New York, so excited, she felt as if minnows were darting around inside of her? It was for the meeting with Maud, the one Eve had to wait all summer for, the one in which—with her entire dissertation in her hand and finally read—they were going to discuss her "defense."

"Is that where professors throw tomatoes at you and you get to hit them back Monty Python style?" Hart had asked, as he ate his Cheerios and milk at the dining room table, while Eve paced.

"That's where your committee tells you how very grateful you should be that celestial beings, such as themselves, are deeming the work of a mere mortal, such as you, 'passable,' although not exceptional."

"Sounds like rip-roaring fun." Sarcasm laced his words. "Can I come and observe the festivities?"

"Not today. Soon, though, I hope."

But, from the second Eve walked into Maud's office, she'd felt as if she'd entered a butcher's freezer, even in the oppressive heat. If Maud's normal aura was a crisp chilly blue, this day it was the glossy black of villains' cloaks in Disney cartoons. Her hair was pulled into a bun—but so tightly it looked like a form of self-punishment—and, she was nursing a swollen eyelid. She removed an ice pack from the wound and explained, abruptly, "allergies," as if annoyed that Eve had noticed.

"Allergic to me it seems," Eve thought, cynical as Hart. But little jokes to herself weren't going to change the mood of doom that had fallen, swift as a guillotine, once she'd entered Maud's office.

"Please do sit," her advisor gestured to the only other seat in the room, as she gently rubbed her eyelid with her slightly arthritic index finger. Looking at her now, Eve assessed that she could probably play a wicked Beethoven's Fifth on the piano without even a wisp of hair escaping from her obedient bobby pins.

"Well," Maud drew out slowly, pressing her eye into her fingertips. "What I'm going to say is bound to disappoint you."

Eve sat there nodding, one of those Mexican dolls whose head is attached to its body by a spring. But only certain words or phrases made their way from her ears to her brain; her advisor's displeasure was so loud, it blocked out noise like a 747 flying overhead. Eve heard: "You seem to have *entirely* lost your focus. Suddenly, problems have cropped up of a fundamental nature, both structurally *and* thematically." And: "the thinking in the last few chapters, I'm sorry to say, is quite trivial. I had not realized how trivial much of the study has become, in fact, until I saw the work, all in one piece." Then: "I would have to suggest re-drafting in quite an essential way. You need to rethink your *methodology.*" And: "The comparisons to twentieth-century feminists that you make are all but trite, and the use of trendy scholars is too easy. Really Eve," and here she practically sneered, "you do write with a certain style, but unfortunately, you seem, of late, to have lost your intellectual prowess." Eve imagined Maud grinding dead baby's bones in her teeth. "It is my job, as your advisor, to save you the embarrassment of going to committee with your work in *this* shape."

As Maud turned her eyes to her desk, to other matters, to more important papers from true scholars, it hit Eve. She would never complete her doctorate under Professor Forster's tutelage. But why? She mumbled something about "touching base" once she'd "whipped" her thesis into shape. Then, she'd backed out of the office with the humble expression and glazed look seen on the faces of exchange students, confused by the rudeness which passed as conversation in this part of the world.

Once outside, she stared, dazed and aimless, like a survivor of the blitz, having crawled out of her cellar, to view her home in ruins but the earth still in one piece. Once on her bus, she dozed as exhaust fumes swirled into her brain, doing their dirty work on what was once Eve's prized possession and now was just the mind of a *trivial thinker.* At home, Eve paid the baby-sitter, listened to her sleeping daughter's patterned breathing, then left a message for Hart. Feeling feverish—aware that rage had elevated her temperature—she crawled into bed, tightened her body into a fist, and waited for Hart. In the background the dog whined soulfully.

Hart's voice rang out from the other side of the apartment, "Eve, are you all right?" But, she had drifted into a bleak, headachy state and said nothing in response. Hart ran towards the bedroom, shouting: "Eve," and, once he spotted his wife, asked more softly, "what did that bitch say to you?"

For the rest of the afternoon and evening, Eve was as useless as another infant, mute and curled up, hands on her chest. Hart was nursemaid; at one point, he actually rocked his wife in his arms, and, later, he heated up a bowl of chicken soup for her. He said, "Just tell me what happened. Please, Evie." But, then, he dropped it. When the long, early afternoon finally turned to a dusty gray, Hart whispered in his wife's ear, "I've never seen the fight go out of you like this. It's not like you. You're supposed to be screaming, ranting, venting." It dawned on Eve, then, that her husband might be more afraid for himself than upset for her. Gemma began to cry and he asked, "Should I give her a bottle?"

"Yes," Eve said.

And that was the night she stopped breastfeeding for good.

In the morning, Hart asked in his most tender voice (one she hadn't heard in awhile), "Should I stay home today?"

"Do you have work?" she asked.

"Eve, *please*. Yes. I should be finished with this project at the end of next week."

She didn't want to ask him what impending disasters he anticipated after these few days were up. "Then, go," she said.

He caressed her cheek with his warm fingers but Eve retreated, slinking back into bed. "You need to work," she said. "We're poor, in case you've forgotten."

"No. You wouldn't let me even if I could."

"Don't blame me. I'm not the one who stole our entire savings. Look, I'm sorry. Just go. I'll be nicer when you get home. I promise."

For a long time after Hart left the house, Eve lay in bed waiting for Gemma to cry. She was afraid that if she allowed her emotions to stir, all her feelings would fly out in a burst, like magician's birds, startling her with their quick spectacular appearance. Eve remembered the last glimpse she'd caught of Maud before leaving the college, and rubbed her hands over her face to erase the image.

She tiptoed into Gemma's room and found her daughter awake, lying on her back, staring at her mobile of pastel-colored bunnies. She was gurgling, self-amused, like someone else's child.

"Hi, little bunny," Eve whispered and lifted her up. Cradling her daughter, she went back into her small dark bedroom and picked up the book on her night table. It was a leather bound copy of Jane Austen's work—a birthday present from Graham, years ago—and actually tried to read it aloud to Gemma. But the words skidded across her vision as if they were written in ice. "Never mind, sweetheart." She kissed her daughter's eyes; and the moisture from her own tears speckled Gemma's cheeks. "We'll find something else to do."

Eve sat in her tee shirt and sweatpants for most of the morning and flipped from one talk show to another. Gemma was propped up on the rug in a sitting position; she giggled as she toppled over and then practiced inching herself up again. Eve considered calling Hart, then Annie, but her finger punched the numbers by itself.

"Hello, Maxine Sterling," her mother announced with the newfound authority she'd acquired since launching her show.

"Ma."

"Eve? Is that you? You sound a million miles away. Something's wrong with this line."

"Ma," she repeated, weakly.

"WHAT HAPPENED," Maxie shrieked. "IS GEMMA ALL RIGHT?"

"Yes, Ma, calm down. I'm sorry. She's fine. She's right here. She's almost sitting up by herself."

"Really? I always said that child was a genius!" She sighed. "So, what'sthematter?" she asked. Meaning: now. This time.

"I saw Maud."

"Oh, GOD, what happened?"

As Eve retold the story, tears sprouted anew, and she wondered if this would happen, for the rest of her life, at the mention of her wrecked career.

"She can't do it, Eve. She can't get away with it."

"She can do what she wants, Ma."

"No, she CAN-NOT," Maxie articulated. "And here is why: I don't care what you think but, I am coming with you to speak with someone in *authority*. I have given generously to that school and I don't mean just paying your tuition. I received my own doctorate there and send generous

178

amounts during each alumni drive. I am a semi-celebrity now. I wield some power now. *I expect* to be compensated."

"Okay," Eve agreed, meekly, feeling as if she were three years old and hiding under the umbrella of her mother's hoop skirt. "But this isn't about *you.*"

That last part, she whispered, and Maxie didn't seem to hear. "I told you not to work with that woman, Eve, didn't I? I told you she sounded like trouble from the first time you described her. All right, you're young. You thought it was important to work with a *woman.* She impressed you. I sensed *something* when I met her at your wedding—I didn't want to tell you, to upset you—some bitterness in her. This Maud person is single, right? She's never been married or had children? Who knows how hard it's been for her to get where she is and what she gave up to get there."

"Mom, she isn't jealous of me, if that's what you mean. *Please.*"

"How do you know that, Eve?"

"You've been telling me that people are jealous of me since the first grade when Loretta Steinberg stuck her nails in my neck. And it turned out she was manic-depressive. You're my mother."

"It doesn't matter. We'll get you away from her and YOU WILL FINISH."

"Okay," she said, wanting only to believe in Maxine's godlike powers.

"Look, I have to go. I have to do *some* work. But make an appointment with the president of the school. Right away and I'll take the time out to come in with you."

"The president? I don't think his secretary would fit me into his schedule. I'll find the right dean to speak with."

"You find someone with clout, that's all. DO YOU UNDERSTAND? You make sure the person has some CLOUT."

"Okay, Ma."

"OOO-kay. God, does it ever end?"

"What does that mean?"

"*Crisis.* Kiss Gemma for me."

Maxie, looking large and forboding in her brown linen skirt and matching vest, marched into the dean's office. In a commanding tone of voice, she announced her presence to Lily Hijinx, his tiny, thin-lipped secretary.

"Name, please," Lily said with disinterest.

"Sterling. This is Eve Sterling."

"And you are?" The secretary raised her penciled eyebrows.

"Maxine Sterling."

Eve winced, suddenly conscious of how appalling it was that she'd shown up at the office of the dean of the graduate division with her *mother!* "What's happening to me?" she thought. But, it was as if she were a marble thrown down a hill, randomly rolling without a course.

Ms. Hijinx's mouth curved down slightly, into a frown, but she said, "Please have a seat."

They sat on wing-tipped chairs decorated in yellow and red plaid. For the next ten minutes, Eve watched Lily Hijinx type forms at rapid speed. Maxie whispered words of advice in her ear: "DON'T be nervous. DON'T be defensive. DON'T sound guilty."

That morning, Hart had leaned over the breakfast table and, for the first time in weeks, looked directly into his wife's eyes. "What are you doing, Eve?" he'd asked. His voice was as startled and stern as if she'd been strolling down the aisles of the A&P with her hands down her pants.

"Drinking my coffee," she'd said.

"Eve!"

She responded to the bark in his voice by starting to cry.

"Shit," he'd said and shook his head. "Try not to fall apart on me. We've got a baby to raise. I know this is a horrible time for you, but why are you meeting your mother at the dean's office? How's it gonna look, trotting in there with your mother? You're thirty-one years old. Listen, why don't you let me drive you to the city? I'll wait in the car."

Another pang in Eve's chest. His offer meant he had no paying work that day. "No, thanks," she'd said softly. The day after she delivered Gemma, Eve had managed to take a walk through the maternity ward. On the other side of the floor from her room, women were laboring. She'd heard one scream out in agony: "Oh, Mommy." She had thought, then, about how true the cliché was: pain transformed a person into a small and vulnerable creature. That feeling, instinctively, made you want to crawl back into your mother's lap, and that's what she was doing now. It just so happened that *her* mother—caretaker to the cable audience's needy—had a rather large and influential lap these days.

The dean, a tall, handsome man with cornflower blue eyes and wavy brown hair, finally emerged from the inner office. His arm shot out and Maxie automatically extended her hand. He shook hers with his own large, long-fingered one.

"Charles Eagleton," he said, glancing from Maxie to Eve, a slightly bemused look on his face.

"I'm Eve Sterling," she asserted, convinced that without a push, she would be the child who deliberately sits in the back of the class while her mother would be the one, in front, with her hand constantly raised.

Dean Eagleton shifted his gaze from one woman to the other and gave them (what Eve could see was) his self-acknowledged charming smile. "Yes," he shook Eve's hand. "Ms. Sterling, glad to meet you. Won't you both come in."

His office was in a state of disarray: his desk was cluttered with papers and his bookshelves overstuffed with books. He sat in another wing backed chair and stretched out his long elegant legs in front of him, under his desk. "Well, ladies, how can I help you?"

Eve recited the drill as Dean Eagleton nodded slowly.

"Ah, the pesky English department again," he said when she'd finished. Two hands together, he reached his arms into the air and then landed his palms on his head.

"Is the English department pesky?" Maxie asked, flashing the dean a smile.

"Well. . ." he returned her smile, pleasant as a diplomat. "You have to understand the setup of the University. It's not unlike a feudal system. We have almost no laws. Each department has its own set of rules and standards to which students must adhere. He sighed. "The English Department, shall we say, gets more than its share of complaints in this office. Well, with the exception of Psychology, but that's another story."

"Please don't get me started on psychologists," Maxine interjected.

"That sounds hopeful," Eve said.

"Don't jump to conclusions just yet," Eagleton said. "Despite my elevated title, my influence only goes so far." He sighed again. "Why don't you tell me your story and then we can try to find the most politic way of solving it."

Eve launched into her attack on Maud, trying to remain as objective as possible, modulating her voice so that it didn't break out into one long whine: *shefuckedupmy wholelife!* "So you see," she said wrapping up her complaint with a clear, conclusive statement (just as she taught her remedial students to do), "I had no indication of Professor Forester's discontent with my work up until her unexpected dismissal of my entire thesis. I have been working steadily, handing things in regularly, for more than two years without a problem. I've always been an exemplary student." Eve could feel the wrath swelling inside and sat on her fingertips as if to prevent leakage.

"Yes, yes, I see," he said abstractedly, hands still on his head. "Frustrating, yes. She didn't harass you in any way, did she?" He repositioned his hands, folding them together on his desk. "I mean sexually harass."

"No, of course not! Why?"

"It seems to be the only foolproof defense around here, for the student, I'm afraid. Anything else is tricky."

"You mean, anything else a professor can get away with?" Eve asked, wanting to pounce on his chest, knock him over, and stick her nails in his perfect blue eyes, Loretta Steinberg style.

"No, of course he doesn't," Maxie said.

"I'm afraid, I do, Mrs. . . . I'm sorry, your name just flew out of my head."

"Maxine. Maxine Sterling."

"Right. Sterling. . . ." His voice trailed off and he looked disoriented. Then, suddenly, he snapped his fingers. "That's it. I knew I recognized you from someplace. You're the one with that cable show that runs in Spanish and English, aren't you? I saw your show a couple of times. Saturday morning? Well, well, well . . . I'm in the company of a television personality!"

Maxie grinned and shifted in her chair, edging herself closer to his desk. "I'm not exactly a television personality, not in the ballpark of Oprah. Not yet anyway."

"I was very taken by your program," the dean said, the mood, in the room, having abruptly switched to a giddy one.

Maxie's smile broadened and there was a glint (a flirtatious glint?) in her eyes. "I'm very flattered that you would even take the time to watch the show. It's quite well produced, I think. I, *personally,* can't take any credit for that. But it's such a specific topic, not your average talk show. Not that I'd expect you to catch the more popular talk shows."

"No. I never have the time off to watch them in the afternoons, naturally. Although," Dean Eagleton sighed here (sharing Maxie's talent for melodrama, Eve noted), "sometimes I think spending my time that way would be more productive."

Maxie nodded sympathetically. "Administrative work can be so frustrating. That's why I've avoided it all these years. But, of course, you're in a different league than I am. I mean, I'm just a social worker, although I *do* have my doctorate. I've always told Eve how—if I'd started earlier in my life—I'd have loved to have been a college professor. I always revered my social work professors. They seemed to have the best life." Big sigh.

"Teaching can be immensely gratifying, if you have receptive students. I'm sure with your show, you could get a visiting professorship somewhere. It's quite eye-opening. You know, your show. . . ," here he paused, looked directly at Maxie with his wide blue eyes and rubbed his, nose nervously with the tips of two fingers.

Oh God, Eve thought, he's going to reveal something personal about himself!

"Well, it's embarrassing to say. . . ."

"Go ahead," Maxie coached. "I hear embarrassing things everyday."

"I didn't catch your show by accident. It hit home, so to speak. My wife . . . well, I should say soon-to-be ex-wife battled with . . . ," he stumbled.

"Infertility," Maxie offered gingerly.

Dean Eagleton was blushing—a lovely coral. How had this conversation avalanched so far out of control? And where did Eve fit into this poignant, private discussion (between patient and shrink)?

The dean coughed into his fist. "Well, we certainly have gotten off the subject, haven't we?" He grimaced. "Yes, let's see about solving Ms. Sterling's problem. I do have one suggestion. Do you know Professor Wellington, Gray Wellington?"

"He's an eighteenth century scholar, isn't he?" Eve asked, daring to intervene. Having never taken a class with Wellington, she had trouble conjuring up his face, of distinguishing him from a pack of nondescript, benign male professors who had been tenured for years. But, an image cropped up in her mind: a brown ruffled suit on a bony frame, charcoal hair, a warm smile, legs crossed and pants hoisted up so that thick crimson socks peeked through above sturdy walking shoes.

"Yes. He has a book on Richardson and several articles on Sterne. I think he may have done some work on Austen, as well, if memory serves me right. Anyway, I do know he is quite interested in Austen and would be open to a slightly radical approach. He is a personal friend of mine and a very steady sort. You might try him with your topic; tell him it was my idea. Put it this way: you are at intellectual odds with Professor Forester. I'm sure he won't find that startling."

"Oh, that's good to know," Eve said.

"Yes, but, I can't get into that. There is one catch!"

"Oh?" Eve asked, waiting for the clap of cymbals, forewarning the doomed end of her sad, sad tale.

"He is away until January, teaching in Scotland for the semester. You'll have to reach him there, at the University of Glasgow, and you'll probably have to wait to get started working with him. Naturally Scotland is too far for any extended correspondence and, in fairness to him, he is exempt from the responsibilities of this university."

"Oh God, a whole semester wasted." She felt her jaw, her stomach, tense with this realization. She thought of Hart, how desperately they needed to change their situation. Now, more time would be wasted before she could go on the academic job market.

"Better than an entire degree, huh? You might ask the English department for his telephone number and address. They should have it."

"We'll see about that," Eve said, smug with disillusionment.

"Dean Eagleton, thank you so much." Maxie smiled luminously.

"Whatever I can do to help," the dean smiled in return, beauty contest style. He stood up. "Don't hesitate to call. Let me know how things turn out. And I'll keep tuned into *Mornings with Maxie.*"

"Thank you," Maxie preened. "I like a satisfied customer."

The dean laughed, nervously, as Eve elbowed her mother.

As they were shuffled out the door, Eve realized that the dean had never even *questioned* Maxie's purpose in accompanying her to his office. Hart had been right, of course: with her mother there, Eve had allowed herself to slip into the role of child and, worse, of minor player in her own life's drama. The good Eve, sitting on one shoulder, echoed her husband's question, "How could you let her come with you? You're thirty-one-years old." But her evil twin sister, perched on the other shoulder, just sneered, "Because you're a failure as a mother, an academic, a wage-earner—in every way."[1]

"That is confidential information," the chairman's assistant scolded. "We are not at liberty to give it out to students."

"But I was instructed to contact him by Dean Eagleton," Eve said into the phone, careful not to bark at insolent Debbie Dole who—with her perpetual beehive hairdo, rhinestone studded harlequin glasses, and thick calves covered by the tight ankle straps of spiky pumps—had always struck her as a nasty anachronism. "Besides, I'm a doctoral student working on my thesis with Professor Wellington. *Naturally,* I would need his address."

"Naturally, then, he would have given it to you," Debbie Dole said snidely.

Eve slammed down the phone. "I'll simply have to call the nice, ineffectual dean again," she told Mr. Knightley who was perched on the window ledge with his back arched. Eve tried to lift the cat into her arms, but sensing neediness, he leapt out of them and scooted out of the living room.

Lily Hijinx was little help, as well. "Dean Eagleton is at a conference and will be out of the office till the end of the week," she said.

Eve hung up the phone; despair was looming around the corner ready to leap, a sprightly thief. Then, Eve had an idea. Perhaps they are more accommodating in Scotland, she thought, imagining Professor Wellington—ruddy cheeked in a plaid skirt, knee-high socks, and golf shoes— standing at the podium in a lecture hall. All that ale must make for more congenial student/teacher relations, she figured, dialing the operator to determine the area code for Glasgow.

A half-hour later—with a just-awakened Gemma wailing in the background—Eve reached a lilting female voice which informed her that the department was "closing shop" for the day.

"I'm trying to get in touch with a Professor Wellington from the United States who's there visiting for the semester," Eve pleaded. Rubbing her right temple, delivered a silent prayer to the gods and her daughter to forgive her this transgression. Eve could not hang up on this woman, from another continent, in order to reassure her baby that the waking world was a safe and steady one.

"Wellington, you say? Doesn't sound familiar," the British secretary said. "Hold on. Where do you say you're calling from, love?"

"New York. He works in New York."

"Very good. Hold the wire, then." Eve heard rustling and some muffled voices.

She held her hand over the mouthpiece of the phone and cried, "Coming sweetheart." But, as was becoming the norm, Gemma had already begun to placate herself. Her fierce sobs had quieted into complaining whimpers intermingled with cooing. Finally, the woman said, "Yes, he's here for the term. But he's on holiday at the moment."

"Holiday! He just got there." It was September in Scotland, wasn't it?

"Just a short one, through the weekend. Up fishing a bit in the highlands with Professor Deering and Dean Monroe. He should be back, Monday next. Can I leave him a message, then?"

"Yes," Eve said emphatically. "Please tell him to call me *collect*. That's very important. Reverse the charges."

"Right love. Who shall I say is calling?"

Who, indeed? Eve wondered. But, she proceeded to give out her name and telephone number. "I'm a doctoral student, tell him. Tell him *Dean Eagleton* suggested I call him. Have you got all that?"

The lilting voice declared, "I have every word. Don't you fret."

Eve began fretting the moment the line went dead.

The next morning, the ringing phone jarred Eve into consciousness. Her first image was of Professor Wellington in knickers, on a 1940's-style black rotary phone. She pictured him calling her from a two-hundred-year-old Scottish pub, a claustrophobic place filled with damp old wood. But it was Annie.

"Have you heard about Dee?"

"My God, no," Eve exclaimed. Had her her ex-friend been found strangled in the dank, dark green vestibule of her six story walk-up? "Did something happen to her?" Eve inched her way up in bed, glancing over to see rumpled sheets in her husband's place. Rain was spitting its drops on the window. In a minute, Eve knew, the reality of her life would alter her vision, like a funeral veil falling over her eyes. As had happened every day since her meeting with Maud.

"It certainly did. She's had her poetry manuscript accepted by *Viking.*"

"What?" Eve bolted upright. For a moment, she felt lost: Rip Van Winkle having slept half a lifetime away. But, according to the glaring green numbers of her digital clock, it was only 7:53. "She's published a few decent poems in journals with names like *Red River Expressions.*"

"Didn't she have a couple of things in *Poetry* last year?" Annie asked.

"That's not the point. And, how do you know this? You two aren't even friends." Listening to the intercom, Eve could hear Gemma's short shallow breaths signaling that her daughter was in the restless sleep right before awakening.

"I ran into her yesterday at Zabar's."

"At Zabar's? What the hell was Dee doing so far north? She never travels north of 14th Street."

"Well, here's the juicy part: apparently she's in love with some journalist who writes for *Newsweek* and lives around there."

"Oh, don't believe a word of that. For Dee, serious is someone she'd take her clothes off for." Eve fell backwards into her pillows. "I. E., male."

"In any event, she said to say 'hello.' She sounded pretty contrite. For Dee."

"How nice of her to extend herself like that. Do you know how many times she's seen my daughter, Annie? Never." She paused, letting the implications of the word—

its unequivocal rejection—impress her friend. "She's *never* managed to even meet Gemma. And, do you now what she sent me, two months late of course, as a baby gift?" Eve recognized Maxie's rant in her own voice. "Another black teddy with a garter belt! What an appropriate baby gift that is!"

"I don't know. Maybe she's trying to get back in your good graces by sending something just for you. She really seems to want to hear from you. I thought you'd be glad to know that."

"She has a phone. Maybe she can have her agent send me a notice about her new book."

"Eve," Annie said in a measured tone, "Dee's an essentially messed-up person. You used to realize that about her and it didn't matter."

"Well, now it does. What I wouldn't give to have a book coming out. I wish *I* could stop being wife and mommy for awhile and deal with editors, agents, publishers, lovers."

"Hey, what's wrong?"

"My life is really screwed up right now. I didn't want to go into it."

And, why not? Because her friend had chosen to share her deepest disappointments with Maxie.

Tit for tat.

"And why are you calling me so early with this news, anyway?"

"You know me. I'm up doing my exercise tape at 5:30. And, I won't have another minute all day; I'm just so busy. I thought you'd want to know, to make amends. Also, I wanted to tell you what's happening with the adoption agency. But, you know what? I have to run. Let me let you go and I'll call you later, okay?"

The image of a Chinese opera popped into Eve's head: Annie, Dee, Hart and herself, with painted faces, holding red and gold paper fans over their mouths. All their seething emotions would be sung in the appropriate, impassioned style. Just not to each other.

Letters

Guangzhou, China
December 13, 1996

Dear Eve,

Finally, a beautiful hotel and a chance to rest. Tomorrow, we anticipate receiving Sage's exit visa. Then, after a good night's sleep, we'll be off to Hong Kong, then San Francisco, then home! Since arriving in this country, this image has stuck in my head of us running a race, gasping, our arms outstretched, the finish line not yet in sight.

The agency booked us here at the White Swan Hotel, on Shamian Island. Our room overlooks the Pearl River and it's a breezy 62 degrees outside. Audrey Rothman, the Social Worker and Executive Director of Little Miracles Adoption Service, recommended that all new parents familiarize themselves as much as possible with our children's native country. But the river and temperature are all I've absorbed, I'm afraid. It's strange how resistant I am to explore this city. It's true, I'm exhausted. But, I also have this nagging feeling that I couldn't possibly admit to Arthur (and, probably wouldn't even be telling you, but somehow, it's easier in a letter) that I don't want to get to know Chinese culture. I want Sage to be part of my world, part of me. God, that sounds so unbelievably selfish! I scold myself, "Annie, this is such an obvious case of denial." But, I seem to want to be in denial for a little while, at least.

Arthur says that I stare at Sage for hours on end, she's such a darling, quiet, fat little thing. It's as if I can't grasp her, her presence here, the fact that she's mine. I'm not like you, I'm no good with words. How to explain this feeling? I'm hoping that when I get home, you will be there too and we can talk about it.

Did I ever explain how lucky we were to adopt Sage? According to the Chinese, we're too young (not being 35 years old). But, it seems that exceptions can be made in some cases. Sage was left on the front steps of the orphanage at only a week old and there is no record of her family or her birth. Apparently, this is not unusual here. But the doctor at the orphanage suspected that Sage was deaf. Audrey explained to us how, often, the diagnosis on infants proves to be wrong. Still, you can imagine how nervous this made me—the thought that I might have to raise a handicapped child. Even now, I'm not sure why I didn't just back out. It was as if I just knew that Sage was the right child for me. In fact, by the time we came to pick her up, the doctor had changed his mind about Sage's condition, giving her a clean bill of health. You can understand, though, that I'm still anxious to get her home and checked out by the topnotch pediatrician we've found for her.

I keep thinking about Sage's biological mother and wondering how she could leave this amazingly beautiful baby. Didn't she love her? I tell myself that she was the second child of a couple who would have been punished to the point of impoverishment by the government if they'd kept her. But, more likely, she is a victim of her sex. Didn't John Lennon say, "Women are the niggers of the world"? Now, I know, firsthand, what he meant.

Love,
Annie

"Such violence of affliction indeed could not be supported forever; it sunk within a few days into a calmer melancholy; but these employments to which she daily recurred, her solitary walks and silent meditations, still produced occasional effusions of sorrow as lively as ever."   —*Sense and Sensibility*

"AND SUDDENLY—FINALLY—my life resembles literature. Only the wrong genre. It's Yeats' 'Second Coming,' or one of those fifties' plays by an 'angry young man' or a post-modern, experimental novel in which the narcissistic heroes reflect on the anarchy and godlessness of a declining civilization." Eve was writing in her journal, four days after having called the University of Glasgow, when the phone rang. She was expecting to hear from Hart who had a late meeting with a potential client in southern New Jersey.

"Collect call from overseas, a Professor Wellington," a British accent reported.

"Oh my God," Eve said. "Yes, yes. I'll accept."

There were a few minutes of static on the line in which Eve's breath stuck in her throat and she wondered if she'd lost the connection. Finally, a voice said in a clear and neutral tone, "Ms. Sterling. This is Professor Wellington. How may I help you?"

For a moment, Eve froze, stunned that finally it was time to deliver the speech she'd been whispering aloud to Gemma as she diapered, fed, and rocked her to sleep. Then, she forced herself to envision her Oral Exam during which four men and Maud had listened as Eve rattled off answers to their questions, engaged in laughter, kicked off her shoes. All her life, she'd rallied under academic pressure. Now, Eve began talking rapidly but with a sense of purpose, thinking all the time that this was the one conversation that could determine the shape of her future.

"I can't tell you how much I'd appreciate it if you'd take my project on," Eve concluded, picturing her nose turning as brown as Amanda's doggy one.

"Well, Ms. Sterling, have you spoken to Professor Forster about this dilemma?"

"No." This was one question she hadn't prepared for. "I don't really know what there is to say. She made it clear she wasn't interested in my topic, anymore."

"Nevertheless, my dear, there are politics involved here and she *did* dedicate a lot of time to you." More static on the line; then, she heard a sniffling sound and throat clearing. "Ms. Sterling, I really can't make any promises from this distance. Previous commitments prevent me from taking on new projects while I am here in Scotland, although, I will say, it sounds like something that *might* be up my alley. I suggest you take the first step while I am away; write Professor Forster a gracious note explaining that due to 'intellectual differences,' it would be better for you both if you ceased working together. Then, when I return to the U. S., we can discuss the possibility of my commencing in the role of advisor. Is that understood?"

"Certainly, Professor Wellington," Eve said, despondent again.

"Very good. In the meantime, if you wish, you can send me a copy of your proposal, but not the draft of your thesis. However, understand, I can't offer any guarantees. We'll just have to wait and see."

"Okay. Thank you," Eve consented, throwing fate to the wind, like a mail-order bride. After hanging up the phone, she put her face in her hands and shook her head. "That could have gone better, don't you think?" she asked her audience: a baby, a cat, and a sad-eyed dog.

"I should have married a neurosurgeon and changed my name and registered at Bloomingdale's and worried about layettes for the baby," Eve wrote in her journal the following morning while sitting at her kitchen table gulping down coffee. "Just like my mother who married a doctor.

Only now, Maxie is practically a household name." There had been articles about her in the September issue of two national women's magazines. *Mirabella*'s "A Portrait of Three Outstanding Women of our Time" included a black-and-white airbrushed portrait of Maxie, looking thinner and more glamorous than she ever did in life. *The Ladies Home Journal* feature was entitled "Maxine's Miracle Babies." Their photo was much more conservative: a color picture of a smiling mom in a Christmasy red and green suit.

"My life," Eve continued, "feels like a parable about a daughter who gives up her enormous aspirations so her mother can succeed, succeed in ways the daughter never imagined possible. I am drab, without direction, and like a cliché: woman standing over a sink full of dishes wondering where all her youthful ambition has gotten her. It has gotten her in debt. We're in debt all over the place. Darcy was never in debt. That Elizabeth Bennet knew what she was doing, all right. If he had been an American Jew, he would have been a surgeon."

Hart was not Darcy. He was so tired, he was fading faster than a two-hundred-year-old pencil drawing. The weary recognition that he no longer regarded himself as an artistic/commercial photographer, but as a delinquent adult, had changed him in immeasurable ways. Having to act the part of the traditional male—rock-solid husband, involved parent, sole breadwinner—was killing his spirit. Over the last few months, Eve had come to realize that in Hart's mind, she was the partner with the drive, the one who was following a path as clearly laid out as the yellow brick road. Well, this was the part of the story where the road led to the wicked witch's castle. The sky had grown dark and those huge, screeching monkeys were flying in the way of her journey. It was up to Hart to play hero, to save Gemma and her from annihilation before all the sand slipped through the hourglass. But, not surprisingly, he was not happy in this new role.

"Anything interesting?" she asked her husband, putting down her journal and looking at him, head buried in the

"Help Wanted" section of the Sunday paper. "Hart, I'm talking to you."

"I heard you, Eve. I'm preoccupied."

"Right."

A typical, abbreviated dialogue, of late. Amanda was at Hart's feet. Occasionally, he would pet the dog. More than he did for his wife these days.

Hart, have you noticed that the baby's on fire. No, that he'd react to—he loved Gemma. Hart, your wife is on fire.

Find yourself a nice, rich fireman. I'm preoccupied.

After awhile, she shuffled off to their bedroom to lie in the dim light and glance up at the sloping beams. Inhaling deeply to keep the panic at bay, she dialed Annie's phone number. "I think we're in real trouble," she said hoarsely. "What should I do?"

"I'm not sure; I'm not thinking clearly. Todays one of my Clomid days. But, I'll tell you what: why don't you ask Hart to take care of Gemma and spend the afternoon with me, in the city? You can promise to watch her tonight so he can work on his job search. We'll go to brunch, walk around the Upper West Side, go to bookstores. You could use some lightness in your life."

"Okay. That sounds great, actually. Really great. God, I miss all that, Annie."

They met at The Metro Cafe at noon. It was a bleak, overcast afternoon, the kind of day that drags people back into a dreary sleep. The bus's sudden halt roused Eve at Port Authority. Her eyelids felt fragile, like paper ready to crumble from age.

Annie, too, looked worn despite her crisp, biscuit-colored blouse tucked neatly into a long denim skirt. She had cut her curly, tawny hair to shoulder length so that it could be tamed. She put her arm around Eve's waist. "Who ever thought motherhood, or the attempt at motherhood in my case, would be an endless finals week?" Then, once they'd sat down, she added, "You look so sad." Annie rubbed the bridge of her nose, one of her gestures that indicated concern. "Talk to me, please."

Eve searched for answers in the dark liquid of her coffee; she thought of the future dancing before her, like the sugarplum fairies are supposed to do for children. "Hart's been in this depression for a couple of months, since he resigned himself to the fact that he has to find a job and stop freelancing."

"Bad timing between Gemma and your fallout with Maud. Does he know how truly depressed you are?"

"He knows how *upset* I am about Maud. But, he's in this place all by himself, jailed."

Annie sucked her lips in and nodded. "What's he doing about it?"

"He's looking for work, going on interviews. He's miserable, but what choice does he have? We need the money."

"Do you think he resents Gemma? Not her, exactly, but the fact of her."

Gazing at her paper napkin, Eve shook her head. "No, Hart's the most devoted father I've ever seen. It's *me* he resents. As if he'd rather be raising Gemma himself and I'm in the way. But, of course, that's not feasible since I'm the free nanny."

"Okay, how bad *are* things? Is he working at *all* right now? What's it really like between the two of you? No exaggeration."

"He's working a little. And. . . ." Eve rubbed one eyelid where the headache was brewing. "We're very distant. I don't think we've had sex more than a few times since Gemma was born." She hated this feeling that, suddenly, they were on such uneven ground: Eve living close to a temperamental river, Annie, high on a hill where no harm could reach her. "Anyway, he's ready to take the first solid offer he gets."

"Good," Annie pronounced, adamantly. "That's good. A *devoted* father needs to feed and clothe his child."

Eve looked directly into her friend's face, into her determined eyes, and realized that she had been judging Hart all along. She and Arthur seemed to sort responsibilities the way one sorts white from colored laundry. Arthur was the money maker; Annie was the potential child-bearer turned adoptive mother. Although an "emotional middle-C"—according to Annie—her husband was known to woo her with his off-key rendition of "My Funny Valentine." And Arthur did beam with pride and a hint of arrogance when he announced that his wife held a Ph. D. in psychology. But, there were clearly stated rules in their family: Arthur would never stop providing in an ample and good-spirited manner and Annie would be the primary parent, to the point where infertility was her sole burden.

Their marital style reminded Eve of a mother's sense of justice: one cookie for you, one for your sister. But what if you are ravenous and your sister didn't particularly like vanilla wafers? Now, she realized that trying to satisfy their "grand passions"—hers for literature, Hart's for photography—struck Annie as unrealistic and immature. Perhaps she was right, Eve thought. After all, it was their quest for a purist's sense of fulfillment that had turned their lives into a chaotic jumble of unpaid bills, abysmal moods, life without a map.

Annie was nodding, vigorously, as she swallowed a hearty bite. Eve was her friend, but a juicy clinical problem was still her passion. "As for the intimacy issue," she said, "that's bound to improve once the two of you feel better about your own lives, get some rest, and get used to having a child. Sounds like you guys should consider seeing a marriage counselor. Has Hart ever been in therapy?"

Eve bit down hard on her lip, trying not to lash out. All her life, she'd been on a quest to rid herself of those old images leftover from her childhood: Freud/Dad and his couch. These days, Eve frequently reminded herself how Freud's patients had hefty bank accounts. Hart and she would be in a different class, in nineteenth-century Vienna, the kind of people with whom the good doctor could not be bothered. "No. But, as you know, I don't think therapy is necessarily the answer."

Annie lifted her gaze from her coffee cup to her friend's eyes; her own were a cool blue and there was a flicker of a smile on her lips. "Therapy isn't *always* the answer; but it sometimes *can be*. But let's not go down this old road."

"Right. How about you? How're the adoption proceedings going?"

"Okay. Slower than I'd like. I've been so crazy lately; I actually called a psychic hotline." She laughed. "Can you imagine? Me? I probably spoke with an illegal immigrant making minimum wage. But, the weird thing is she said a child would come into our lives soon and I never even mentioned wanting a baby." Annie shrugged.

Eve sized up her friend: all starched and manicured in soft pink, only the most modest jewelry—a thick gold wedding band, a sapphire engagement ring, and tiny opal earrings. Annie lived on two planes: the world of analytical thought and that of concrete objects. While she excavated the mind with the rigor and enthusiasm of an anthropologist, she was searching for tangible things, fossils from which one could piece together a childhood, a personhood. The idea of not being able to control her future was just as terrifying for her as it was for Eve. "Oh, Annie. What are you going to do?"

"Do? I don't know . . . exactly." She looked up, tears in her eyes. "She said our life would change dramatically, for the good, in a few months' time. And, like a moron, I want to believe her."

Eve nodded; and, for a few seconds, they sat in silence, glancing out at the sky: a tapestry of melancholy grays and blues.

That evening, Eve waited for the nightly storm to brew between Hart and her, just as surely as if it had been predicted on all major networks. She was beating two eggs around a bowl with a wooden spoon, when her husband— holding their daughter against his body—asked, "What're you suddenly so happy about? Did Wellington call again?"

Eve shook her head. She finished scrambling the eggs and slapped them on a plastic plate with a slab of bread: a dinner for someone incarcerated, she thought. Then she placed the meal on the butcherblock table with a fork and a glass of orange juice and headed for the kitchen. "I didn't have time to shop. Sorry."

"That's okay." Still standing, he shifted Gemma into the nook of his left arm and scooped up the food with his other hand.

Eve said, "It was just so great seeing Annie, even though she's worried about being infertile. She actually called that psychic hotline to hear good news. Maybe I should try that."

A deep-throated, nasty laugh, followed by: "Jesus, Eve, you're not going to fall for that are you?" The new sarcastic Hart, not the man whose joyful eyes brimmed with tears at the wedding altar. He threw his fork into the half-eaten eggs. Gemma looked up at him, imploringly, and began to whimper. "I thought you were a rational person, a scholar, not someone who'd throw money away on such bullshit."

"I wasn't serious and even if I was . . . . could you please show some concern about something besides money?" Eve took her plate away from the table and headed for the sink. "Guess my mother was right about your money problems eventually sabotaging us."

Hart followed her into the narrow space that masqueraded as a kitchen. They were all crammed together into this tight capsule, like astronauts, far from their home planet. "Why don't you just get it over with. Give it to me, Eve. Everything that's wrong with me. The consensus you and your mom have come to after much discussion and analysis of my faults. Since it's the two of you who are really married."

Gemma was howling now—such an animal sound—and, instinctively, Eve began to rinse out a bottle to fill with formula. She couldn't remember the last time her daughter had eaten and was waiting for Hart to make a nasty comment about that, too, her poor mothering skills.

"Hart, *please,* Gemma is screaming and I have no energy to fight. My mother just worries about me, that's all. You don't know what that feels like, to have parents who care, who are involved. When was the last time your mother even asked how you were doing? Does she even know how depressed you are? That your work is suffering?" The conversation was like trying to run a comb through hopelessly tangled hair, the more you tugged, the more deeply entrenched the comb became.

"No. And it's none of her business. Why would I tell her what a failure I've made of my career? It's not as if she's going to offer to help us out financially. But there is something in between her dismissal of me and your mother's constant interference."

Eve placed the bottle in Gemma's hands and squeezed out of the room without looking at Hart's face which, she knew, was as ugly as he could possibly make it. "You can't stand the idea that people are rooting for me, can you?"

"You're mother isn't rooting for you, Eve. She's controlling you!"

Eve turned around, nearly spun, and shot out, "Okay, Hart. You've made it obvious how you feel. Why do you even stay with me?" She ran into their bedroom, slammed the door and cried, not wanting to hear her husband's answer. After awhile, she calmed down and lay on the bed. The apartment was quiet except for the squeaking of the floorboards as Amanda lumbered down the hall. Eve knew she was avoiding much that needed to be scrutinized, but simply couldn't face all that Hart had seething inside. The best she could hope for—when one of them finally opened the door—was that they would speak to each other in civil tones. As evening darkened into night, Eve thought vaguely about the time-space continuum, wondering about the concept of going backwards, through the years, until you hit the exact right moment when everything began to go wrong.

"Hart?" Eve said, nearly whispering, later that evening. "Can we talk?"

"Uh?" he answered, this strange man, her husband. He had clicked on his computer and was inserting a disk. Gemma had just fallen asleep; this was the time of Hart's deliberate separation.

"I think we need to talk." Eve imagined herself pounding on his chest—applying the CPR she'd studied when Gemma was born—to help start his heart beating again.

He turned toward his wife, his face slack and slightly yellow, his eyes unrecognizable from lack of light. "Okay," he said.

For a few minutes, Eve just stood in the entrance to the living room, tentative and still. "Say something," she finally pleaded. Married life had turned out to be another country, someplace deeply foreign and cold: Nuuk, Greenland, where inhabitants were used to the hazards of icy living.

"You're the one who wanted to talk, Eve." He slouched into his seat so that not even his body language was his own.

Eve walked in and sat on the ugly plaid rocking chair she yearned to replace. "What is it that I can do to help you fight this bleakness? I feel as if I'm living with a black hole. You let all your anger fall inside you and absorb it, but you have no way of letting it out."

"You haven't exactly been a prize to live with since the crisis with Maud, either. You've been pretty damn awful, as if *your* life is all that matters. Why would I even want to talk to you about my problems when you're so wrapped up in your own?"

Hart just stood there, arms folded, a sneer on his face. An autumn wind battered against the window. Eve turned to watch as the branch of a half-naked tree knocked against the glass as if seeking refuge. "You're right. I am. But, that doesn't mean I don't care about your life. I love you, but you don't give me a chance. You shut me out."

He drummed his fingers on his arm. "I can handle things on my own. And, maybe, all your problems, *your* needs, make me feel like I can't even share anything with you. You're so self-involved, it's a wonder you ever agreed to get married."

There was nothing left to say. Eve rose slowly, controlling the manic fear that could easily rip loose into hysterics, sobbing, breakdown. For over an hour, she sat on their bed waiting for Hart to come in the room, to soften. But he never came.

All night, Eve lay in bed, studying the sloped pine ceiling, fingering the buttons on her flannel nightgown, feeling the ache around her eyes intensify. It wasn't a matter of her guilt, of Hart's righteousness. The core issue was that they were both grappling with the same emotion: loss. In marrying and having a child, she had lost control over everything. And, so had he.

She dozed on and off. Images of herself slipped in and out of her mind like rapidly changing slides: in her old apartment writing her thesis; with Dee drinking cappuccino and laughing in Telly's Place; alone in their dark, moldy bedroom, Hart and Gemma having moved out. Finally, in a pre-dawn fog, she crept out of bed into the morning chill. Gemma was on her back, in the crib, open mouthed, her olive cheeks flushed with rose: a replication of Hart's sleep face. Eve touched her daughter lightly and whispered, "I love you, Pea." The wood floor felt cold on her bare feet as Eve shuffled to the kitchen to make coffee. All the blinds were down in the dining room and at the table was Hart, his head bobbing over his neck, newspaper ads scattered before him. The whistle of the kettle woke him. "Up early?" he asked.

"I guess so," Eve mumbled, but didn't stop walking.

"Listen," he said, standing at the doorway to the kitchen. There was that warm streak in his voice again which reminded Eve of being close to him, hearing this low familiar sound, smelling the musk in his neck, all her muscles relaxed. But she would not let him in. "You always said I was tactless," he said.

"Tactless? Try cruel."

"Come. Take your coffee into the bedroom." He led Eve to their bed, then sat, his head in his hands. "I don't know, Eve. I didn't mean to be cruel." He took her hand and wrapped it in both of his own: tulip petals folding around its flower. "I haven't meant to take out how I've been feeling on you."

"Maybe you were right about one thing. Maybe I should never have gotten married."

"That's not true," he said, shaking his head. "Eve, I love you. And, I really envy how focused you can be, even if you're a pain in the ass, sometimes. I'm . . . I don't know. Fuzzy." He dropped her hand, stood up, began to pace. "It's *me* I'm angry at most of the time. It just comes out at you, I guess."

"Why are you so angry at yourself, then?" Eve asked, sidestepping out of his way, to make a path for him. Movement, even this smallest amount, was good.

"Here I have a wife and a child and I know, consciously, that I need to get my ass in gear, to protect my family. But, there is this little voice in my ear: the rebel. Look, I want to do the responsible thing. I'm a good guy." He sighed. "But, I'm not a company man. Never have been. I'm creative, a loner. I've always wanted to work alone. I'm a photographer."

"Of course you are, Hart. You're a wonderful photographer. Just a poor one." She touched his hand. "Well, I haven't been making money either. I feel like a failure, too." Eve couldn't help but smile. Finally, she let herself sit down on the bed. "We sound like the picture of mental health. What now?" She slid back, and felt her head and neck float down into the feather pillow, relaxing for the first time in days.

He smiled, his old crooked smile. "It might be fun to see you in a trailer home, eating white bread and butter, with one of those huge vaccination marks on your arm."

"Too late. I've already gotten all my shots."

"Oh, Evie. Everything is such a mess. What are we going to do?"

Eve thought of the last month, their marriage: like the shell of a cicada that hangs onto a house after it has died. They felt alive now, this current streaming between them.

"Maybe we should stand outside the subways with a cup," Hart said. "You can read from your dissertation and I can sell my photographs."

"Sure. I'd give to us rather than starving children from gun-torn streets."

They laughed and Eve knew that, for now, at least, the cold front had moved out of their house, of their lives. But they would have to work hard at keeping themselves warm.

Brookfield, Connecticut
USA
December 15, 1996

My darling Granddaughter,

Please come home for Christmas. This will be my first one in 31 years without you. Can you even fathom being someone's mother, much less grandmother, for so long? I can't! If it sounds as if I'm working on your guilt, I am.

Honey, I have no way of knowing if you've even gotten my letters since I haven't heard from you. Mrs. Grunwald at the Post Office assured me that the mail is very reliable to England (it's not as if I'm writing to you in India, which, I quote: "would be like putting my message in a bottle and sending if off to sea"). I can only conclude that either you have no use for your silly old grandmother or you're down-in-the-dumps. I'm hoping it's the former, but suspect you're suffering from the latter.

Okay, you wheedled it out of me with your silence. If I tell you this story, you have to promise never to repeat it. Only because I'm ashamed of it, not because it's such a great secret. Well, I trust you, honey, so here goes:

Way back in the Stone Age, when I was close to your age, I'd finished the biography and was feeling very proud of myself. After it was published, Bart Engle, at Simon and Schuster, asked me to go on a tour to promote the damn thing. It was for a couple of weeks, so your grandpa decided to come with me and get a peek of the Midwest and West. (We'd sailed all the way to Europe for our honeymoon but had never seen our own country—always doing things ass-backwards, I guess!) Your mother was four years old at the time, happy in her nursery school and with her nanny Cheryl Smith: a nice girl from Oregon whose family could be traced back to the Mayflower. Also, Hannah and Bernie lived nearby and promised to check up on her every night, after work. So, we stupidly decided to leave Maxine home. Stupidest decision we ever made.

Writing about what happened is still painful, all these years later. Poor Cheryl—a tiny little thing, not much older than a girl herself—was killed instantly in a car accident; she was hit by a drunk driver only five minutes from our apartment. Maxie was in the back seat, and thank God, Cheryl had always been careful to belt her in. Still, she punctured a lung and cracked four ribs. Our daughter lay in a hospital bed for a solid week while Hannah and Bernie tried to track us down. It was the first time during the entire trip that we hadn't checked in. Just our damn luck, right? I honestly can't remember, or maybe your father would say I'm "in denial," but I don't know why we didn't call. Honey, the question has haunted me everyday for over fifty years. Maybe we were just too damn exhausted and, self-ishly, stupidly, figured we'd be home soon anyway. You know, we were never much for talking about things, not like your mom and dad. But, I wonder if your mother remembers what happened to her.

I haven't forgiven myself for leaving Maxine, not to this day, especially when I think of what could have been. I loved that tour. But I never wrote another word. After what happened, well, it was as if I was paralyzed to write. Guilt just sucked the creativity out of me. I know I always claimed teaching was my real vocation. But, honey, that just isn't true. I loved writing that book; even now, eons later, I remember how much. So you see, Eve, sometimes life has a sneaky way of forcing us to rearrange our priorities. Come home darling and we can be co-conspirators. I'll listen to everything you have to say.

All my love always,
Grandma

London, England
December 13, 1996

Dear Professor Forster:

 After carefully considering the ideas you delineated in your response to my dissertation last September, I came to the conclusion that we have different visions of the direction in which my thesis should be headed. While I certainly appreciate the academic merit of your criticism, in the end, I do not believe it would benefit either of us for me to continue my studies under your tutelage.

 Subsequent to our meeting, I had the opportunity to speak with Professor Wellington who showed interest in my approach. Since, at this point, I feel I need to work with someone who more closely shares my academic viewpoint on this project, I thought it best if I changed advisors.
 I thank you sincerely for all your time and help over the last two years. I wish you the best.

Very Truly Yours,

Eve Sterling

"My mother means well, but she does not know—no one can know—how much I suffer from what she says."
—*Pride and Prejudice*

THE BOOKSTORE OPENED at the beginning of November to surprising fanfare. Aside from helping to run the place three out of six days a week, Eve would be in full charge of book inventory. The leaves were spinning, spiraling in the wind, on Eve's first day opening the shop. It was a cold morning with the last of autumn's brilliant exhibit on display: a palette of mustard yellow, carmine, and plum colors graced the trees in one last grand gesture. Already, though, the ground was littered with nature's cast-offs, the browning discards that cracked like fish bones when you stepped on them. Despite the gusts leading the dying leaves in dance, the sky was icy blue, the clouds long streaks of pure white; there was no sign of rain. In her burgundy knit sweater and matching corduroy booties, Gemma struggled to sit upright in her stroller and laughed aloud. Eve told her daughter that she loved her, then listened as pebbles crackled beneath them—pieces of the sidewalk that had loosened—on their half mile walk to *Armour and Lace*.

When they got to their destination, Eve propped Gemma up on a fuzzy salmon-colored blanket and surrounded her with plastic bath books, a teething ring, her Ms. Bear and various toys in primary colors. "It should get interesting when you start walking, Pea," she said as she kissed her daughter's thick black tuft and then sat her on the floor. Gemma bit down hard on the bright green key and gave her mother a look of intense satisfaction. Eve didn't care what anyone else recently observed about her "good nature"; her baby was a smaller version of herself. As if to prove her mother's point, Gemma rolled over onto her belly and began crawling speedily along the floor, alternately squealing and shrieking in frustration as she tried to lift her body into a standing position. "Wait until you get to the dissertation," Eve said.

She played with Gemma for twenty minutes after opening. Then a customer—a middle-aged woman in army boots, with a thick gray ponytail—approached Eve. "Do you carry *The Complete Jane Austen?*" she asked.

Eve smiled and nodded. Just maybe: it was an omen, a blessing.

Jo showed up a bit later with two cups of cappuccino. "Kiddo, I know how much your degree means to you," she blurted out. "But, I wondered if you might want more of an investment in the store. I think you could use the cash, if *Armour and Lace* does well. We could, maybe, work something out."

"What do you mean?" Was it possible that Eve's good safe sky could recede further into the universe?

"I don't exactly know. I'm in the thinking stage," she said, waving her spoon expansively in the air and, then, landing it in her coffee. "But, I thought maybe you could come in on the business in some bigger way." Spoon out again, dripping hot liquid, she added, "I *know*. Don't say you have no money. I wasn't talking partner. I'm thinking: manager. Maybe for a 30% profit, if that sounds fair? But it would be time consuming." She eyed Eve intensely, for a second, then shrugged. "Think about it. We'll both think about it."

"Thanks, Jo." But, she already knew: she'd given up her teaching job; Hart had depleted their savings. She had no choice.

"This isn't charity, kid. A word of advice. Put your grand plans on hold until you're thinking clearly again. Give yourself time to settle into this marriage/motherhood thing. Okay, I said my piece, I'm going into my office. Enjoy your freedom."

As Gemma's nap coincided with the slow part of the day, Eve read. First she dutifully skimmed through feminist theory: Treva Goldberg's *Epistemology of the Sexually*

Chained, Alison Hoxman's *Cultural Chaos: the Role of the Woman in Postmodern Fiction,* Delia Hubert and Terry Strauss' *Syntactical Configurations in a Feminine Mode: The Fluid History of Women Writers in the English Language, Vol. One.* Eve ran her finger over the periwinkle spine of a new biography on Austen. But it was increasingly painful, the knowledge: this might no longer be her field of expertise.

Later that afternoon, Eve swapped her Hubert and Strauss for Ruth Holden's *The Mulberry Park Murders.* When the wind chimes pealed, Eve looked up, startled, to a sight she hadn't encountered in months: her husband with light in his eyes and a grin on his face. He was carrying four yellow roses wrapped in white tissue paper.

"I called in the machine from Ron's," he said, by way of explanation. Ron was one of Hart's only loyal clients left, the editor of *Hair Life* magazine for whom Hart shot pictures of lanky models from the neck up.

"What's up?" She asked, tentatively, leaning over on the counter. "Here to pick out a book?"

"Not exactly," he said, cupping Eve's face in his hand. His grin grew. She thought of how he loved it when the street lights on one city avenue suddenly turned green, all in a row.

She leaned forward, into his touch; it had been months since they'd made love. Who would have thought that the energy between them could alter so rapidly, after marriage, like the weather on the cusp of a new season? "Here to check on Gemma?"

"Not exactly. Although I would like a peek." With that, he crept behind Eve and peered into the puffy-cheeked face of his baby, who was sleeping in her port-a-crib.

"So?" Eve repeated, after he'd cooed and kissed his daughter twice. "Why are you looking so pleased as punch?"

He rubbed his hands together, conspiratorially. "I thought you'd never ask. Bob Joll, from the advertising firm Joli and Weltz, called me last week . . ."

"Last week? You never even mentioned it."

Hart touched the frayed edge of his sweater vest and stared down at it. "I know. I had an interview there. I wanted to keep it to myself for awhile to see how it worked out. I didn't want to disappoint you."

She twisted her wedding ring around her finger, inching it on and off. "Hart, do you think—in my wildest dreams—I ever imagined myself working in a bookstore? You know, it was painful for me to even talk about *thinking* about it? But, I'm trying to share stuff with you."

He sighed. "I know." He just stood there, head bowed.

"Anyway, Bob Joli called . . ." Eve did a circular motion with her hand. "And?"

"And . . . well, I didn't get the job in the graphics department." Hart paused.

"Is that supposed to cheer me up?" Eve hissed, in a lower register. A young woman in spandex pants, platform shoes and an oversized black men's coat had walked into the store and was browsing through the Lesbian and Feminist Theory section.

"No," Hart said in a normal speaking voice. "But, he did give my name to the producer of *Eyewitness News,* daytime edition at ABC. Seems there's a position open in the editing department over there."

"I don't understand! What does that have to do with *you?"*

The woman in the large coat walked over to the desk, with a silver nose-ring and appalling pumpkin colored hair. Her husband pretended to show interest in the Historical Fiction section while Eve wrote up a book order for two Jeanette Winterson novels. After the customer left, Hart approached Eve with a grin. "Hi, Ms. Businesswoman."

"Cut it out," she snapped.

"I'm sorry. I just think it's cute. *You* as a businesswoman."

"I'm not a businesswoman, Hart. I'm a *clerk.* Working out of desperation." She put her hands up to her face, but he kissed her cheek, anyway.

"I was just trying to lighten the mood."

"I thought we were talking about you. About ABC.

About this mysterious talent of yours that I hardly knew existed." Eve's feelings were jiggling like dice.

"You knew, you knew," Hart waved away her doubts, magnanimously. "I told you I freelanced as a video editor for a few years before I started getting paid as a photographer."

"So?"

"So, I got a call today to come into ABC next week for an interview. Seems Joli highly recommended me."

"I don't understand. You said that you were looking for jobs in the graphics department of these companies because *that* was your backup skill."

"What can I say? You married a true Renaissance man."

"Well," she mumbled, piqued. "Congratulations."

Hart nuzzled his cheek next to hers. "Try to be happy. It could help us out tremendously. You could go back to working on your dissertation."

"Yeah, if I had one to work on." She rubbed her temples, headachy. "Look, I'm really happy for you. Really. Just . . . no more surprises, like with the wedding money, okay?"

"Okay. I'll work on being honest with you even when I screw up, even when I'm afraid that you'll be angry." Hart took her hand, kissed it, and said, "And, you work on not telling your Mom everything and, not relying on her so much emotionally and financially. Is it a deal? I have to go. I have to get to the darkroom downtown and do some developing. I'll be home by dinner. You okay?"

"Of course," Eve muttered, but once his back was to her, added, "Hart. I hope you get the job. You know that."

He turned around and threw her a kiss. "I know."

After Hart left, Eve felt odd. "What's wrong with you?" she demanded of the rows and rows of books, the shelves of black, white, and pink lingerie, tempting as button candy. "Your husband is finally acting happy and responsible and you're miserable. You can't even feel glad for him. You *are* a selfish bitch." Three customers sauntered in, two asked questions which distracted Eve. "When am I going to feel myself again?" she wondered, once the last woman exited with *The Freudian Guide to the Universe*.

Eve dialed her mother's number at the hospital in a haze. "I'm addicted," she thought, "I don't need counseling, I need a twelve step program: *Mamma's Girls Anonymous*. She said aloud, "Ma, I was wondering if you could help me out with something?"

"When *haven't* I?"

Eve ignored her, panic climbing from her stomach to her throat. "I'm thinking of going to Glasgow for a few days, to talk to Wellington in person. But, it's expensive and I'll need someone to help me out with money."

"By someone, could you mean me?"

"Yes, Ma," Eve said, humiliating herself in the familiar way.

"I don't know," Maxie said, in her "Eeyore" voice. "Do you think that's such a good idea, you're just showing up like that? Is he going to want to see you?"

"He won't be able to turn me away after I've made such a . . . big effort. It's not like he's around the corner."

"But, is that a good way to start the relationship? Ohhh, never mind, it would do you good to be pro-active. After all, it's your husband's fault you had to resort to working in that *shop*. You know, Eve, you're weren't raised with money problems. *I* was. I knew that Hart's amorphous career would someday haunt you, but I didn't want to say anything before you got married. I thought about it, believe me, but *I* didn't want to be the one to cause problems. Now, I don't know what you want me to do. Just listen passively, just take it without ever saying a word, like a sheet of glass? Okay, maybe you thought working in that little store there would distract you from this Maud business for awhile. Fine. But, I hate the idea of you *having* to work there, and with Gemma, shlepping her there. . ."

"Ma, I won't get into this. And, please don't pick on Hart. He's trying very hard to get on his feet. He just had an interview that looks very promising."

"Well, *good*. It will certainly help matters if he gets a steady job *and* it will make him feel better about himself. Listen, since you called, I want to run this idea by you. Gan

213

you talk? An editor from St. Martin's Press was on the show last week." She paused to chew—with her usual gusto—on something which made a loud crunchy sound. "She asked me afterward whom I had a book contract with. She just *assumed* that I was working on a book. Isn't that funny?"

Eve was trying to balance the phone under her neck along with cradling Gemma who was sucking fiercely on a bottle, already afraid that the world wouldn't accommodate her greedy appetites. "Hysterical."

"I told her I wasn't working on anything, *of course*. I'm totally exhausted trying to balance the hospital with my show. As it is, I've had to cut my hours down at the hospital," Maxie said. "Anyway, the editor seemed surprised, genuinely surprised. So," another pause to munch. "Wha'da you think about it? Are you busy there?" Maxie asked, as if the possibility had just occurred to her. "I can talk to you about the book later." A grandiloquent sigh. "Anyway, I'm sending out a blank check. When do you plan on going?"

"I don't know, Ma. I have to see when Hart can watch Gemma for a couple of days."

"Just don't let your husband get his hands on this money. I'm making it out to you. But, it's for the airlines, Eve, not to pay off your husband's debts. Do you understand?"

"Yes, I understand," she said and sighed, recognizing clearly—for the first time—how tirelessly Maxine worked to pit her against Hart.

"So, how is it managing the bookstore?" Hart asked, tentatively, Saturday morning, two weeks later. They had set the alarm for a few minutes after seven. Gemma still woke them twice a night, so that they had become conditioned to existing in a quagmire of slow, muddy, head-thumping fatigue. Their daughter would be up, anyway, within the hour, and they wanted to spend some precious time alone together before Maxie's show aired and their twenty-hour day began.

"It's okay; you know, a distraction and some cash. But, it's not the same as having my career. The problem is: I'm feeling desperate to get my focus back." She still hadn't approached the topic of going overseas, not when they hadn't had a fight since the phone call from Joli and Weltz.

Hart began humming "Money Makes the World Go Round," from *Cabaret,* tapping his foot in rhythm. "Want pancakes or eggs?" he asked, while glaring into the poorly lit refrigerator.

"Pancakes are fine, thanks. I'm going to take my coffee in the living room."

Eve couldn't help but lie down on the couch, balancing the mug on her loose-skinned belly. The sky was still a pale shade of gray, the sun nowhere to be seen. It was nearly impossible to unglue her eyes permanently, to throw herself into—what was once—her characteristically focused fervor of thought and activity. Eve wondered, as she often did, if family life was a drug meant to sap a woman of purpose and momentum. Listening to Hart clank the pots and pans around in search of the right utensils for his breakfast, she dropped one arm to the floor and scouted around for the remote control with her hand. The floor was wood panelling, faded in spots and in desperate need of a profes-sional polishing job; in the center of the room was one of their old, now threadbare, oriental rugs. From this position, Eve could spy every piece of dirt: dust, lint, and crumb. "Oh! Money makes the world go around. The world go around. The world go around," she sung—off-key—into Amanda's fetching doggy face.

The remote control was wedged between the arm of the couch and the cushion. Scrambling to sit up, Eve felt unco-ordinated and heavy, like a sea lion clambering up the side of a rock. Finally, she positioned herself snugly against the stained black pillows, sipped her lukewarm coffee, and flipped through the channels until she came to the one in which her mother's show appeared in English. There was a woman—for whom a stroke or some sort of partial paralysis had frozen the right side of her mouth—speaking in choppy phrases about sewing a baby blanket. "Whew," Hart said, "The ratings must be through the roof on this show." He'd entered the room with breakfast laid out on the pink plastic tray that had Gemma's name painted in yellow, a gift from his sister Elyse.

"Nice looking breakfast, hon." Eve placed a peck on her husband's cheek.

Hart slid down beside her and bent down, reaching for a plate of whole wheat pancakes soaked with raspberry jam.

"Do you experience bloating, irritability, headaches before your period? I do," an actress on a commercial confessed in a lilting voice.

"I'm going for more coffee," Eve said, "so I can experience even more irritability. Call me when the dirge begins."

Maxie was dressed in a brown linen pantssuit with an apple-green scarf draped across one shoulder, on which was embroidered an enormous monogrammed *M* in gold thread. She emerged from her chair and walked closer to the studio audience, smiling in that odd, fake way she'd perfected: a cross between sympathetic therapist (the mouth) and haughty Hollywood star (the eyes). "Welcome everyone. Today's show is entitled 'Tough Choices' and deals with women's particularly difficult and uniquely twentieth-century burden of having to cope with juggling high-power careers with worrying about their own fertility."

Maxie gave her opening monologue, in her most comforting tones. "For the first time in history, women are struggling with the unusual problem of balancing their hard-earned professional accomplishments with this fairly new phenomenon of having to quote/unquote schedule motherhood. Many worry that they may have forfeited their most fertile years to their careers. Women on the fast track often have trouble fitting children into their busy lives; many wrestle with guilt over their distinctively *female* predicament. Yet, the conflict is becoming a familiar one: they may yearn to start a family precisely when all the difficult years of school and/or work just begin to pay off, when their career clock *clashes* with their biological clock.

Today, I have with me three women, all distinguished in their respective fields, who have grappled in their own ways with this issue. Please welcome: Dr. Priscilla Kelly, a renowned cardiologist, our own beloved Dr. Sarah Anne Schwartz, and Eloise Lawrence, staff writer for *The Wall Street Journal* and author of *Superwomen: A Twentieth-Century Fairy Tale,* hot off the presses from St. Martin's. Priscilla, why don't you tell us your story first," Maxie instructed, gently, "as much as you feel comfortable with. . . ."

The camera zoomed into Priscilla Kelly's round, blue eyes, and hard smile. Then it drew back to present the whole person: blanched skin, but delicate features, feathery penny-colored hair, long turquoise earrings. She looked like a female Robin Hood, skinny and tall in a green tee-shirt dress, a leather jacket and short, black boots.

Just beneath the surface of Priscilla's tough-girl mask, there was the shadow of something else: a long battled sorrow. "As you said in your very generous introduction, I'm a cardiologist and Associate Professor of Medicine at Einstein Medical Center in New York, divorced, no children. I'm infertile, most likely a result of waiting until I was almost forty to try and become pregnant."

For awhile, there was silence, a long, uncomfortable pause that would have had producers from other talk shows clutching their clip boards, shouting frantically to break to a commercial. But not Adrienne. As Maxie often boasted, "She trusts the genuinely therapeutic atmosphere on my show." Finally, Priscilla shifted in her seat, tucking one long leg underneath her, and said, "The problem is, unless a woman is a prodigy and finishes her medical training very young, getting really established in my field takes much of her childbearing years. Children are hard to squeeze into the equation. I obsessed over the issue of having a child for over a decade. But, my ex-husband told me 'Don't throw away your career; wait until you're secure in your field.'"

Maxie nodded, encouragingly. "Do you feel your husband was against the idea of having children?"

Priscilla shook her head, causing the long earrings to slap the sides of her face. "No, Henry wasn't against having children. He just understood how much my career was taking out of me and how much it meant to me. He's an ophthalmologist, and works long hours himself. He knew that I was afraid to interrupt my success, afraid I'd never get on my feet again."

"Is that what persuaded you to wait before trying to get pregnant? *Fear?*" Maxie probed, with Olympian importance in her voice.

Priscilla coughed into her fist, then looked into the camera, her eyes squinting with anger. "I *thought* about it all the time. But so many people in my field, men and women, dissuaded—not only me—but all the women I knew, in the medical profession, from having children before they were through with all their training. Many of them lost respect for those colleagues of mine who didn't wait. There is a feeling that women who choose to have a family are not as serious, not as dedicated."

There was another, more significant pause in which the camera panned the faces of a disapproving audience.

"Let's hear from Eloise," Maxine suggested.

Ms. Lawrence smacked her lips together and twirled the ends of an orange and yellow paisley scarf, then smiled. "As we discussed, Maxie, I am here as a representative, shall we say, of a dissenting, unpopular opinion. And, that opinion is simply this: to achieve excellence in one's chosen field—if, indeed it is a field which requires long years of study and commitment—one must often sacrifice other options. That's really what my book is all about: that women *can't* do it all."

"Soooo," Maxine said, then paused dramatically. "Let me see if I understand you. Are you saying that women with ambition should forfeit motherhood? Maybe that's why my *own* daughter got pregnant while still in her doctoral program and attributed it to an accident. So that she didn't have to make that awful choice."

"Shit!" Eve screamed.

"Jesus," Hart said, stunned.

During Lamaze class, the nurse had said, "The contractions can be painful," in a voice so placid it erased the meaning of her words. Her mother's betrayal was done in the same insidious way. It was as if all Eve's trust was as flimsy as a fly's wings.

Maxine was bobbing her head in superiority. The camera zoomed in for a sadistic close-up of her face: every pore seemed temporarily revealed, her eyes and smile twinkled lustfully. "My oldest daughter, Eve, is an academic. I have a statistic here which states that women in academics have children at the lowest rate of all professional women. But it's unfortunate that women, from all walks of life, are being given the message that if they want children, they have to give up their dreams. So, Eloise, would you say that you're in favor of the so-called 'Mommy Track?'"

Eloise cleared her throat and smiled condescendingly at Maxine. "No matter that feminists and other idealogues may misconstrue my meaning, I am not advocating for any political or social agenda. What I *do* suggest in *Superwomen: A Twentieth-Century Fairy Tale* is *this:* a human being can only accomplish a certain amount in a lifetime. A woman, or a man for that matter, needs to determine her/his priorities. Fulfilling one's desire often means limiting one's possibilities. *That* is just reality. *That* is what used to be called maturity."

Maxine smiled back, her conciliatory smile, and then gazed out at her audience. "Well who among us could disagree with that? And so women, we have a *dilemma.* Just as my own poor daughter's worklife, her dreams and aspirations, suffered—*maybe irreparably*—after the birth of her child, so must many women's. It is hard for most women to juggle everything. In fact, the possibility of 'juggling,' *successfully,* may be a myth of our own making." And here, she stared into the camera and enunciated carefully: "Dr. Lawrence may be right."

Eve shook her head and began pacing, trying to outrun rage with movement. "This is a nightmare. How could she talk about me like that?"

Hart said, "I don't know, sweetheart. I don't know. Christ, Gemma's up." In fact, she was wailing; it was as if

219

she'd tapped into her mother's miserable brain and was articulating her pain.

"Take care of her. Please, Hart. I need to go out for a walk."

Without bothering to turn off the television, Eve bounded down the stairs, old wool coat in hand and hit the bitter air, without breaking stride.

It was sometime in the early evening—when the world had just turned black and bitter cold again—that Eve made her decision. It had been an oddly quiet day after the shock of the morning. For the first time since her mother had begun *Mornings with Maxie,* Eve hadn't congratulated her after a segment aired. Eve figured she'd call—frantic to make amends—but, the telephone hadn't rung. In the afternoon, Hart had bundled Gemma up in her down jacket, purple fuzzy hat, and fur lined booties, and taken her to the park. The apartment had been eerily silent and, Eve had lain on her bed, imagining that she was back in her tiny studio in New York, with the bay window and makeshift curtains, all those dreams ago.

It had flooded her—in a rush—what she'd lost: that good, muscular quality that had shaped her life. Trust that it would be a success. For so long now, she'd experienced herself as amorphous, all sense of purpose leaking out of a flaccid body. What she'd evolved into was: someone's wife, mother, daughter, the essential kernel of her being buried under the weight of these roles, like the pea beneath the princess's colossal bed. There had to be a way to dig herself out. For awhile, she tried to read but, her mind was too weary from obsessing over her predicament, like a thumb rubbing a worry stone. At one point, she heard Hart and Gemma return from their outing; as they were dutifully quiet, she chose not to greet them.

Eve lay there until evening; periodically, she opened her eyes and wondered—just for a second—what she was doing in bed. Then, it flashed in her head: an image of her mother's laughing face atop the body of the witch, from *The*

Wizard of Oz, flying off with Toto in her bicycle's basket. Sometime, late in the afternoon, when the sky outside her window had faded to a bleary gray, Hart entered the room. "Eve, sweetheart, are you getting up for dinner?"

"No," she said, slinking further into the refuge of sheets and blankets, her back to her husband. "How's Gemma?"

"Fine, fine. She's in her crib."

"She shouldn't be napping now, she'll never sleep tonight."

"She isn't. She's playing with her Busy Box."

Only Hart could perform this miracle. With Eve, a trip to Gemma's crib—before her daughter was appropriately drowsy—translated into a crying jag so formidable she could imagine social services pounding on their front door. The truth was: Hart had earned the most gold stars for being the calmer, more patient, parent.

The telephone rang. "Don't answer it," Eve said instantly.

"Okay. I'll let the machine get it. You know it's her, don't you? How can she even have the nerve to call? What could she possibly have to say?" After meeting with his wife's silence, he asked quietly, "Do you want some tea or something?"

"Okay. Peppermint. I'll do it." If she let Hart believe that her wrath at her mother had transformed Eve into an invalid, he'd wait on her unrelentingly until, finally, his own indignation at Maxine would turn on his wife.

By midnight, the house was quiet, save for the melancholy whine of violins crying out of the radio on Hart's end table. Eve tip-toed from the bed, careful not to touch her husband. When she got to the living room, Eve saw the red light on their answering machine blinking in warning. After turning the volume on low, she listened to the one message.

"Hi everyone. Hi my beautiful granddaughter. Did you see the show today? I hope you're not mad that I mentioned you on the show, Eve. It wasn't planned! It just came out spontaneously! And, you know, I thought about it afterward: a lot of women could benefit from your experiences, Eve. How would you like to come on the show? *Just think about it.* I'm booked for the next few weeks; how about after the New Year?

Oh, guess what, Adrienne got a call from the network. Seems there's some interest in my show expanding. Something about a new, more general theme. Less grim. What a hoot, huh?" Big sigh. "I don't know if I'll do it; it would mean taking a leave from my job at the hospital. Well, let's face it! It might be nice to take a break from saving everyone *else's* life for a pittance. What would you think about your mother being on CBS with David Letterman?!"

If you believe that life can be divided neatly into "befores" and "afters," then it was this message from her mother that catapulted Eve into "after." With perfect composure, she pushed the button to erase Maxine's news, then dialed the operator for information. "British Airways please," she said in a husky voice. She jotted down the available times and rates, then rummaged through her desk for her appointment book; on October 1st, followed by a sketch of Oscar Wilde, was Wellington's phone number in Glasgow. It was too early—Scottish time—to bother him. But, Eve resolved to wait until a suitable hour and trudged off to the kitchen to fix herself a pot of coffee. The house was filled with night sounds: Hart's intermittent snorts, Amanda's more regular canine snores, accompanied by the even more mournful cello music now emanating from the radio.

Eve stopped to peek in on her daughter. "Hi little moonbeam," she whispered, stroking Gemma's hair with only the tips of her fingers. It was nearly impossible to imagine this beautiful creature having once been inside of her, gestating in a mess of blood and uncertainty. Had she been the appropriate nest for such glorious creation? "Mommy has to go away for awhile," she whispered. "But when she comes back, she'll be a much better mommy, I promise."

When Eve checked on airfare, she'd done so for one adult and one infant. But, she realized, now—with a tear into her heart—that it'd been foolish to consider such a plan. Abducting her daughter from her home would make Hart look like an unfit father, when he was the very opposite of that: a wunderkind at parenting. Eve wanted her daughter to have the most magical of childhoods, one in which she could believe in the power of Tinker Bell's pixie dust to transport her to Neverland, Dorothy's shoes to deliver her over the rainbow, and Mary Poppins' love to mend her aching heart. "Daddy can give you that," she said, ever so softly.

Eve waited on the couch—with Mr. Knightley curled upon her feet, faithful animal—and sipped a cooling cup of coffee. She envisioned her replacement: a buxom woman with milky skin and the requisite twinkle in her eye. Perhaps it was the lateness of the hour which lulled Eve into a dreamy sense of security: all would turn out fine, her abandoned daughter would be blessed with an upstanding mother figure in her stead. That is, until Eve could fulfill that role properly herself; she would return as soon as this deadly sense of suffocation abated: when her thesis was rewritten, a promise secured from Wellington, and her academic life restored. In the meantime, she would work diligently through the pain of missing her daughter; the miles between herself and her family would prove a buffer. And the old dream of excellence, focus, and achievement would be hers again.

At nearly two in the morning, Eve reached for the telephone and dialed, overseas, to Wellington's office in Glasgow; on the fifteenth ring, he picked up. His voice was low and startled, "Yes?"

"Professor Wellington, this is Eve Sterling, the doctoral student who'd been working with Professor Forster, the one whose dissertation you said you'd look at when you returned home . . . ?" She was breathless.

"Yes, Ms. Sterling?"

"I hope I'm not bothering you, Professor. . . ."

"It's quite early here, you must realize. I happened to come in to get some work done on my book before the department arrived."

"I won't take more than a minute. I just wanted to tell you that I planned on being in . . . the British Isles . . . this winter, soon in fact, and was hoping I could see you, to discuss my thesis. I'm very anxious to get back to work."

"I see." He paused. "I'll be in Scotland until Christmas week and extremely busy. I'm afraid I won't have a minute until after New Year. But, I could make time then. I'll be in England, in fact, for the following term, at London University."

"Oh! I could meet you there . . . ?" She was clutching onto the telephone wire tightly and crossing her fingers.

"I suppose so. I suppose you could, if your plans include London. And, if the timing is all right."

"Yes, yes they do. I was planning on going to London," she babbled. "And, the timing is perfect, actually. I'll first be going to the nineteenth-century literature conference in Bristol. I'm giving a paper there actually."

"Well, if you are here after the holidays, I'm sure we could arrange something."

"That would be wonderful! I *really* appreciate it."

"Hold on. Let me get you the address and telephone number there. Actually, if you'd like me to have a look at your paper for the conference, I might have time for that, to get a jump on things. You might try sending it DHL, if that's all right with you?"

"Oh, yes! That's all right."

After hanging up the telephone, Eve realized how truly exhausted she was. She plodded off to bed, then curled into a question mark. The last thought that crossed her mind, like a shadow, was: Can I leave my baby until I finish my thesis? Am I really such a monster?

In the dream, they were living in the basement of a tenement without windows, lit by fluorescent bulbs, with moths beating their wings against its dull casing. Eve's daughter was howling and she raced down a long hall in search of her; she darted from room to room until she found Gemma wedged into a drawer in an old wood dresser that smelled of mildew. When Eve picked her up, her daughter felt limp and oily—like a cooked sausage—and out of her mouth came an inhuman scream. I've killed her, she thought, just by my touch. A few hours later, she awoke to the pearl white sky of early morning; tears were pasted tightly to her cheeks.

Eve's life now became a list: make airline reservations; place an ad for full-time childcare; leave a message for Mom to help with baby-sitting until an appropriate nanny can be found; pack; go. The next two days passed in a daze; somehow, she managed to keep her plan to herself but she did pass on the news about her mother's show expanding. "Please Eve, don't talk to me about her right now," Hart had said, "I'm too angry to even hear her name."

The night before Eve left, she finally told her husband. "At first I'd arranged to go for a short time; but Professor Wellington can't see me until after New Year's. So, I want to give a paper at this conference in Bristol to help my credibility with him. And, I figure, I'll really need the next few weeks before going to Bristol to work on my thesis, work on it day and night, without interruption. This is my last chance."

"Eve, what are you talking about? This is crazy!" he said, reaching for her. "Listen to me, are you in shock because of what your mother did?"

Eve shook her head slowly, backing away from her husband, her eyes burning. "No. It's not just that, Hart. It's everything."

"What everything?" he asked in an unnaturally loud voice, as if she were hearing impaired instead of unglued.

"You know, everything."

"You mean me and Gemma? Why are you taking out the unforgivable things your mother and Maud did on us?"

"I'm not. Things started to fall apart when we got married."

Hart slapped the wall as if it were his wife. "Are you having a breakdown?"

"No." She swallowed hard. "I don't know. Listen to me, Hart," she begged, desperation crammed into her throat, like vomit. "We weren't prepared when we got married. We have no money for one thing, and both our lives have fallen apart. I've lost all my confidence and that can't be good for our marriage or our daughter. I need my old self back."

"So, let me get this straight: you think it's because of me, because of your daughter, that Maud rejected your thesis?" He was shouting now. "You bought that bullshit that ridiculous journalist person said on your mother's show?" When Eve didn't answer, they were both silent. Then, he asked, his voice a notch higher, "I hope you don't have any thoughts about taking Gemma with you on this fantasy trip?"

"I did," she whispered. "I wanted to. I love her so much, Hart. But, then I thought about you, about how unfair it would be."

A smirk distorted his face but, Eve knew it was from terror as well as rage. "Unfair? I'd get a court order to prevent your leaving with her! How about that?"

When she didn't answer, when all she could do was stare at a liver-colored stain on the already filthy yellow rug, Hart jeered, "Who's paying for this trip?"

"Don't worry, not you."

"What kind of mother would just leave her baby?"

"A bad one," Eve whispered.

Hart began to pace, his hands in fists. "Okay, okay. Let's look at this great escape plan of yours. Who do you expect to take care of Gemma while I'm job searching *and* working?"

"I've put an ad in the *Reporter* for a childcare person. Just until I get back. I spoke to a couple of women who called; and I left the names and numbers of the ones who seemed nice on a notepad on the dining room table. They really did sound good, Hart. Also, I've left a message for my mother both at work and at home asking her to pay since she can afford it and knows we don't have the money." Eve put her hands above her head as if to stop an avalanche from burying her under rubble. "She owes me after humiliating me on her show."

"She thinks what you're doing is acceptable? Leaving Gemma?"

"I didn't speak with her directly, but it wouldn't matter if I had." She shook her head. "She can't stop me."

That's when Hart slumped over just as surely as if he'd been punched in the gut. When he looked up into her eyes, he was crying. "I thought we were working it out. I thought we—Gemma and me, people—came first with you, the way it does for me. How could you do this?"

His question reverberated in Eve's mind even as she whizzed away in a cab to Newark Airport before the first light of morning.

Late December, 1996
Bristol, England

"She began now to comprehend that he was exactly the man who, in disposition and talents, would most suit her. His understanding and temper, though unlike her own, would have answered all her wishes. It was an union that must have been to the advantage of both . . . ."
—Pride and Prejudice

It snowed—a nasty, slushy snow—in Bristol on the first day of the conference. Eve was scheduled to give her talk at noon; she had a return bus ticket to London, leaving the next day. It was impossible to think of mingling, of having to bolster herself up in every conversation with wine-sipping, tenure-track participants who'd bemoan the condition of the job market at the same time that they'd thank God for their own good luck. Already, on her way into the hall, she'd witnessed a glass enclosed case filled with books published by several of those speaking at the event.

Hortense Dudley of Girton College, Cambridge, presided over Eve's panel. Round-faced, with clipped gray hair and a simple beige shirt and cardigan to match, she was tiny in stature, old but agile, and extremely cheerful. She rubbed her chafed hands together in excitement as she introduced the program: "Jane Austen's 'miniature delicacy' versus Charlotte Bronte's 'Speaking Acquaintance with that Stormy Sisterhood: Contrasting Feminist Visions.' I hope we're all in the right place?"

When it was Eve's turn to speak, she felt a brief flutter of panic in her stomach, but then read with appropriate gravity. She appeared completely in sync with the rest of the scholarly crew, so that no one guessed that she was suffering from something other than scholarly self-importance. "Emma is a novel which flaunts female independence and entitlement in a world where the predominant thinkers of the day were clearly threatened by women who claimed

228

even the slightest bit of power. Thirty-five years later, Charlotte Bronte renames 'passion' as 'that stormy sisterhood.' Her objection to Austen—at least in part—is that her predecessor does not demonstrate the fierce emotions often associated with women, including—perhaps most importantly—rage." Eve paused to inhale; she couldn't seem to take in enough air. "What makes Emma unusual, even by today's standards, is that she is a woman endowed with self-esteem who possesses and enjoys power, boldly asserting, 'I always deserve the best treatment, because I never put up with any other.'"

"How wonderful," Eve thought.

Her voice echoed in her head as she read. At one point, she looked up from her paper to see him standing there, relaxed but alert, in his tweed blazer and wool pants. His wispy yellow hair was shorter than she'd remembered and his face paler, rounder; he'd put on weight. Still, his eyes were that startling blue, the color heaven promised to be. He didn't move from his spot as she read, finding it piercingly hard now to draw in enough breath.

After the last speaker read her paper on 'Feminist Visions,' he approached her with an intimate smile on his face. "Hi," he said, blushing a bit. "You look great, sexy. Motherhood agrees with you."

"Thanks, I think. You look good too." It was true; Graham exuded an unshakable ease with himself and the world, a seductive sense of entitlement that comes from being born rich, privileged, and loved.

He kissed Eve lightly on the cheek. "Do you have time for a drink?"

She averted his gaze but said, "Sure."

Driving over the gorgeous Clifton Suspension Bridge, at night, with Graham, there was a moment when time lost its meaning. She caught him glimpsing at her, while he caressed his sandy blond mustache, and her pulse galloped. There was still that breath of sex between them, as if Eve's relationship with Hart was as shaky as a pyramid of cards.

They stopped at a pub near Eve's hotel in Bristol. People were mulling about, chatting, smoking, joking, laughing loudly. The waitress wore a silver cross hanging from a chain in one ear, tight turquoise pants and a black spandex shirt. "What can I get you loves?"

"Gin and tonic, please," Graham said. Eve looked at him and they smiled at each other. The first time she'd seen him was at a party; he had been holding the same drink with a cool slice of lime in it. His choice of alcohol and his outfit—his Ralph Lauren jersey and leather backpack, the brown moccasins with no socks, so she could see the light hairs peeking out between pants and shoes—made her think 'money.' He asked, "Seem like old times?"

"Not exactly."

He grinned now, one small hand, half-covered by his wool sweater, cupping his head. "I enjoyed listening to your paper."

"Thanks."

"Umm," he said, while sipping his gin, then, "what does your husband . . . I'm sorry, what's his name?"

"Hart," she said, quietly.

"What does Hart think about your being here sans lui?"

"That's not such a great topic of conversation. Let's stick to work."

"Okay," he said, his mustache wet from his drink. She had the urge to lick it.

When she'd finished recounting the last encounter she'd had with Professor Forster, he took her hand in his and said, "Oh, E. J.," (he was the only person who'd ever called her by this nickname), "That's horrible. She screwed you royally. You did the right thing coming here to speak with Wellington. I took a class with him once; he's a nice guy. Just be super prepared for your meeting."

"Right," she said, as a knot of anxiety tightened just above her collar bone.

At the hotel, he walked her to her room. She actually invited him in. They both avoided looking at the bed but, he touched her lightly, on the back of her neck, then ran his hand down the slope of her ribs into her waist.

"Stop," she said, "I can't." Eve walked away from the bed, purposely; his body smelled too familiar. "Things aren't working out the way they're supposed to, right now, that's all."

"E. J. you're not just talking about the thesis." He followed her, and she thought of what it used to feel like between them, the combination of lust and competition.

"It's that . . . and other things. I have other people to consider."

"What things?" he said, his breath on her mouth. Graham ran his hand through his hair. "You want your old life back, I can tell."

Eve kissed him; his lips were so light and his breath clean and slightly sweet, like tonic water. It amazed Eve how she could compare the shape and pressure of his mouth on hers to Hart's, the sheer otherness of Graham ignited something so illicit inside of her. If he had asked, if he had tried to seduce, he might have had her. She let him put his hand under her shirt, on her breast. For a moment, it was all she desired: to stop thinking and yearning and working so hard. But, then, she pictured Hart, lying on the couch with their daughter asleep on his chest; she knew that, if she didn't stop herself this time, she'd lose everything. "There's only so much I can ask him to forgive me for," she thought and backed away.

He looked at Eve and smiled his sweet, slow smile, the crinkles at the edge of his eyes more noticeable. They were both remembering a familiar battle:

"You can't really believe that Rabbit is man's idea of a hero, can you?" Eve asked. "Have we really sunk that low?"

"He's one of us: ordinary folk. But even Lancelot was cheating on his King. The most noble characters are not only boring, they're not realistic. They lack passion."

"I don't agree," she insisted. "If you aim so low, where are we as a civilization? You have to set high standards for people." Eve would never relent.

"Why?" He looked up at her and grinned. "So they can fall from grace?"

Now, without saying a word, he walked to the door in his cream-colored, wool sweater, his beige jacket resting in his arms.

The last thing Eve said to Graham was: "It's amazing how I've always held other people's characters to such a high standard, yet required so little of my own."

The dawn was awash with fog. Eve had rarely experienced this sort of dense, cloudy gray, the kind that hides objects only inches from your line of sight. Later, she knew, there would be an icy rain—maybe hail—and pale, polite Londoners rushing from the streets to their cars, buses, or to the Underground. She wished she had the energy to dash out to the corner shop, to load up with whatever appeared half-way edible, then to return to the room, pack up her lap top and her mountainous notes and head for the airport. But, as it was, she hadn't moved from her bed for two days. Not since she'd called Hart—right after her close call with Graham—and told him she was coming home. "Don't bother," he'd said and hung up. All she'd eaten—as far as she could remember—was what was left of a box of crackers. She'd been dozing on and off. A few times she'd attempted to watch television; but the reception was terrible and the British accents depressed her. "This is not your country," their voices seemed to say.

The morning was so raw and the hotel so badly heated that Eve lay shivering under the one thin blanket, wondering what had happened to turn London into her penitentiary. She'd been to the city with Graham, but that had been in summer. A wholly different thing. And, of course, back in that other life, she'd been spared the image of Gemma's dark, round face. Now, Eve made a peculiar noise: something between a sigh and a squeak. The sound triggered a memory of her mother and, she wondered which magazines Maxie's wide, fake smile was captured in this month. "I miss my baby," she said aloud, just to hear a human voice; then, she rolled over slowly, every molecule in her body exhausted from the effort of movement.

Eve was studying the ceiling when he knocked. The picture of her daughter with her arms extended vanished as she opened her eyes. For a moment, she figured she'd imagined the tapping on her door. Then, it happened again. Since she was staying in a third-rate place, she doubted that an employee of the hotel had any services to offer her. And if there was a message—a phone call she'd missed—wouldn't they just ring her room? A chill raced up and down her arms. Something had to be wrong for anyone to break into her seclusion.

"Yes?" she said in a thick voice.

For a second, there was no answer. Then, "Eve?"

Stunned, she reached out as if there was another body in the bed who could offer her support. "Hart? Is it you?"

"Yes. . . . It's me."

Without noticing that she was merely wearing a dirty tee-shirt and underpants, Eve flung open the door so that she was in full view. But, the only person standing in the hall—astonishingly enough—was her husband.

At first, her relief must have been what a drowning person feels after being yanked out of the water. Once she's done gasping for breath, she can begin to anticipate that moment when living will revert to being a habit. But, then Eve noticed the terrible sadness in Hart's eyes. She squeaked, "Where's Gemma?" just before her knees buckled. Hart lifted his wife easily—as if she were light as a cat—whispering in a gruff voice, "She's fine. She's home with your mother. God, when was the last time you had a meal?"

Then, when Eve was back in the cocoon of her bed, he said, "Henrietta died yesterday morning, suddenly, from a heart attack." Eve began shaking both from the impact of his words and the fact that, while she'd been lying in bed, 3000 miles away, her husband had picked up the telephone to the sound of her mother's voice, cracked with grief.

Hart had flown to England to retrieve her. No one believed that she would have returned otherwise. Hart cried out of a combination of rage and relief from having the burden—the knowledge of Henrietta's death—removed from him. But Eve's tears were disconnected from her, incidental as rain; she was a plaster-of-paris sculpture of herself.

The plane was scheduled for evening, the funeral, the next day. It was amazing how little there was to pack.

Eve couldn't grasp that she'd never see Henrietta again or talk to her grandmother about everything she revealed in her last letter. Her last letter. Eve thought about how her grandmother had tucked away all her longing so neatly, as if it were possible to fold desire into a hatbox or the toes of one's shoe. And, she thought: now, she would never be able to ask Henrietta how—for all those long years—she'd managed that trick.

"She was vexed beyond what could have been expressed—
almost beyond what she could conceal. Never had she felt so
agitated, mortified, grieved, at any circumstance in her life. She
was most forcibly struck. The truth of his representation there
was no denying. She felt it in her heart. How could she have been
so brutal, so cruel . . . . How could she have exposed herself to
such ill opinion in any one she valued!   —*Emma*

AS A GIRL, Eve had spent every Christmas day with her
Grandma Henrietta and Grandpa Isaac. When they lived on
East 78th Street, they'd serve duck in orange sauce off of
blue and white china with pictures of the American
Revolution painted on them. Because the family was
Jewish, the gifts—gorgeous in their silver and red wrapping—would be neatly piled under the baby grand piano
rather than under a tree. The smell of the duck mingled in
the air with Henrietta's lavender perfume and the rich odor
of chestnuts which Uncle Bernie pretended to hide, tucked
into his fur-lined jacket. Aunt Hannah's first words, after
greeting everyone, were always, "You know I'm hopeless in
the kitchen." And she'd hand Henrietta a bakery box of
Christmas cookies, part sugar with red and green sprinkles,
part yellow half-moons with chocolate melted on each
corner. The Goodman's hypocrisy was blatant: they
embraced Christmas, and winced when—once a year, on
the High Holidays—they entered a temple to hear a sermon
spoken in a language they didn't understand.

Gemma's first Christmas was nothing like Eve's had
been. Two days before, Grandma Henrietta was buried in
the frozen earth while the family watched. Maxine, pale and
grim, helped Uncle Bernie to steady tiny Aunt Hannah.
Shivering in her black knit coat and veiled hat, Hannah
witnessed her sister being lowered into the ground, an old
woman's confusion stealing the light from her now glassy,

nearly colorless eyes. Grandpa Isaac stood between his two granddaughters, looking brittle as a twig figure. His long, pale, weather-beaten face was down-turned, his hand, thick as a cow's tongue, alternated between squeezing Eve's and shaking in her grasp.

Her father spoke so softly that the words made no sense to Eve; the faces of her family members appeared fuzzy. At her funeral, Grandma Henrietta had finally become a Jew. The same rabbi who'd married Eve conducted the services and, at Maxie's house, no pork would be served. No one mentioned that Christmas was only three days away. "I love you Bĕe. I'm sorry," Eve addressed Gemma, silently, watching as her daughter's sweet berry breath came in even measures, asleep and protected as she was in Hart's arms.

During the burial, Gemma wailed from the shock of the cold; Hart and Eve were the first to leave. The air was ash colored and heavy with impending rain. Sober and blurry-eyed, in his rumpled navy suit, Hart drove slower than usual to the Sterlings'. "Listen," Eve began, but was too dispirited to continue: *listen, I'm so sorry, I love you, please, please, if you can't forgive me, give me a second chance.*

When they pulled into the driveway, the first drizzle leaked sadly out of the sky. A storm was coming. "Hart," Eve said, staring ahead as the water hit the windshield and ricocheted off. "I don't think I can go in. I can't face my mother right now."

Hart raised his eyebrows into a sharp triangle, then shrugged. "Do what you want."

Eve stared at the weeping willow on the front lawn to her childhood home, its top-heavy body arched over from the burden of branches. The slam of the car door echoed inside the old Dodge. She shut her eyes to ward off the flood of sorrow, and rocked slightly, trying to intellectually catalogue all she was grieving for.

At some point, she heard a knock; it was her father. She rolled down the window, but couldn't bear to look up. "Please come in, Eve. You have to come in now." His voice was both a plea and a reprimand. She did as she was told, feeling humbled next to her father's distress.

The house smelled of rug cleaner, roses, and pot roast. Eve's instinct was to duck into the front bathroom, but Olivia was guarding the entranceway like Charon waiting to ferry her down the river. "God," her sister said, arms crossed, eyes narrow, "you look like a Holocaust survivor, Eve. I heard the food in England was bad, but not *that* bad." When Eve just stood still, eyes focused on their parents' plush carpeting, Olivia's whole face became a frown. "You could thank me, you know."

"For what?" Eve asked, flatly.

"Who do you think was taking care of Gemma while you were off on your European jaunt?"

"Who? *You?*" Disbelief washed over Eve, another shock. That's when she realized what her fantasy had been: her mother tossing aside everything to tend to her granddaughter. Self-delusion was a hard vice to outwit. "Why?"

"Mom *paid* me to be your nanny. Out of guilt." Olivia smiled, eyes scornful. "So, it looks like I'm out of yet another job. Until law school next year, hopefully. I have to admit I'll miss that little cutie."

Another jab. Was it possible that her sister—with her newfound ambition and nomadic yearnings—was a better mother than she?

"Hi." It was Maxie: eyes red-rimmed and skin puffy, grayish as if deprived of sufficient oxygen. Eve felt like Jonah swallowed by the whale. "We need to talk, Evie." An old woman, a friend of Henrietta's, tapped Maxie on the shoulder, who spun around, all sad smiles, and crooned, "Ida, dear. How are you? I know, I know, it's an awful day for all of us."

Eve managed to slip away.

"I understand why you did what you did," Olivia said, as she grabbed her sister's arm. "I wanted to tell you that I'm barely speaking to Mom, that I'm on your side." When Eve didn't respond, Olivia shrugged. "It surprised me, but taking care of your daughter made me realize that I'd like to have a Gemma of my own someday."

"She envies me," Eve thought. "What chamber of my slow-witted mind finally grasped this concept? Like Emma

237

Woodhouse, I am truly clueless." But where was Ms. Austen, when you needed her, to sculpt the perfect solution to the heroine's problem?

"Call me if you need to talk. And really—not to sound like Mom—but if you don't start eating again, you're going to get sick."

In the car going home, Eve gathered all her resources to whisper, "Do you want a divorce, Hart?" She envisioned herself, seated at the desk in London, her Jane Austen notes before her, feeling terribly lonely and disoriented, desperate for her husband. But, if Wellington had responded more enthusiastically—if he'd even acknowledged the paper she'd sent him—would she still regret her trip to England?

"What do you want me to say?" He sounded almost menacing, reminding Eve of how he used to imitate Darth Vader, back when they still knew how to joke.

Since arriving home, her own voice had taken on the breathiness of a ghost, of someone permanently gone. "Just what you want to do."

"No. No, you *don't."*

Eve's tear ducts were on overdrive; she figured she'd be crying on and off for months, maybe years, until she was emptied of all feeling. "I just want to know what you're planning to do, Hart."

"Planning. I'm not *planning* anything. I think I'll just act as I feel, be spontaneous." Still, he would not look at her. "You should know about *that."*

"What I did was completely selfish. But, I wasn't gone that long, not irreparably long, was I? Can't we. . . ."

"This isn't about how long you were gone; it's about your intentions."

Eve wiggled the heel of her black pumps, then slipped off her shoes; her feet were aching as much as her heart. She wanted to ask: do you think we'll ever be okay? Will you ever forgive me? But her fear was greater than her longing. And she was just too tired to talk anymore; it was as if a virus had seeped into the most intimate part of her: the very marrow of her bones.

For the rest of the ride home, they listened to Gemma's breathing and the mournful dancing of the rain on the windshield.

The holiday season was upon them. Eve's insights on Jane Austen lay frayed in her desk drawer. She imagined her unfinished dissertation, a mound of chipped yellow paper, packed away in an attic to be discovered by Gemma's great granddaughter, a successful scholar. In the meantime, she bowed her head to Ms. Austen as she suffered through her life, nothing like a comedy of manners, and badly lacking the author's brilliant wit.

On December 24th, Eve received two cards: one from Dee and one from Graham. Dee's card was a photograph of a red bowl with sprigs of holly in it. She had written: "I'm so sorry about your grandmother, but I'm glad you're home. I miss you. Love, Glassman." It filled Eve with remorse. She thought of her old friend: her sharp green eyes ringed with feathery lines, her yellow-stained fingertips, her face encircled in cigarette smoke. Eve hadn't found the courage to call her from London; she vowed, now, that she would phone her after the first of the year.

She took the card from Graham as it was meant to be: a brag, a peacock preening. The outside was a drawing of a pastel blue dove with a pink rose in his mouth but, when Eve opened it, an announcement for his book fell out; it was called: *An American Vision: Cheever Country,* which told her nothing about theme or substance but everything she needed to know. More important than Graham being her former lover, he was now officially a success. Eve waited to rev up inside, like an old car waiting for its engine to catch, so it could take off. Despite all that had happened—the alienation from her husband and mother, the death of her grandmother—her hunger for accomplishment still needed to be fed. Like a beast, it was relentless in its appetite.

Christmas morning was dank. The landlady had refused to insulate the windows, pleading poverty and, now, a frosty wind sneaked in through every available crack. Even in her sweatsuit and woolly socks, Eve was cold. "This place is a dump," she murmured over her morning coffee.

She bit into an apricot scone with raspberry jelly, the special treats she'd bought for the holidays. But the fruit tasted dull, the dough heavy. She put it down, unable to eat. Before the thoughts could form in her mind, they were out of her mouth, "Maybe we should move."

Hart stared at the soft globe of his fried egg; he didn't pick up his fork. Eve could practically hear his heart racing as he sat perfectly still. "Good timing" was all he said.

"I just thought we could . . . start over." She drew in her breath. "Maybe what I did was truly unforgivable. But you did things, too. You lied to me about the money and hid what was happening to your work. I'm not saying this is your fault. Of course, I'm *not*. But couldn't we start over, fresh?"

Hart stood up, kicking the chair back into the table. "I'm going to check on Gemma, it's not like her to sleep so late."

Eve followed her husband into her daughter's room. "Please talk to me, Hart," she pleaded with his back.

He whipped around, startlingly fast. "Ssssh," he demanded, causing Eve to gasp and stumble backwards, hitting her head on the door frame. When she yelped in pain, Hart grabbed her by the upper arm and pulled her out of the room. "You will not screw up my daughter any further with your *narcissism* and *angst*."

Eve ran to her bedroom and locked herself in. For a long time, she lay on top of the blankets and traced the veins in the ceiling with her eyes. Finally, she dozed, staccato images flashing in and out of her mind: herself walking down a narrow street, suddenly turning into Jane Austen, hurrying and laughing, with a manuscript in her hand. But, then the dream zeroed in on the book, suddenly opened to reveal the author's inscrutably elegant handwriting: "No one who had ever seen Eve Sterling would have supposed her born to be an heroine. Nobody has even found it possible to *like* Eve." Then she awoke, awash with grief.

The phone rang and, she heard her husband's voice; muffled by the door between them, it sounded serene, rippling like lake water. Finally, he knocked on the bedroom door. "It's Annie," he said in a wholly different tone.

"It's so *good* that you're home," her friend exclaimed. "I know this is last minute, but, can you come into the city today? We can really talk and you can meet Sage."

"Yes, oh, yes. I have to meet Sage! Let's have lunch out, just like old times."

There was almost no light coming from the window on this grim afternoon and The Metro Cafe felt warm and protective as Eve imagined a cocoon might be. A secret place where your heartbeat slowed down. Annie had arrived earlier and ordered a chocolate croissant and coffee; she looked thinner, more angular, and wearier than Eve had ever seen her. "Just take a peek at my baby and then we can get down to business," she said, after kissing her friend's cheek.

Eve tiptoed to Sage's carriage: an elaborate blue and white number with a canopy covering the baby from dust, sun, and other carcinogens. This magnificent piece of equipment was tucked diagonally against the wood table, so close not a molecule of air could inch its way in between. The baby was extremely chubby, lying on her back, in a white parka, with one fat fist curled up under her neck. She had that beautiful black Chinese hair that looks bright as ink, and feathery black eyelashes that touched her cheekbones.

"She's beautiful, Annie, really."

"Thank you. I feel free to agree since I had nothing to do with it." She bit into a croissant and smiled. "Thank God I don't have pregnancy weight to lose. I practically starved to death in China; looks like you could say the same about the U.K. Oh, I'm so exhausted, I don't even have the energy to lecture you, much less eat healthfully. I'm planning to blimp out during these three months home with Sage. Okay. Order. Then tell me everything. About Wellington, about Hart. How's he taking you being home?"

Eve spun her wedding ring around her finger several times. "He's so angry. I've never seen him like this. He's been sleeping in the living room."

241

"You're depressed," her friend, assessed and clucked. "It'll pass."

"How cavalier."

"It *will*—not right away—but it will get better as soon as you and Hart make up." She clasped Eve's hand in a therapeutic gesture. "You know what I think? Can I tell you what I honestly think?" When her friend nodded, tentatively, she divulged her theory (not without a tinge of glee, Eve observed), "I think your deeply ambivalent feelings about Maxie pushed you into going to England. That your leaving had more to do with unfinished business with your mother, then it did with you and Hart. Maxie's developed this relationship with you where you both expect her to rescue you. So, when she discussed your problems on T. V., it violated that relationship."

She glared at Annie as if seeing the arrogance glittering in her cool blue eyes for the first time. "Christ, Annie, what's with all this free psychoanalysis? My fucked-up problems with my mother are not why I went to England. I went there to revive my dying career."

Annie smiled in that encouraging way: helping the patient to make the correct connections. "Just like my mother," Eve thought. "Well, of course. But, don't you think your rage over your dependence on Maxie propelled you there?"

"Has motherhood made you so desperate for work, you need to take *me* on as a patient? And, after you had us all fooled that having a baby was the most important thing in your life . . . ." Instantly, she sunk her head in her hands. "Shit, I'm sorry."

"It's okay," her friend said, all cockiness gone. "You're right, I got carried away. I'm sorry for what I said, too." In a firm voice, she added, "But, you're *wrong* about me. Being a mother *is* the most important thing in my life."

Tit for tat.

"I guess I should tell you," Annie said, gazing down at her paper napkin, once the exaggerated effort of settling in was exhausted by them both. "Your mother is going to show up in less than half an hour."

A fly had landed on the table and the sound of him rubbing his wings together seemed horribly magnified. "What?"

"Look, Eve, I made a mistake." She lay her palms open on the table. "I definitely did the wrong thing, here. But Maxie has called me several times since you've gotten home. She's so broken up over your grandmother's death. And, I think she figured the money would help ease things for you, help make amends."

"What money?"

"Oh, I thought you knew! I should just let her tell you herself."

Eve stood up. "I'm leaving."

"Please don't go," Annie covered her face with her hands. "Try to understand, Maxie was the only one who helped me deal with things. She even helped me figure out how to get Sage. Just stay and talk. . . ."

Eve felt the tears, sharp as bee stings under her eyes, and thought how allegiances had changed.

The apartment was warm, with an amber glow coming from two torch lights in the front room that Hart had splurged on the weekend after he'd gotten his job offer. While Eve was away. They gave their home such a rich secure feeling, as if the walls were cradling one another, excluding Eve from their embrace. Hart was in the kitchen making himself dinner and whistling, actually whistling. As soon as he saw Eve standing in the dining room, he stopped. Gemma was strapped in the snugli to his chest, her long legs dangling out the sides like a beetle's from its shell. This practice of cooking with their daughter in such close proximity to the fire was something she'd forbidden. But Eve's credibility was gone now.

"Hi. What're you making?"

"Stew," he grumbled. "Beef stew."

Another surprise. She had never seen her husband prepare or eat such a thing. "Really?" she asked and sat down on one of the pine chairs whose beige cushions had been stained from cranberry juice and baby formula. Hart said nothing, but kept stirring, the smell of tomato sauce, onion, and meat wafting through the air, deliciously.

Eve rubbed between her eyebrows from where the headache would originate. "Hart, I want to work on our marriage, to make things better. . . ."

His back stiffened, and when he turned to her, his eyes were as devoid of light as stones. "Really? *Good for you.* What did you think would happen when you came home, that is, if you were even planning to come home? If I hadn't gone and fetched you, if your grandmother hadn't died. . . . Do you think I'd feel all cuddly towards you because you were gracious enough to return for Henrietta's funeral?"

A shiver ran through Eve, and her headache was in full force now. "No, but it seems as if you'd given up on us," she dared to say because there was no point skirting the issue.

Her husband said nothing, and the silence was enervating. Finally, she stood up. "Is there anything I can do to make you less angry?"

"Why? So you can leave at any moment, when the whim hits you, when your angst gets to be too much? Who are we, Gemma and I, to compete with your own private angst?"

"I've learned my lesson," Eve said, beseechingly. "You and Gemma are the most important things to me."

Hart walked back into the kitchen and began ladling out stew into blue ceramic bowls, wedding presents. And, Eve noted how, even now, hurt and betrayed, her husband was still nurturing her, unconsciously perhaps, but there it was: his true character. Suddenly, she realized that the words she'd been saying *were* true: she loved him, she *was* sorry. Couldn't her desire to be in London, waiting for her own life to begin again, co-exist with this love? "What if I promise to make it up to you? What if I could show you how devoted I can be?"

Hart glanced up at her, his face clear of cynicism or rage for the first time since she'd arrived home. He shrugged. "Then, we'll see," he said, just as the phone rung.

There was a feeble cough chugging its way through the wire and into the receiver.

"Eve, the lawyer will finalize it in the next few weeks," her father said, stiff, reproachful. "But I thought it might help ease tensions at home," he coughed again, cleared his throat, then added, "after your . . . I don't know what to call it . . . escapade. Anyway, Henrietta left a good deal of money to your mother which I was more than happy for us to keep. But, your mother insisted I divide it between you and your sister. It seems Olivia needs tuition for law school and, well, Mom thought it would help out you and Hart. It's not a million dollars, but it should be enough to get you back on your feet."

As her father spoke, in a low monotone, Eve imagined a dollar sign hanging in the air, more inviting than mistletoe. She wished she could kiss Hart, but he'd already retreated to the kitchen. She would offer the gift to him as a sign of faith, of trust in their marriage. She thought of how money should be bottled, like perfume, to be dabbed behind the knees and on the wrists, alluring and haunting. Bewitching as a ghost.

On New Year's Day, Annie's prayers were answered. Her period was a week late, enough time to pull out the little plastic beaker from its box with the hopeful-looking woman on it, and test her fate. In the blue five a. m. light, she stood on the cold ceramic tile of her Riverside Drive bathroom, in bare feet, and waited. She stared at the vial with such intensity, it was as if she believed she could will the liquid inside to turn pink just from the power emanating from her eyes.

She relayed this information to Eve so early that the sun was still slowly presenting itself, proud as a diva in the sky. The phone call woke Eve from a profound slumber and a thought flew into her mind, "Hart's got a divorce lawyer." But the voice on the phone was giddy with joy; "Arthur doesn't even know yet. Eve, you're not going to believe this. . . . I'm really pregnant. That crazy phone psychic was right. I did the test five minutes ago," she said, her words light as gauze sighing on a clothesline. "I haven't even told Arthur yet. Isn't this crazy—when we have an infant asleep in the next room! Two babies at once!"

Eyes still closed, Eve smiled, savoring the old, delicious conspiracy of friendship. "Thank you for telling me about the baby first. I have a secret for you, too. But, what I'm about to tell you can't go any further, okay?" She rolled over on her side and cradled the phone under her arm, the way she had with Gemma in those first weeks when her daughter was a fragile sparrow, her mouth always open. Next to her, the sound of Hart's breathing eased gently in and out.

"What is it? Good news I hope!"

"I'm thinking of using Henrietta's money for a down payment on a house. It's my idea, but it's for Hart's sake. He actually seems to be enjoying his new job, although he won't tell me about it. But, I'm hoping that if we actually put down roots, he'll stop worrying that I'll just pack up and leave again."

"Oh, Eve! You've finally come to your senses and given up on the fantasy of moving to Broken Arrow, Oklahoma?"

"I guess," she laughed, slightly hysterical. "I'll have to settle for teaching Jane Austen to plumbers at the local YMCA. At least my job at Armour and Lace is still there for me if I want it."

Just the previous day, she'd stopped into the shop to discover that so much sorrow can happen in the world in one month's time. Jo was more biting than ever: "Nice of you to drop by," she'd said, "What are you trying for the Kate Moss look, anorexic heroin addict?"

"Hey, ease up on the compliments."

"You'd be a bitch, too, if your husband was shacking up with Oksana Biaol. Yep, a week ago Saturday. Richard took me out to dinner and, between the coconut soup and the Pad Thai, confessed that he'd met a graduate student in Russian Literature and was planning to move in with the little bitch."

Eve shook her head, up and down, open-mouthed.

Jo looked her up and down, and asked, "Have you gone truly bonkers? Because, you look a bit touched. Well, I hope not. Because I could really use a partner, someone invested in the store, right now." She touched Eve lightly on the arm, and added, "Don't leave Hart, again, unless you're absolutely sure you never want him back. Fuck the clichés. It's not possible to repair your marriage when one person commits an unspeakably selfish act."

In Jane Austen's novels there is always closure: intricately embroidered pillows, they are completed when one last stitch ensures that none of the solid stuffing will sneak through the tightly sewn threads. In life, of course, there is no closure except for death; but Eve thought otherwise when she saw the house on Ferelly Road. She prayed this was the answer, the first step to repairing her marriage.

White mist spun through the sky like apparitions, traipsing their long, lanky, disproportionate bodies from telephone poles to housetops, from storefronts to street lights. In the car, Eve held her breath as if speech would cause the mist to dissipate, leaving them with another bleak, stone-gray winter afternoon: a reflection of her marriage. Houses—rambling and boxy, neatly manicured and overrun by weeds, wide-eyed windows madeup with pink and lavender shutters—passed before her eyes, in rapid succession. Each one struck her as more enticingy than the last. When Hart parked outside the home they were scheduled to see, she gasped without a second thought, "I love it."

The wind smacked Eve as she rose from the car, and she wound her scarf around her head like an old Russian woman. "Winter is going to be unbelievably awful this year," she said. Her husband hugged his daughter to his chest, but allowed Eve to huddle with him, momentarily, against the shivering chill.

The house was eighty-three years old and three stories high; it had sloping ceilings on the top floor, four cramped bedrooms, and a wood staircase that creaked in two places. "The refrigerator looks as if it's about to celebrate *its* eightieth birthday," Hart complained.

Afterwards, they sat in the car in anticipatory silence. Finally Eve said, quietly, "You could convert the basement into a darkroom and I could have my own office. I'd work on the top floor and be able to look out on a backyard with a deck."

"That's a nice thought, but as you may not have noticed, I'm too busy with my job and Gemma to take photographs. And, as important as your dissertation is, I don't think we should make a decision on a house merely to accommodate it."

Eve peered at her feet as if they had the most interesting story to tell. "You're right. Anyway, I've been thinking of giving it up and working at the store full-time."

Hart looked askance and snorted. "That's absurd. I know you too well. You'd never give up on anything you really want."

Eve glanced up into her husband's face, but was unable to determine if he'd just flung an insult at her or complimented her on her tenacity. It was her single-mindedness, the one thing she was trying desperately to change about herself, her old badge of honor, which she knew both attracted and repelled him.

Staring straight out the windshield at a patch of sunlight hatching from a cloud, he said, "Tell me what happened with Wellington."

There was no malice in Hart's voice, so Eve exhaled slowly. "There is nothing really to tell. He didn't even contact me about the paper I sent him."

Hart shrugged. "He was probably busy with his own book and his teaching duties and just fell behind. You have to remember, Eve, that the relationship is totally unbalanced. The man doesn't even know you yet. Just write him and explain why you had to leave, why you couldn't meet him. Death in the family. He can't fault you for that."

Suddenly, the very mechanism of breathing startled her; Hart was interested in her again! Of course, it would be lunacy to think all was forgiven. Still, Eve felt the first surge of hope since she'd been home. "And you wouldn't mind that, my working with him?"

He turned to face her, but would not make eye contact. "Why should I mind?" Out it came, like a humming wind that can whip itself into something more menacing with little warning: "What I mind is having a wife who takes off for Europe with no notice, who doesn't take marriage and family seriously enough to stick around and work through problems, even if those problems are real crises. All those nights you were away, you know what I thought? I thought: if she ever even bothers to come back, she'll never be there for Gemma and me, not if it gets too hard."

"Things felt too hard," Eve whispered.

"Well, that's the difference between us. *I* wanted to be married in the first place, so nothing has felt too hard."

"Except forgiving me."

"Maybe. Maybe, you're right."

Panic flowered in her chest, a poisonous plant. "Then, why did you agree to house-hunt?"

Finally starting the car, Hart said, "For Gemma."

That evening, she watched the sun set, a carmine ball, so beautiful, and thought: "We will begin this new year as strangers, Hart and I." Silence and anger hung between them like sullied clothes. Her husband had fallen asleep in Gemma's rocking chair, and she lay in their bed, covered by two quilts, as heavy and as tightly packed around her as the sand used to be when Olivia covered her body with it at the beach.

When she was finally exhausted enough to sleep, the house invaded her dreams. In one, her grandmother was walking from room to room with a dust cloth in her hand. She was cleaning her own country French furniture: dining room table with cushioned chairs in indigo, oak hutch with wedgwood china plates and tea cups upon it. Eve knew that hidden in one of the teacups, she kept the keys to the hutch; locked inside the left cabinet was a bowl made of carnival glass filled with saltwater taffys. When her granddaughter was a girl, Henrietta used to put the key in a cup on the highest shelf so that Eve couldn't spoil her appetite with sweets. But whenever she left the room, Eve would stand on a chair and search, frantically, in hopes of pocketing some of the chocolate and carmel ones. Henrietta almost always outsmarted her, but occasionally, Eve found the prize and dashed off to the bathroom to devour five or six taffies at a time.

The next night, her grandmother spoke to Eve in a dream. "Buy the house," she said. "The ghosts in it are from a fine family. The father was an appellate court judge; they speak five languages. They're teaching me Portuguese."

Despite his reservations, Hart agreed to make a bid. "I feel powerless to argue with ghosts. Especially ones who are financing our purchase," he said, sulking. "But, we'll have to make absolutely sure there's no structural damage, nothing major." He crossed his arms and shook his head. "It's just so old."

"But in excellent condition," she piped in, reciting the realtor's jargon. "And, what about that great extra room in the basement? It could be your darkroom. *All yours.* Gemma and I would never bother you there. And, we could even plant. How about sunflowers?" Eve had already imagined a row of them, swaying like gospel singers, their faces turned upward towards her window.

"Gardens require gardening. Remember, I'm a city boy."

"People change, evolve." She grinned.

The yellow tulips whose heads popped up each May, the wild raspberry bush, even the pine deck that overlooked the backyard, none of these cluttered up Eve's fantasy life the way that attic room did. She imagined how it would someday be, far in the future: the morning sky, a swirl of light blue and white, the birds perched on the roof next door, squawking in greeting to each other, Gemma lulled by her swing, and Eve at her desk, spinning out fine work, as if it had only been the loom that was missing and not the craftsman.

It would take months for all the paperwork to be signed and the house ready to be occupied. They would be moving during the summer. Despite the rift between them, Eve and

Hart were preparing to loop themselves more tightly together by committing this act.

"By then, Wellington will be back," she said, a rock lodged between her lungs. They were lying in bed listening, on the intercom, to Gemma breathe. Hart had finally given up the couch; but at night, when the light went out, his back became the symbol of their separation.

"And you'll go speak to him," he said, his voice low and even, stirring.

"It's just so humiliating. I tracked him down in Scotland, I schlepped to another continent, for God's sake. I asked him to do this great favor and, now, I'm not even there to meet with him."

"Eve, he doesn't care." Hart raised himself up on one elbow, his eyes glaring down at her, shining in the dark. "To be honest, he's probably relieved."

Hart stroked her lightly on the neck; it was the very first time he'd touched his wife since she'd returned home. Shocked, she lay very still to prolong this brief moment of connection. She could smell all the fragrances of his day mixed with his warm musk. "I am a sponge," he once said of his oily complexion. "I pick up the scents of the city." Now, he said, "He's a person with other obligations. He's not necessarily bad news. Not everyone is Maud."

For awhile, there was silence and Hart's breathing grew deep. "Hey," she said. "You're such a nice man."

"Too nice," he said.

"Maybe. But, I love you." Eve leaned into her husband, the old energy crackling between them like fireflies. Yearning terribly for his hands to touch her neck again, she took a risk, laying her head down on the soft underside of his arms. "Now, will you tell me about *you*, about your new job, for starters."

"Oh, well, maybe later." There was hunger in his voice; and, when he rolled over, she could feel the heat of his breath on her face. Then, he cast his arm around, like a fishing rod, reeling Eve in.

Making love, Hart was his most rigorous, as if he wanted to peel off her skin with his teeth, to get to the meat of her. Afterwards, Eve lay in bed naked, not caring that black winter was howling outside, and that the windows did not fit squarely into their frames.

Before he'd even opened his eyes the next morning, Hart said, "It's time to call your mom."

The muscles in Eve's jaw clenched so tight, she thought of Charlie McCarthy with his wooden mouth slapping open and closed. "I can't, not yet."

"She just lost her own mother." He kissed her to the sound of their daughter crying. "And, it's time to get on with our lives."

Eve rolled into the musky shelter of her husband's skin, finally feeling safe again. "Does that mean I'm forgiven?"

"I don't know. Just a little. It means we've turned a corner."

She threw her arms around her husband's chest and kissed the soft patch of his throat. "That's enough then, for now."

Letters

From the Desk of Maxine Sterling, D.S.W.

Woodmere, Long Island
Jan. 2, 1997

Dear Eve,

Grandma Henrietta left you most of her books, her framed diploma (her Masters from Columbia), and oddly, her diaries. She always said you were an offshoot of herself, the scholar. There was a note attached to one diary which read, "For Eve's personal research." There was something else, all wrapped up, so I don't know what it is. You know how my mother liked to seal things so tightly, just like you—well, I'm sending this package as well.

I'm still so sorry about what happened, and would like nothing better than for good feelings to be restored between us. You know I only want the best for you, that I always have. I just get so carried away sometimes, I end up doing the wrong thing for the right reason. Evie, I didn't mean to hurt you, I swear. But, in the meantime, I'm concerned for your family, Gemma most of all. I'd like to arrange to come and to see her soon. (I was over every weekend while you were away and I'd like to think she got attached to me).

Love,
Mom

P. S. Call and congratulate Olivia. She just received notice that she was accepted to B. U. law school, early admission.

Eve took it out of its manila envelope: a brown leather notebook, peeling at all four corners. The pages were ancient, yellowing, and delicate as moth wings, and the handwriting—in scratchy black ink—was tight and tall. But, the note clipped to the first page was in her grandmother's bold sturdy script:

"These were my mother's poems. I never talked about them (or her very much, for that matter. Maybe because I'm such an old crone, my memory started to fade with the invention of the wheel). But, she left them to me when she died and, now I'm leaving them to you, Eve Jael. One thing I do remember is that I had a joke when I was young and discovered this habit of my mother's, quite inadvertently, as she hid it from Hannah and me. (She was a proud, tight-lipped woman, my mother, even a little intimidating, if you can imagine your witch of a grandmother finding anyone intimidating!) She told me it was poetry she was "scribbling," but never a word more. I called myself "Bronte's daughter"—although, I can't for the life of me tell you why. (Maybe, I was studying Emily Bronte in school? Who the hell can stretch their mind so far back without getting a hernia.). Now, they are yours, because only you can determine their true literary worth (if that even matters). Please continue the tradition, 'Bronte's great-granddaughter.' (Or, Jane Austen's, if you prefer!)

All my love, forever, Grandma."

Finsbury Hotel
158 Gross Drury Lane
London, England
December 21, 1996

Forwarded to the U. S. A.

Dear Ms. Sterling:

As circumstances would have it, I will be remaining in Scotland for another term rather than traveling on to the University of London. I hope that this change in my plans won't inconvenience you too much. As things stand, it couldn't be helped.

I'm afraid it has taken me a long time to respond to your letters. I've been more than busy with my classes here and my book on Sarah Fielding which must be sent to my publisher before spring. But I did want to contact you, before more time passed, to let you know that I was finally able to read the paper you gave at the conference in Bristol. I must say that I was quite impressed by it. Rather than go into particulars, why don't you just send me the chapters from your thesis, that you worked on with Professor Forster, and we can go on from there.

I hope your stay in England has proved to be a relaxing break, but, that you will soon be back to work on Ms. Austen. I look forward to reading your thesis and expect to help you complete a successful study. You write with much clarity—and passion, I might add.

Sincerely,
Gray Wellington

"Marianne Dashwood was born to an extraordinary fate. She was born to discover the falsehood of her own opinions, and to counteract by her conduct her most favourite maxims."

—Sense and Sensibility

PUSHED BY THE wind from the ceiling fans, the prehistoric-looking palm trees swayed as sensuously as Hawaiian dancers. The soft swoosh of the fans was the only perceptible noise in Ramona's, that and the few muted sounds of people working in the kitchen. Eve had arrived early, on this glorious April day, having woken up to find the sky a surprisingly clear cornflower blue, so crisp she thought that the Maine sky had travelled south overnight. They packed a tired Gemma into the car with her bottle bag stuffed with toys, leaving out her tape recorder with her favorite Neil Young tape inserted. Right after Hart buckled her in, Gemma's eyes flew open; she grabbed the red plastic mike attached to the white and green machine with the words *Fisher Price* painted on it. "My toy!" she exclaimed. It was her first sentence.

Eve gasped, "She's a genius!"

Gemma squealed with delight. "My toy! 'emma's!" she repeated.

"She's your daughter all right," Hart laughed.

"There are worse fates than a sense of entitlement," Eve said after slapping her husband lightly on the arm.

"I never thought any differently," he answered. "Look where it's gotten you."

Ramona's was bathed in a golden sunlight, the mural of the dancers half-shadowed, revealing only splotches of brilliant color. But Eve knew what they'd see when the restaurant's lights came on: dark shirtless men with their buxom partners in billowing multi-colored dresses. The painter had created a brilliant juxtaposition: this one moment of exuberant motion captured in the still, never-changing group of images.

"Do you think I can pull this off?" she asked Hart, who was attempting to waltz with a giggling Gemma in his arms.

"Sure," he said, mid-swirl. "What's to pull off?"

She thought for a moment, then said, "Appearing gracious. Not acting angry at my mother. It's not as if she wants us to move into the house; I thought she'd go down fighting."

"Let's face it, the real reason she's giving this shindig isn't to celebrate our buying the house. It's to beg for your forgiveness. I have to tell you Eve, I never would have thought you could go this long without talking to your mom. But it's time to start."

"Maybe," Eve said, rubbing her thumb so hard against the index finger of her other hand that it turned a purplish red. "But a public reconciliation, I don't think so."

"Don't sweat it," Hart said, slowing down his dance and kissing his wife on the cheek. "Your mom will be busy working the crowd. You'll deal with her after the party."

"Can I do it? Can I forgive her, Hart?"

"I forgave you, didn't I?"

"I don't know. Did you?"

"Whatever residue of anger there is will fade. It's fading even as we dance."

Annie, Arthur, and Sage Louise were the first to arrive. Annie's face was bloated and so pale it was nearly translucent, a thin blue vein on either side of her nose suddenly standing out, like river markings on a map. In the second trimester of her pregnancy, a tiny belly was starting to emerge, poking out from her navy smock dress.

"I feel like Beulah the Whale," she said by way of greeting and fidgeted with the matching headband, trying to push back her bangs.

"You're a vision of loveliness," Hart said. He planted a quick kiss on her cheek.

A sacked-out Sage dangled—arms around her father's neck, open-mouthed—on his chest. "It's a boy," Arthur blurted out into his daughter's perfect hair.

"We just got the test results back yesterday," Annie said.

"Henry," Arthur said. "He's going to be named Henry, after my grandfather."

Eve hugged her friend and said, "Oh, I'm so happy for you. Let me get a good look at that little pumpkin."

Olivia showed up next, in a smart pea-green dress that complimented her eyes. She had changed her hair; it curled softly around her ears and had returned to her natural chestnut color. The usual look of exasperation was missing from her face but when she smiled "hello," she still did so with the caution of one raised as royalty to keep her guard up. "How much money do you think she blew on this?" she whispered to Eve. Still competing.

"Quite a lot, I imagine."

"And has it worked? Is all forgiven?" Eve shrugged and her sister said, "Your daughter seems to have exonerated you. Oh, let me pick her up." Olivia cooed, "Aunt Livy. Remember me? I'm your Aunt Livy." She touched her nose to Gemma's and suddenly her face relaxed and a wide smile burst forth. "You know who she looks like? I'll tell you who she looks like! It's so obvious, I can't believe you haven't noticed! She looks *exactly* like me!"

Spontaneously, Eve kissed her sister quickly on the cheek. "Thank you for being her surrogate mother while I flipped out."

Olivia blanched, then smiled. "It's okay. I wanted to. I liked it. Mom didn't even have to bribe me, in her usual intrusive way."

Maxie's "few" friends appeared in a flock: nurses, secretaries and other social workers from the hospital, Adrienne and her assistant from *Mornings with Maxie*, then couples she'd known for twenty years, colleagues of Daniel's with their spouses transformed from doctors' wives into speech therapists and art teachers. Uncle Bernie and Aunt Hannah pulled up in a cab; dwarfed and frail in coats that were now too big for their shrinking bodies, they leaned on each other for support.

"That's us in sixty years," Hart whispered. "Let's hope." He then rushed out the door of Ramona's to help them navigate their way.

Surprisingly, two weeks before, Hart had hinted that they should invite his parents, and Eve had relented. They showed up early, of course, decked out in their finest: Manny in a cobalt-blue silk shirt and alligator shoes; Norma in Halloween colors: a black leather mini, tied tightly at the waist with a wide orange belt. "Good to see you, Sonny," Manny exclaimed, sounding sincerely happy. A couple of months ago, he had sent Hart a note in which he asked, "We haven't heard from you since Gemma was born. What went wrong, Sonny boy?" Preoccupied with the disaster of his own life, Hart hadn't bothered to answer. Now, he shook his father's hand and even smiled as his mother clutched him to her chest, teary-eyed. For the first time, Eve faced the Orbachs without anger. That they were small-minded and narcissistic, that they had loved Hart selfishly, and without concern for his essential self, struck her as sad in an oddly nostalgic way. But their deficits no longer posed a threat. For here stood her husband: smiling his off-center smile, flecks of green and yellow sparkling in his deep brown eyes.

Dee actually showed up to an event early. She looked lovely in a twenties-style dress: champagne-colored, spaghetti straps holding it up, fringes swinging just above her knees. Her hair was longer than ever; it hung halfway down her back, black, but now laced with strands of gray. She approached Eve, eyes squinting as if keeping them open was too tiring. "Hi there, Sterling," she said in her muted, gruff voice. Eve expected her to make a crack about her "little overseas junket." But she didn't. She said, "Thanks for inviting me. It's great to see you."

"It's great to see you, too. Listen, thank you so much for your letter. I wrote you back but—I was in a state—and never mailed it."

259

"Don't worry about it."

"So . . . how's the new man in your life? I heard he works for *Newsweek.*"

"Right," she said. "Come and gone. Don't forget you were out of town for an extensive stay. My love life can be measured in thirty-second sound bytes."

"Oh, I'm sorry."

She shrugged, and smiled. "Don't be. I'm grazing on greener pastures."

"And, the work . . . ."

"The work is going better than I ever expected. My poetry book, *Myths of Love,* is coming out in the summer. I'm renting a loft in Soho and having a huge bash. You and Hart are invited. And what about you, Sterling?" She shifted all her weight from one high-heeled pump to the other. "I heard you are considering returning to the life of erudition and back-stabbing."

"Thinking of it. Wellington contacted me. He really liked my work." Eve grinned. She deemed that thirteen years of scholarly ambitions wouldn't just evaporate into the air, that Jane Austen had reared her perfect head once again. "But, we bought a house. Obviously, you know that, because you're here." She spoke deliberately, careful not to reveal too much; it would take time before Eve and Dee could reveal their lives easily again, like crisp new books opened wide until their spines nearly snapped. "After the dissertation, I'll just have to see. We're not moving so fast for any one job."

"Yeah, well, it's great to see you've relaxed enough to get off that unbending track you've been on your whole life. You'll figure it out. You're an ambitious woman." They smiled at each other, and Eve noticed the lines etched into the crevices around Dee's lips. They flattered her, making her look wiser and earthier; all she needed now to be truly beautiful was a white streak in her hair, flaunted as a emblem of courage. Dee motioned to Hart who was lifting a laughing Gemma into the air. "Anyway, look at all you have."

"Yes, I'm so lucky."

"You know, that's the first time I've ever heard you say that."

"Well, the cliché is true: you don't know what you have until it's almost gone."

Dee touched her friend's hand. "Sounds like you've discovered you had the power to return to Kansas all along. Isn't enlightenment grand? Certainly must be better than spending your birthdays alone, grading those ridiculous papers. Shit, Sterling, you used to live as if you were doing penance for some crime against God."

"No. It's like you said," Eve smiled, "I'm ambitious. Just like you."

The noise level in the room rose, like a firecracker ascending and then bursting in the air. Maxie had arrived. Her mouth opened in a surprised O, as if she were about to scream, as if she hadn't arranged the event and orchestrated her late entrance to get the appropriate attention. Tears welled in her eyes; she raised her hand to her cheek. Applause filled the restaurant; it sounded momentous, the thunderclap at the end of an opera.

Eve felt a warm hand on her shoulder. "You'll forgive her . . ." Hart whispered and the tiny hairs on the back of her neck tingled. "Now that you're really starting your own life."

"I hope so. I hope you're right," she whispered back, then shook her head and laughed, "God, just look at my mom."

Eve felt as if her heart had cracked open, a pomegranate revealing its luscious red juice. Even with all the people between them, she could discern how her mother's eyes shone in gladness at the sight of her daughter. As if she, too, sensed the drama stamped into her heritage, Gemma unleashed a loud squeal. Hart lifted her into Eve's arms, embracing his wife as he did. And, for one brief moment, they created a nearly perfect circle.

Epilogue
1998

"I hope when you have written a great deal more you will be equal to scratching out some of the past."
> —Jane Austen in a letter to her niece, Anna

IN THE DREAM, it was Grandma Henrietta's talk show—*Bronte's Daughter*—and the set had been refashioned to include a mess of flowery lilac and pink material. There was a lot of commotion from the audience before her big entrance: leg stomping and clapping as if the hostess were a Christian healer in some backwoods southern town. When she finally emerged, her spirit was a lustrous golden color and a gauzy texture; she was laughing as she tried to get her slippered feet to touch the floor, unsuccessfully. "Who knew anyone in this family could have this much fun," she said.

Suddenly, Maxie came racing through the auditorium—the one in which Eve had appeared in *Giselle* in junior high—shrieking, "Wait! You can't hand it in like that!" Eve, on stage, gazed down at the manuscript which lay in her hands; frayed lined papers, with copious, illegible scribbling, were sticking out from the black binder. "They won't be able to publish it!" Maxie screamed, frantically, scarves flying from around her neck, one tied to the next, like a magician's prop.

Henrietta's cackle was witchy. "My book is coming out *this* month."

"But you're dead," Eve said.

"It's still getting published before yours."

"Don't listen to her," Maxine shouted, fading as Henrietta's shimmering celestial body gelled into flesh. "*We'll* get it done. Don't worry."

It was a relief to wake from such a dream. In the last month—ever since The University of Nebraska Press had sent her the book contract for *Redeeming Eve: Female Entitlement from Austen to Lessing*—Eve's nights had been plagued with visions. Mostly they were of Maud, larger than life, towering over the city, her eyes like the shutters of a camera clicking their disapproval.

At 6:30 in the morning, the phone rang in their bedroom; Eve was already zipping the back of the vanilla-colored silk dress she'd bought for the occasion. "Guess who?" Hart laughed, as he towel dried his hair.

"Hi Ma," she said as soon as she picked up the phone.

"Hi," her mom whispered, secret-agent style. "I'm calling to wish you good luck. Although, you don't need it."

"Thanks."

"I finally sent you a video of my grand apology show. You know, just for safekeeping. Whenever you hate me, you can watch and remember how humble and kind I can be."

"Ma. . . ."

Sigh. "I know, it's *your* day. I've had the radio tuned into WNYC all week. I'm on the cordless and going downstairs to turn it on right now."

"The show isn't on for over two hours."

"What can I say? I don't want to miss it. I'm just going to sit very quietly, on the stool, in the kitchen, until it's time."

Eve laughed. "I have to get out of here, Ma, or you'll be listening to elevator music instead of the interview."

"Oh, I'm so excited! It's just so *nice* of that *nice* Professor Wellington to arrange for this! Who knew that an academic could actually have any contacts in the 'real' world. Well, I have to hand it to you: your instincts were right about this man. Oh, Eve, don't forget to bring your book with you to the studio!"

"Gee, it's a good thing you reminded me," she said, sarcastically. "Although, I doubt I'll even need it. It's a panel, Ma. I don't know how much I'll even get to say."

"'The Future of Feminism: Changing Constructs for a New Millennium.' I love that idea. Do you mind if I steal it for my show? Just kidding!"

Eve elbowed her husband who whimpered loudly, in imitation of their daughter. "I have to go. Gemma's up."

"Okay, sweetheart. Kiss her for me."

"I will."

"Good luck, Evie. Ohhhh! I'm just so proud."

"I know you are."

After hanging up the phone, she kissed her husband's cheek. "You better hurry and get dressed. I'll wake her."

Hart cupped her face in his hands. "Nervous?"

"Yes," she said, sliding her foot into a white sandal. "Very."

"Sweetheart," he kissed her lightly on the lips, "I think you'll be great. I'll be ready in five minutes."

Eve glided down the hall and into her daughter's room, light with anticipation. She snapped the bottom of the window shade and it crawled up into itself. The morning was clear, cloudless, and windy. Eve glanced down at her two-year-old daughter sprawled out on her new bed, with the ladybug decals pasted on its pine headboard. Hart sneaked up behind her; he was shirtless, but his jeans and loafers were on. "I'll get her ready. Go have a quiet cup of coffee. Meditate. Look over your notes."

"Thanks," Eve whispered. She walked downstairs to the living room: a hunter green couch with leaf patterns; a mustard, rust, and green wool kilim rug; an antiqued pine coffee table and two torch lamps with wood veneer shades. Nothing from Eve's graduate school days. Her bound manuscript sat on the coffee table. She took a deep breath and picked it up, not bothering to read over the familiar, marked pages. She already knew everything she had to say.

In Fidelity
M. J. Rose

Still suffering from the pain of her husband's infidelity, Jordan Sloan is also haunted by the long-ago murder of her father. When she learns that his killer has been paroled she fears his revenge. Although everyone thinks she's being paranoid, Jordan knows better. But as she struggles to prove to others that her fear of Mallory is justified, only she is aware of the dark secret of her relationship with him. All the while, a mysterious new client seems intent on contributing to Jordan's unravelling...

From the author of *Lip Service*, *In Fidelity* is a riveting and intricately woven novel in which M.J. Rose once again explores the dark corners of the human psyche.

Praise for *Lip Service*:

'A blend of erotica and suspense that will make your skin flush and hair stand up on end'

The Book Report

'packed full of tips...'

The Sun

'There's something disturbingly truthful about this novel'

Northern Echo

'Wow. Watch this one ...'

The Bookseller

Iron Shoes
Molly Giles

Kay Sorensen can't shake the feeling that she's 'stuck' in her life. She's a failed musician, disappointing daughter and resigned wife and mother. She envies her friend Zabeth – who seems to have the most vibrant sex life in the San Francisco Bay area – and the mysterious Charles Lichtman, with whom Kay feels destined to have an affair.

She has been unable to move out of the shadow of her glamorous and wickedly impossible mother, Ida. But now it seems that the illness Ida has almost revelled in is finally killing her. Having lived on courage, cigarettes and sarcasm for years, Ida still refuses to compromise. But, as infuriating as her mother can be, Kay is starting to realise that she is also the glue that holds their family together...

'storytelling at its best. Molly Giles's readers are blessed. Spread the word'
Amy Tan

'Giles gets inside her characters' heads, this touching novel will draw you in. Top read.'
Company

'wicked, affectionate, and amused. *Iron Shoes* can dance'
Frances Mayes, author of *Under the Tuscan Sun* and *Bella Tuscany*

Three Women
Marge Piercy

Suzanne Blume has survived two marriages, financially supported two children through college and her teaching duties at a Boston university allow her just enough time to take on important legal cases and spend time with her closest friend. Life in her forties has also yielded some unexpected pleasures – she is enjoying her first sexual relationship in years.

But her neat, buttoned-up life starts to unravel when her daughter Elena returns home, angry and unemployed. Can mother and daughter rebuild their fragmented relationship? And what of Suzanne's own mother? Having devoted her life to men and politics with passion, fiercely independent Beverly is now coping with the effects of a stroke and is also forced to share Suzanne's home and rely on the conventional daughter she has never had much time for…

Marge Piercy, the critically acclaimed author of *Woman on the Edge of Time, Braided Lives* and *Body of Glass,* weaves one of her most compelling novels yet.

Praise for Marge Piercy and *Three Women*:

"Every new novel by Marge Piercy is cause for celebration"
Alice Hoffman

"Vividly imagined and deeply satisfying"
Marilyn French

The Angels of Russia
Patricia le Roy

On a study trip to Leningrad, literature student Stéphanie meets Sergei, an enigmatic young dissident. Stéphanie had fallen in love with a fairy tale image of Russia – full of palaces and aristocrats; Sergei offers to show her just how different the reality is. Even in the supposedly enlightened days of Gorbachev, Sergei is in constant danger because of his political beliefs. So when he asks Stéphanie to agree to a marriage of convenience so that he can leave the country she is unable to refuse him.

Stéphanie finds herself increasingly attracted to her mysterious new husband. But when Stéphanie introduces Sergei to her aunt Marina, a Russian who defected to Paris whilst accompanying her father on a political mission, he appears to know more about Marina's past than Stéphanie. Could Marina be the real reason why he has come to Paris? As it becomes increasingly clear that Sergei is harboring more than one secret, Stéphanie is forced to question whether their first meeting was as accidental as it seemed…

Praise for *The Angels of Russia*:

"A sweeping contemporary historical romance…gripping, surprising…page-turner"
The Times Literary Supplement

"Pacy thriller…fascinating: full of surprises and strong characters" *The Bookseller*

Four Mothers
Shifra Horn

Translated by Dalya Bilu

While Amal is despondent at being deserted by her husband after the birth of her first child, her mother, grandmother and great-grandmother rejoice that she has born a son. For the older generations realise that the birth of a healthy boy means that their family's curse has been broken.

Motherhood proves to be Amal's initiation into the secrets of her family's history and the lives of her four "mothers": Mazal, whose ill-fated marriage brought about the curse; her daughter Sara, with her power to heal; Sara's daughter Pnina-Mazal, the unwanted child whose talent for knowing others' thoughts brings her joy and sorrow; and her daughter Geula, Amal's mother, whose intellect and idealism prove to be both a gift and a burden.

Beautifully imagined and lavishly told, Shifra Horn's lyrical debut novel, spanning five generations of women and one hundred years of life in Jerusalem is a masterpiece of storytelling in the tradition of Amy Tan and Isabel Allende.

"You will find yourself unable to put the book down"
London Jewish News

"Spanning the generations Shifra Horn spins a magic web"
Jewish Telegraph

"A rich and magical tale" *The Bookseller*